The

Highest Bidder

By

Kimberly Hunter

Getting kidnapped was bad enough, but when Trey Morrison gets sold off to the highest bidder and drugged to boot, well, he knows his day has gone from bad to worst.

Or has it?

Going undercover to take down a madman, Renjiro Takeda has rubbed elbows with the world's vilest men. But spotting Trey on the auction block makes him throw all caution to the wind and buys him.

Little does he know that his new purchase will set into motion a chain of events that neither him nor Trey will be able to escape.

It's a life or death situation for the lovers. And winner takes all.

Regarding E-book Piracy

The Highest Bidder

Published by K. A. H. Publishing

Chapter 1

"And now gentlemen, I have a very special treat. A rare delight just waiting for the right owner," Howard Rusk said with avaricious glee. He waved his hand, gesturing to the small stage behind him with a flourish. "I present to you… Joshua."

The curtain rose slowly, building the anticipation. Gasps and groans could be heard from the audience of select and affluent gentlemen as the prize was revealed. For sitting center stage on a raised dais was a naked young man. He was placed on a black satin pillow on his knees, his hands tied behind his back. A black leather collar was around his neck, a length of silver chain attached to a D-ring connecting them both to pull his head back and show off a well-formed, hairless chest and abs. His shoulder-length blond hair was tousled, the strands glinting like rare gold coins. His creamy pale skin seemed to glow with a pearlescent luster. Eyes closed, his face was arrestingly beautiful; the cheekbones tinted a delicate pink, full lips cherry red and slightly parted. His expression was one of dreamy bliss. If he'd had wings, he would have resembled an angel come down from heaven. But what drew the eye more wasn't so much the young man's beauty as it was his rather impressive erection. Standing straight and proud from his body, the young man's cock rose like a column of rose tinted ivory, the mushroom head glistening under the lights with his arousal.

Rusk heard the small audience go wild but there was only one man he watched, one man whose reaction mattered. And from the look on his face as he gazed upon young Joshua, he had baited his trap well. Now it was just a matter of reeling him in. There's a saying about revenge being a dish best served cold. Betrayal, however, that was best served with a smile.

Holding up his hands, Rusk gestured for silence. "Gentlemen, please!" Once the room was quiet, he continued, "For those of you who are familiar with our policies know that any information about the PET is given only to potential buyers." Murmurs began with that statement. "However," He began loudly, silencing the audience once again. "However since this is a special treat I have arranged as a thank you for all my esteemed guests, exceptions have been made"

Walking over to Joshua, Rusk stood behind his naked form, greedy eyes wandering over the young man's delicious body. And it was delicious, seeing that the drug they had given him was still keeping him manageable. Rusk grinned maliciously then began to run his hands over the softest and smoothest skin he had ever felt. It was too bad he couldn't keep Joshua for himself. But the moment his contact called about the young man, Rusk knew he would be invaluable to his plans. And considering that the young man was also a virgin, well, if his plans went awry, there were certainly others who would be more than eager to take Joshua in. Still, he had seen the look on his betrayer's face when Joshua was revealed; the trap would be sprung without a doubt.

"As you can see, Joshua is exquisite in face and form." His wandering hands getting a response, just as he knew they would. "At twenty-three, he's just the right age for some." A disappointed moan came from the front. "My apologies, Mr. Shimata." He knew the old man's penchant was for young boys with hardly any hair on their balls. "A college student, Joshua has never had a lover, male or female. I'm afraid his only experiences are the frequent hand jobs he has given himself," he tsked with mock sympathy as he continued to rub and fondle the silky skin under his hand.

Being in the business of supplying his clients with the best, Rusk had made it a priority to do thorough background checks on his products. The more information he had, the better chance of a good sale. A happy client was a repeat client. And the less loose ends to deal with didn't hurt either.

Murmuring in the audience grew as the implications of that statement sank in.

"Do you have proof?" Asked a distinguished gentleman with silver at his temples and an un-Godly expensive suit draping his toned form.

"Of course." Rusk smiled, gesturing to a tall black man at the edge of the small stage. "This is Dr. Nubu, the personal physician of our Nairobi guests. He was kind enough to examine Joshua. Dr. Nubu."

The doctor rose and inclined his head respectably toward Rusk then faced the audience. "I have given Joshua a through exam. He is free of disease and is in excellent health. And as stated, untouched and intact." He nodded to the audience and Rusk again, and then took his seat.

Rusk waited in silence for the audience to talk among themselves, his hands continuing their explorations as Joshua began to writhe and moan. A fine sheen of sweat began to glisten on his silky skin.

"I'll give you what you want soon, my lovely," he whispered silkily into Joshua's ear.

"Please," came Joshua's raspy plea, his beautiful skin flushed, toned muscles straining as he tried to find relief.

Rusk chuckled, knowing the drug had Joshua firmly in its thrall. He was a bit surprised at how quickly the young man had succumbed though. Then again, Joshua's sexual experiences weren't exactly satisfying or fulfilling from the accounts Rusk had received, so Joshua's inhibited response was an added bonus to the drugs already potent effects. And if the drug could bring out this kind of response, then a double dose would be even better. Rusk grinned at that, knowing the end result would be sweet indeed.

"Seeing as we have such a rare blossom, I'm afraid the price will be a bit higher than usual," Rusk said, not hearing as many grumbles to that announcement as he thought he would. Of course, he had baited his trap well with the beautiful virgin sacrifice. Now all he had to do was wait.

"And what is your starting price?" Asked a dark-skin man in flowing white robes.

Rusk slowly moved his right hand down Joshua's chest and stomach, making his way to Joshua's weeping cock. "A hundred thousand." His fingers wrapped around the rock hard shaft.

"Oh, God!" Joshua moaned loudly, head thrown back with pleasure.

As the dickering grew and the price rose ever higher, Rusk continued to stroke Joshua's cock, continued to push him toward release. It was all for his prey's benefit of course, showing how responsive Joshua was. Hearing such wonderful sounds of pleasurable agony burst forth the closer he came to his peak. Then it was down to two men, a senator from the US and a Japanese businessman.

"Will you counter Mr. Takeda's bid at nine hundred thousand, Senator Ross?" Rusk asked as he sped up the stroking of Joshua's weeping cock.

"Oh, God! Please!" Joshua cried out, his writhing body glimmering with sweat, his hips pumping.

Rusk could see the naked want on the Senator's face, but in the end, he merely shook his head in the negative.

Smiling with satisfaction, Rusk took one of Joshua's nipples, pinching it as he stroked Joshua's cock faster. "The bidding is closed at nine hundred thousand. Sold to Mr. Takeda."

The moment he said sold, Joshua came, screaming his release as he spurted onto the black satin pillow. Rusk smiled with pleasure. His betrayer would soon know how it felt to be helpless, how it felt to go against Howard Rusk. The trap was sprung.

Chapter 2

Renjiro Takeda had come to tonight's auction with one goal in mind—to get the last piece of evidence to put Howard Rusk in jail for human trafficking.

For three long years, Renjiro had worked undercover with different agencies coordinated with Interpol. He'd rubbed elbows with the world's most dangerous, most ruthless, and most corrupt men it had been his misfortune to meet. But he had made a promise and he intended to keep it.

As was standard procedure, the auctions were by invitation only and held at private estates. Tonight's was held at a private hotel on the eastern seaboard of the United States that catered to the uber wealthy. The perfect location for such a high stakes operation. And it was high stakes. Howard Rusk had been trafficking for years, catering to the wealthy and depraved, getting children as young as toddlers, male or female, all the way up to grown adults. And the requests just kept coming. Tell Rusk what you needed, what you wanted, and he got it. No questions. Just the right amount of money and he delivered. Then there was the small army of guards that he kept close at all times. Despite their reject status, all were ex-military and all very lethal. Those few stupid enough to go against Rusk or try to stop his operation had met with untimely and very painful deaths. That included the last Interpol officer who had been a childhood friend of Renjiro's. They had lost touch over the years, their dreams going in different directions. His friend to law enforcement and Renjiro to architecture, finally taking over his father's multi-million dollar company. Both had renewed their friendship many years later and talked from time to time. Which is why when Renjiro learned of his friend's death, he was greatly saddened. Soon after though, that sadness turned to anger when his friend's Captain explained his death and asked that Renjiro join their team in taking Rusk down. Renjiro was an established and wealthy businessman who had dealings with some of the men who went to these auctions. And the fact that he knew the deceased detective wasn't a problem. They rarely ever met and the few calls they had exchanged were mostly on holidays. Their connection was mere coincidence.

After Renjiro's acceptance to help, it was months before he received an invitation. Rusk was a greedy bastard but he wasn't stupid. Renjiro had never been to an auction nor had he ever voiced any desire to do so. So information had to be leaked, false accounts of Renjiro's rather odd activities and unusual tastes. The bait had worked. And now, three years later, Renjiro's mission was nearly complete. The team needed one more piece of evidence to nail Rusk and the nightmare would end.

"Mr. Takeda, how are you this evening?" asked a well-armed guard in a three piece suit at the entrance to the small conference room of the private hotel.

He smiled. "I'm well, thank you."

"Excellent." The guard returned the smile. "Your usual seat has been arranged, so please enjoy yourself."

"I will, thanks." He casually walked through the doors to see a small curtained stage and ten round tables that had already started to be filled with those eager to see Rusk's newest acquisitions.

Renjiro went to his seat near the back but with a clear view of the stage and sat down.

"Ah, Takeda-kun, how are you?"

Renjiro heard the question in Japanese and stood. "Shimata-sama." He bowed low to the elder Japanese man whom he towered over; the man was wearing his usual black and white silk kimono. "I'm well, sir," he replied in Japanese.

"Good, good. How's business?"

"Just opened a new office in New York."

"Expanding." He nodded with approval. "You need to grow to survive."

"Yes, sir."

Mr. Shimata patted Renjiro's arm. "I will send your father a little something to celebrate the occasion."

"He'd be honored, sir." He bowed low again.

Mr. Shimata returned the bow then moved to take his seat near the front of the stage, his two mammoth bodyguards flanking him. Without weapons, of course. Not that they really needed them.

Renjiro kept his face blank, letting nothing show as he took his seat again. Mr. Shimata was an old friend of his father's, and though he had heard rumors of his illicit relations, he had never imagined that they were true. Nor that he would see firsthand the type of man Mr. Shimata really was. It was because of his father's long friendship that he treated Mr. Shimata with such respect, but it was all for show. The moment he laid eyes on Mr. Shimata at his first auction, whatever respect he had for the man died. A serving girl came around seconds later bringing out drinks for everyone and a bottle water for Renjiro.

"Well, well, didn't expect to see you here."

Turning at the snide comment, Renjiro locked eyes with Senator Orin Ross, a stout middle aged man from the American mid-west. Renjiro kept his seat, seeing no reason for formalities with such a crude man.

"Business kept me away." He shrugged.

"I'll bet," Ross sneered. "More like that new PET you outbid me for."

Renjiro shrugged again, letting the ill mannered man think what he wanted.

The Senator frowned, visibly trying not to lose his composure. "Stay out of my way, Takeda." Then he stalked past to take his seat near two black men with clear African roots.

Renjiro sighed, taking a drink of his water. The Senator was still pissed about losing that young boy, but Renjiro couldn't help it. The kid was barely driving age and looked so helpless and fragile that Renjiro was bidding before he even knew he had raised his hand. He would have done it again if it meant saving one more innocent from a life of depravity.

When all the arrivals were seated and comfortable, all doors were locked and secured, two guards each posted there as well as flanking each side of the stage. It wasn't a show of force per se, just a not so subtle reminder that if you won your bid, you paid, immediately. And of course Rusk was paranoid. Having a price on your head by every law agency in the free world did that to a man.

Renjiro didn't have long to wait when their host finally made his appearance. Of medium height and build, Howard Rusk had the swarthy good looks of his Latin-American heritage and the personality of a chameleon. You never knew how he was going to act in any given situation, and that was what made Rusk dangerous, that unpredictability. He'd been known to shoot men for laughing too loud.

Coming out to mingle a bit with his guests, Rusk wore his signature white and black, white suit and shirt, black tie and shoes. But there was something else about the man tonight that raised Renjiro's hackles. He looked too happy, too cheerful. Not unusual, Rusk was always wearing a smile, but Renjiro's instincts were screaming that something was up. He would have to be on guard just in case his cover went to shit along with everything else.

Seeing that Rusk had spotted him, Renjiro stood, bowing slightly. "Mr. Rusk"

"Good to see you tonight, Mr. Takeda. We missed you last time." He returned the bow with a bright smile.

"Regrettably, I had business to attend to."

"Then no troubles with your PET?"

Renjiro grinned. "No, he has behaved perfectly."

"Excellent." Rusk beamed. "So, what can I get you this evening?"

"Well, I need to get him a companion. I can't be with him all the time, business you know."

Rusk nodded thoughtfully. "Of course."

"So I thought I would get him a little friend to keep him company while I'm away."

"Not a problem." Rusk grinned, patting Renjiro's shoulder "I have several you might be interested in."

"Sounds good."

"Just make sure you don't spoil him with his new friend." Rusk chuckled good naturedly.

Renjiro gave him a malicious grin. "Not to worry, the boy knows who his master is." He made his eyes go cold, face a hard mask. "And his friend will to."

Rusk took a moment to look Renjiro in the eye, apparently approving of what he saw. "Glad to hear it." He then left to continue his rounds of the room.

Once the meet and greet was finished, everyone settled down and Rusk took position on the center of the small stage.

"Again, welcome gentlemen. I have a good selection for your viewing pleasure tonight, so let's start the bidding." He gestured to a guard to bring out the first victim.

After that, Renjiro watched as eight young men and three boys were bid on and sold. He bid as well, throwing off suspicion but was outbid each time. He just wasn't able to bring himself to fake any kind of enthusiasm. It was as if the more times he came to an auction, another piece of his soul died. Unable to help those being bought like cattle by the scum of the Earth and what their lives were going to be like. That thought and others had kept him up many a night, heart heavy, mind troubled as the faces of those he couldn't save flashed through his conscience. But still he came, gathering more evidence against Rusk to save countless others from a life of slavery and hell. It was that thought and the promise he made that kept him going, kept him from losing his sanity. And seeing Rusk pay would be worth the living nightmare of the past three years.

Hearing Rusk's next announcement snapped Renjiro out of his contemplation as a feeling of unease skittered down his spine. It wasn't like Rusk to change anything on the agenda. He liked order and strived to make sure his schedule wasn't deviated from in any way. But once Renjiro saw the beautiful young man on the stage, he understood Rusk's need for a surprise. He also couldn't take his eyes off him.

Not making a secret of his sexual orientation, Renjiro had never made it public either. His private life was just that, private. His family knew of course and his father, while not exactly happy that his eldest son was gay, knew that no matter Renjiro's sexual preferences there was no one better suited to take over the company. And that was proven when after five years, Renjiro had nearly doubled the company's profits and had expanded to four countries, two offices in America alone. Of course, Renjiro was still careful. As the years have passed and homosexuality becomes more acceptable, there are still those that aren't as tolerant, those who could use such behavior to break a company. So Renjiro kept his lifestyle out of the public eye and in the bedroom where it belonged. And the more he saw of Joshua's pale beauty, the more he wanted to put him in said bedroom. Which was quite odd in itself. Renjiro's taste in men didn't usually lean to the Caucasian persuasion. Not that he had never been with a white man. There were the two Americans while in college and that rather crazy affair with a Scot several years ago, but most of his lovers were Asian like himself. Thinking back, none of those men, Asian or otherwise, had ever got him hard with just one look or had his blood surging at the thought of all that pale skin under him. Fortunately, his carnal musings were brought to heel when one of the men from Nairobi stood up.

"I have examined Joshua thoroughly. He is free of disease and in excellent health, and as stated, untouched and intact."

Renjiro stiffened slightly at that statement then nearly saw red when Rusk began to run his hands over Joshua's smooth skin.

"Please."

It was that breathy plea that made the decision for Renjiro. Whatever it took, however much it cost, he was getting Joshua out. After that, he didn't know. He couldn't' really think with his dick aching and the sight of Joshua responding so seductively to Rusk's ministrations. But he knew he had to save Joshua, keep him out of the clutches of these vile men. And he would, countering every bid as Joshua writhed and moaned while Rusk continued to pleasure him. The sight sent Renjiro's senses reeling, his heart pounding with every pump of Rusk's hand until only two bidders remained. He and Senator Ross.

"Will you counter Mr. Takeda's bid at nine hundred thousand, Senator Ross?"

Renjiro saw a burning lust in the Senators eyes then defeat as he shook his head in the negative. Those eyes turned to smoldering hatred as he trained them on Renjiro. He had definitely made an enemy in the Senator. Then Joshua was crying out his release and all thoughts fled of the Senator and his anger. Renjiro watched transfixed by the sight of that luscious body straining, pale skin flushed rose, beautiful face a mask of blissful agony. Renjiro nearly came himself from the sight, his iron control hanging by a thread. That thread almost snapped when Joshua slumped over in an exhausted heap at Rusk's feet. Rusk chuckled, motioning a guard over.

"Take Mr. Takeda's new PET and prepare him to leave."

The guard nodded. "Yes, sir, Mr. Rusk." He reached down and picked Joshua up like he weighed nothing.

He looked so small and fragile in the large guard's arms that Renjiro had to force himself to remain sitting lest he show any weakness. It was a weakness that Rusk would be sure to exploit if he saw it.

"If you'd be so kind, Mr. Takeda." Rusk smiled merrily as he took out a kerchief to wipe his hands, bidding Renjiro to come up to the stage.

Renjiro nodded, glad that after he stood, his suit jacket hid the monster erection that refused to go down. From the knowing grin Rusk gave him, the man already knew. Renjiro gave nothing away though, his face a mask of indifference, body relaxed. Rusk softly chuckled, waiting for Renjiro to climb the steps up the stage then leading him to a small room behind it where a laptop was set up on a table. Renjiro wasted no time, going to the computer and bringing up his banking account to transfer the appropriate funds to Rusk's untraceable account.

"You surprised me tonight, Mr. Takeda." Rusk put the kerchief in his breast pocket and took a seat in the sparse room, crossing his legs at the ankles in a relaxed manner.

"Oh?" Renjiro finalized the transaction, not bothering to turn Rusk's way.

"Of all the men here, you were the last one I would have expected to take Joshua. He's not your usual type."

Renjiro looked up to find Rusk's piercing black eyes leveled at him, the challenge in those dark depths clear.

"I wanted him," Renjiro stated, not bothering to lie. Not much point really.

Rusk chuckled. "And I have the distinct feeling you deny yourself few things, Mr. Takeda."

"Very few." Renjiro grinned

Rusk inclined his head in acknowledgment as the computer beeped. The money had gone through and was now safely in Rusk's account. Rusk got up and went to check the screen, making sure all was right. He then powered the laptop down and closed the lid.

"Joshua should be ready by now. Shall we?" He led Renjiro back out and through the now empty room where the stage sat, to the front of the hotel and a waiting sleek black limo. "A pleasure doing business with you, Mr. Takeda." He held out his hand to shake Renjiro's.

"Likewise." He returned the shake then got in, the driver closing the door behind him. He found Joshua on the opposite seat lying on his side clad in a blue/green silk robe that barely covered him. His breathing was soft and steady in slumber.

His gaze wandered greedily over Joshua's silk draped body, amazed that he looked even more delicious up close. He sighed, knowing he would have to tread carefully. The situation was a precarious one and it didn't matter that he had rescued Joshua; he'd had ulterior motives for it. Motives that even he wasn't sure he wanted to examine too closely. But he did know that he wanted to get to know Joshua better and his gut was telling him that Joshua was special. Renjiro never ignored his gut. So he would take things slow and see where they led. It was all he could do.

"What's our status, Jonah?" He asked the driver when they were far enough away from the hotel. He would have rather have had his earpiece and talked to Marshall about any updates, but it was too risky

"Garret has the jet on stand-by. You should be in the air and on your way to Kyoto within the hour."

"Good."

"And I hope the young man stays asleep. It's easier to explain things after they wake up at the safe house."

"He's going with me, Jonah."

"Pardon?"

Renjiro gave him a steely glare in the rearview mirror, brooking no argument.

"Shit." Jonah shook his head and kept quiet.

Taking a deep breath, Renjiro looked at Joshua once again. He just couldn't seem to take his eyes away for more than a moment and was glad he was still asleep so Renjiro could look his fill. Unfortunately, that sleep period would end and Renjiro would have his hands full, in more ways than one. And it was all because of Rusk's drug. That damn poison he insisted on giving to each of his newly acquired PET's. A well kept secret, the drug lowered your inhibitions while ramping up your sex drive. And for someone like Joshua with very little sexual experience, the feelings could be near overwhelming. Plus, there was no antidote that could counter the drug's effects; you just had to ride it out until exhaustion pulled you under. But in Joshua's case, that wasn't an option. He had never been with a man nor did Renjiro know if he wanted to be. His actions with Rusk were drug induced, so that really didn't count. And still being a virgin at the age of twenty-three did not a homosexual make. Though as potent as the drug was, it didn't matter if you were gay or straight, you'd do anything and anyone to stop the need, the utter craving crawling through your body.

"Mmmm." A sleepy moan sounded from Joshua.

"Damn!" Renjiro softy exclaimed. He had hoped that Joshua would have slept a little longer. Like until they were airborne. "How much farther, Jonah?"

"At least another fifteen minutes."

"Just great." He sighed as Joshua began to stir.

"Problem?"

"Just get us there as fast as you can." He moved so he was sitting at Joshua's hip.

"You got it."

Renjiro watched as Joshua slowly awoke, a pale hand with elegant fingers reached for his head as if he were in pain.

"Jeez, my spinning head." His voice was low and raspy.

"The drug they gave you will wear off in a few hours," Renjiro spoke softly so as not to startle Joshua too much. It didn't work.

"Whoa!" He sprang to a sitting position and nearly toppled over.

Renjiro caught him before he fell to the floor of the limo. "Easy now, easy." He gently helped Joshua back in the seat, almost falling himself as he gazed into the most beautiful aquamarine eyes he had ever seen.

"Who are you?" Joshua snapped, eyes wary as he pulled the robe tighter around himself. The look on his face held more than confusion with his lack of attire and situation. "Where am I? What's going on?" He slowly scooted away from Renji.

"My name is Renjiro Takeda. You're safe here."

Joshua snorted. "You'll excuse me if I don't believe you." He quickly took in his surroundings, face pinched, and lips compressed. Despite his confusion and evident fear, there was fire in those gem bright eyes. Joshua would need it in the hours ahead.

"Fair enough." Renjiro grinned wryly, glad that Joshua didn't seem the type to accept his situation blindly. Unfortunately, with the way he was blinking to stay focused and upright, it wouldn't be long before the drug hit full force. "Do you remember what happened?"

"I got jumped is what happened," he growled.

"Jumped?" A bit shocked that Rusk would go to such lengths, but then he really shouldn't be surprised. Rusk had been known to abduct whole families in broad daylight; one lone man wasn't much of a problem.

"Yeah, my damn car broke down again on the way to school so I pulled over to the shoulder. And no sooner do I get the hood up then some huge guy grabs me from behind and throws me into this big black SUV. It happened so fast that I didn't know what was going on until we were down the road," he huffed out a harsh breath at the recount. "I tried to open the door and make a jump for it, but this other guy snatches me back and sticks me in the arm. Next thing I know, I'm here."

Renjiro nodded with a frown. "You don't remember anything else? Anything at all?"

"Just vague blurs, nothing solid." He shook his head. "Why?" His eyes then widened with alarm. "I didn't do anything stupid did I?" Those elegant fingers rubbed his forehead with clear uncertainty. "Damn, I knew they had probably given me some freaky shit." Then he looked at Renjiro with panic filled eyes. "They didn't try anything did they?"

"No, you are unharmed in any way." Not about to tell him about Rusk bringing him off in front of a room full of men. Now was not the time. And it wasn't exactly a lie. He hadn't been violated sexually. He was still, technically, a virgin.

Joshua sighed with relief. "Thank God for small mercies." He looked down at his attire, or lack thereof. "But why am I wearing this and not my own clothes?"

"Look, Joshua, I..."

"We're here, Renjiro," Jonah informed them, the limo coming to a stop.

"How do you know my name?" Joshua asked with narrowed eyes.

"The explanation is complicated and best told once we're in the air," Renjiro hedged.

"In the air?" Joshua shook his head. "Oh hell no, I don't think so pal." He reached for the door.

Renjiro grabbed him before he got the door open. "Listen to me very carefully, Joshua. Those men weren't merely kidnappers. It's a lot bigger than that and you got dragged into the middle of it. Do you understand?" Renjiro watched that beautiful face drain of color, aquamarine eyes widen, then his shoulders slumped.

"I'm in deep shit, huh?"

"Not nearly as deep as you could have been, but deep enough." He released Joshua with a deep sigh.

"Damn, knew I should have slept in today." Joshua rubbed the back of his neck.

Renjiro chuckled softly. "Don't worry, it'll all work out." He patted Joshua's silky hair. "C'mon, we've got to get going." He got out first then helped Joshua who was a little unsteady on his feet. "Can you make it?"

"Give me a minute, my heads spinning." He held onto to Renjiro's arm for support then quickly snatched it back to use the limo instead until he appeared steady. His distrust was warranted.

"Be careful, Renjiro." Jonah gave him a concerned look, took a quick glance at Joshua as he closed the door, then got back in the driver's seat and drove off.

Watching him go, Renjiro shook his head, knowing that taking Joshua with him would cause a few problems. He would deal with them later. At the moment, Joshua was the bigger concern. He looked down on that golden head, noticing the size difference right off. Renjiro was 6'3" and weighed two thirty; Joshua barely came to his chin and looked half Renjiro's weight. That difference only made Renjiro want to protect him more.

"Okay, let's go." Joshua took a couple of uneasy steps. "So, where we going?"

"My private home in Kyoto." Renjiro stayed close, just in case. It was evident Joshua didn't want to be touched. Still, Renjiro didn't want him falling on his face either.

"Japan?" Joshua's head whipped around in alarm then his knees buckled and he began to fall.

Renjiro caught him before he hit the tarmac. "I got you." He gathered Joshua up and into his arms.

"Sorry, legs feel like jelly," Joshua mumbled into Renjiro's chest, his body stiff. His unease was palpable.

"Not a problem," Renjiro soothed, enjoying how right Joshua's solid weight felt gathered close to his chest, Joshua's head lying over his heart. "The drug is still working in your system and will take a few hours before the effects wear off." His sure steps taking them to the private jet.

"Great, just my luck to get jacked up on something that makes me so weak I have to get carried like a girl," he muttered. "And by a complete stranger at that."

"I'm well aware that you're not a girl," Renjiro replied, hoping the timbre of his voice didn't betray the need raging inside him the longer he had Joshua in his arms. He needn't have worried, the drug was starting to take effect now that Joshua was conscious. Its effects were like the ebb and flow of the tide until it finally crashed over

Joshua. Renjiro needed to be in the air when it happened. As for the stranger comment, he hoped to remedy that. Soon.

"I feel really weird, Mr. Takeda."

Renjiro smiled at the formality. "Please, my father is Mr. Takeda. Call me Renjiro or Renji." A bit surprised at himself for giving permission to use the childhood name. Then again, he'd been doing a lot of surprising things were Joshua was concerned. He'd feel alarmed if it didn't feel right.

Joshua looked up at him with a small smile. "Okay, Renji."

Thank God Renjiro made it inside the jet or that charming smile with the dimple in the right cheek would have been his undoing. He nearly groaned aloud at the sight.

Placing Joshua carefully in a seat near a window, Renji began to buckle him in.

"Uh, Renji?"

"Yes?" He pulled on the strap to make sure it was snug and secure.

"Um, I've never flown before."

Renji looked up into those gorgeous eyes, noticing the uncertainty in them and the slight tremor that shook Joshua's body.

"Don't worry." He gave Joshua a reassuring smile. "The pilot is one of the best and has flown me just about everywhere. I trust him, alright?" He cupped that smooth cheek.

Jerking back, Joshua let out a shaky breath and nodded "Okay, but if we go down in a fiery ball of flames, I'm blaming you." He grinned nervously.

Renji returned the smile, berating himself for the unwanted touch. He just couldn't seem to help himself though. "Fair enough." He then moved to the seat beside Joshua and strapped in as well.

It wasn't long before the jet was ready and they were moving down the runway. Joshua grabbed Renji's hand at take-off, but soon relaxed after the plane leveled out and they were on their way. He took his hand away, wrapping his arms around his waist. His unease was obvious. And not just due to the plane ride. It was time to explain the situation.

"I'm going to get us a drink then we need to talk." He gave Joshua's shoulder a gentle pat.

"Sure."

Renji got up and went to the mini-bar, grabbed a couple bottle waters, opened them, and brought them back, handing one to Joshua.

"Thanks." He took two long pulls on the cold water.

"Better?" Renji took a deep drink of his own water as he sat down.

Joshua sighed. "Yeah."

Nothing to do but begin. "For the past three years I've worked undercover for a coordinated multi-national police effort with the help of Interpol to bring down a man named Howard Rusk who deals in human trafficking."

"Jesus!" Joshua choked on his water, eyes wide.

"I'm not an agent or police officer but a legitimate business man who runs a large architectural firm. I was approached because a childhood friend was a detective trying to take Rusk down and was murdered for it."

"Damn, sorry to hear that."

"Thank you." He smiled sadly. "Ishida and I lost touch after I went to college in the states, our lives going in different directions. We did communicate occasionally, catching up on things from time to time. A year after Ishida's death, his Captain, along with several Interpol Agents, approached me, explaining how they wanted my help and why. They also gave me the facts of Ishida's murder." He frowned at the memory. "I jumped at the chance to make his death mean more than just another of Rusk's victim's."

"I can understand that, but three years is kind of long to take one guy down." Joshua looked skeptical.

"This isn't like the movies." He snorted. "You don't just find out where he is and bust up the party. Rusk is paranoid, extremely so. The auctions are by invitation only and without it telling you where the auction is being held, you're just shooting in the dark. It was months before I received one and months still before I was even allowed to bid."

"Sounds like a class A nut job." Joshua shook his head.

Renji chuckled at that. "Yes, well, considering that he's wanted in twenty-five countries and has connections to some the world's biggest crime syndicates and governments, the paranoia is a given. He supplies what he likes to call PET's, personal entertainment toys."

Joshua gave him a look of pure disgust. "That's just sick."

"That's just business," Renji retorted. "Rusk sees these people as commodities, a business of supply and demand. If one of his clients has a demand for a young blond man." Renji nodded in his direction. "Rusk supplies him. For a fee, of course. Everything and everyone has a price and there's nothing he won't get. I've even heard of him taking whole families and auctioning them off one by one. And it doesn't matter the ethnicity or background, young or old, male or female. If there is a need, Rusk will get it."

Joshua sat back in his seat, face pale. "I don't know whether to start bawling like baby or puke my guts up."

"I did both after my first auction," he admitted ruefully.

"That bad?" Joshua's expression was one of curiosity mixed with concern.

Renji sat forward, rubbing the back of his neck at the horrific memory. "It was that and more." He took a deep breath and let it out slowly. "At an earlier auction, one of the patrons had commented that Rusk wasn't getting enough young boys to choose from. Wanting to keep his clients happy, he got what was asked for." The fear on those young faces would be with him for the rest of his life. "There wasn't a boy over the age of fourteen at that auction and the youngest was barely six."

"Christ." Joshua closed his eyes, laying his head back. It was apparent that he was as sickened as Renji.

"It was weeks before I was able to go to another auction. But I had made a promise to myself and Ishida's memory that I would do what I could to bring Rusk down. Seeing those children being sold to the highest bidder like so much cattle…" He paused to swallow the lump in his throat. "I couldn't just walk away and not do something. I had to help so other children would be safe."

He felt Joshua's hand tentatively pat his shoulder and he looked over, seeing appreciation with a dose of uncertainty in those aqua depths. "You're a good man, Renji Takeda."

Renji sighed at that. "Well, you might not think so after what I have to tell you." He noticed that Joshua's eyes were glassy as he sat back, sweat starting to bead on his upper lip.

"What else?" His voice was breathy as he rubbed a hand over his chest, fingers lingering by his right nipple. The action seemed unconscious.

Renji watched that hand, his own itching to follow it, body beginning to harden with every pass. "As you've no doubt guessed, you were one of the many up for bid."

Joshua snorted. "Yeah, your explanation and my lack of attire kind of gave it away."

Renji couldn't help grin at that, glad Joshua was keeping his sense of humor. Though for how long, he didn't know. It made his grin change to a frown. "Well, there's more."

"I don't know how there could be." His breathing was getting a little heavier, a bead of sweat trickling down his right temple. Renji wanted nothing more than to lap it up and taste it on his tongue. He held back a groan at the thought. "It's obvious that you saved me."

"Not exactly," he hedged. "You see, you were an unexpected addition to tonight's auction, a bonus if you will. And after seeing the stir you caused among the bidders," *Myself included.* "I felt it best if I bid as well."

"What are you saying?"

Renji took a deep breath and let it out slowly. "To keep you from experiencing a nightmare, I bought you."

Those glazed eyes widened. "But I thought…" Joshua shook his head with confusion. "I don't get it."

"Look, Joshua –"Renji needed to hurry before the drug crashed over him.

"It's Trey. My gran was the only one who ever called me Joshua."

"Alright…Trey." He nodded, seeing that Trey suited him much better than Joshua. "You don't just waltz right in there and take someone with guns blazing. Rusk has his own small army. You'd be dead before you could blink. Buying you was the only way." He wasn't about to explain the real reason he had for buying Joshua—Trey—he amended silently. There were some things he just didn't need to tell Trey at the moment.

Renji watched as Trey squirmed a little in his seat. "Okay, well, thank-you. I think." He rubbed his sweaty brow. "And if I could think straight, I'd probably comprehend all this a lot better."

"That's another thing, Trey. The drug Rusk gave you, you're going to be feeling its full effects real soon and I wanted to explain exactly what's going to happen."

"What do you mean?" Trey gulped more water then put the cold bottle to his flushed cheeks, letting out a deep sigh.

Renji huffed out a harsh breath. "As near as we can tell, it's Extasy with a meth base. And it's strong. Somehow, Rusk has been able to synthesize it to its purest form to give it an added boost."

"Just how much of a boost?" Even though he was starting to feel the early effects, Trey seemed lucid enough to understand some of what Renji was telling him. It wouldn't last.

"The truth?"

Trey let out a deep sigh of resignation. "Yeah."

"You'll do anything and anyone to get off." Renji hated to put it so bluntly, but Trey needed to know and Renji didn't have a lot of time to sugar coat it.

"Jeez, that's great, just great." Trey laid his head back on the seat. "I finally decide to accept a date with John Ross Carter, whom I've been secretly lusting after for months now, in the hopes that finally, finally, I'll lose my cherry. But instead of getting sweaty with my fantasy, I get kidnapped and sold to the highest bidder." He gave Renji a sheepish grin with that last bit. "No offense."

"None taken." Renji gulped his own water at the implications of what Trey just revealed. "So you're gay?" Interrupting whatever it was that Trey was about to say.

He blinked at the question. "Uh, yeah, knew since I was fifteen. Why? You a homophobe?"

Renji chuckled. "Hardly since I knew when I was thirteen."

Those gorgeous eyes blinked again, looking Renji up and down. "I've met a few gay Asian men and none have looked like you."

"Really? And just how is a gay Asian man supposed to look?"

Trey gave him another lengthy perusal, aqua eyes darkening with each pass. His breathing was getting harsher as the lust showed plainly on his beautiful face. "Not like all my wet dreams rolled into one man." His voice had deepened to a husky timbre with the admission.

Renji felt his face get warm. "I'm hardly anyone's wet dream."

"On the contrary. Tall, dark, and mouthwatering has always been a star in my fantasies." His grin was carnal.

That made Renji's body tighten further, his own mouth watering at the images of Trey staring in some of his fantasies. But Renji had to put the brakes on. Trey had begun to feel the drug full force, he wasn't in his right mind. With the drug lowering inhibitions, Renji had no clue as to

Trey's real personality when it came to men. Renji didn't want to do something they both would regret. It would be glorious, of that, Renji had no doubt. However, Renji wasn't in the habit of taking advantage. Much as his body was craving he do so.

"Trey..."

"Damn, Renji, I feel like, like..." He moaned as he grabbed his silk covered erection and began to stroke it.

A ragged groan of his own slipped out as Renji watched.

"I feel like my whole body is on fire." Trey's voice was raspy as he reached over with his empty hand and grabbed Renji's jacket, pulling him close. "How long am I going to feel like this?"

Renji swallowed with an audible gulp, his own voice coming out a little strained. "A few hours."

Those beautiful eyes closed, face a mask of pleasurable suffering. "I don't think I can wait that long, Renji." His passion glazed eyes opened. "I feel half crazed now." He then jerked Renji closer and captured his lips in a searing kiss.

Renji was too stunned at the maneuver to pull back, not that he really wanted to. Trey may be a virgin, but he sure as hell didn't kiss like one. His lips were supple and demanding, his tongue going deep as he sought out Renji's hidden recesses. And with a skill that had Renji moaning and wanting more. So much more that when he finally came to his senses, Trey was running his warm hands over Renji's surprisingly naked chest, sounds of appreciation issuing forth with each pass.

Grabbing both of Trey's wrists, Renji pushed himself back. His breathing was choppy and a monster erection strained against his zipper. "We can't."

"Why not?" Trey tried to break free, clearly wanting to finish what he started.

He jerked a little to get Trey's attention. "I won't take you like this, hana. Your first time should be on your own terms, not because of some drug." The endearment slipped out without any thought, but it felt right. Hana—the Japanese word for flower.

Blinking, Trey shook his head, eyes going wide. He jerked out of Renji's hands, toppling to the floor and scrabbling back against the wall of the plane. He raised his knees, wrapping his arms around them and trembling. "God, Renji, I'm so sorry. I...I've never come on to a guy in my life. I don't know what's happening to me. I'm...I'm..."

"Shhh." He cautiously left his seat to approach Trey, like one would a wounded animal. "It's alright. I'm going to help you. But I meant what I said, I won't take you like this." He sat on his knees in front of Trey, careful not to touch. It was apparent Trey wasn't ready yet despite the drug. "And as much as I would be honored to be your first, to make slow love to you, you deserve more. Not a drug induced romp with a man you don't know."

Trey looked at him with startlement. "You want to make love to me?"

"More than you could possibly imagine." He gave Trey a soft smile, reaching over to tenderly take Trey's hands. He allowed it, those blown pupils following Renji's every movement. Renji laid a gentle kiss on the knuckles. "You have nothing to worry about with me, Trey. Strangers we may be, but I swear on my mother's life, I would never do anything to hurt you." It wasn't a hollow promise. From the moment Renji saw Trey, he wanted him. Wanted to hold him, kiss him, make love to him, and care for him.

And most of all, protect him from all of life's horrors. Impossible, of course, but it was how Renji felt.

Trey stared at him, expression uncertain as he continued to allow Renji to hold his hands. Then he let out a deep, shaky breath. "I'm scared, Renji." His body was quaking with no doubt a combination of fear and arousal. "I've never felt so out of control, so needy. I want…God, Renji, I want so much." He choked on a sob.

"Come here, hana." Renji gave those warm hands a gentle tug. Trey nearly leaped into his arms.

He held Trey tight as his tears made wet tracks on Renji's bare chest, Trey's quiet sobs enough to break Renji's heart. "I'll take care of you, hana. Trust me?"

Trey took a deep breath and nodded, pushing away slightly to wipe the tears from his pink cheeks. "I shouldn't. This could all be an elaborate lie on your part. But…even as fuzzy as my mind is, there's just something about you." He gave Renji a penetrating stare then smiled softly. "So yeah, oddly enough, I do."

"I'm glad." Renji reached up to cup Trey's cheek. "May I kiss you, Trey?" The drug may be calling the shots where Trey's body was concerned, but that didn't mean Renji was going to treat this beautiful man like a hook up. He deserved gentleness and careful tending. And Renji was going to make sure he got it.

A shy bob of Trey's head was all the answer Renji needed. Leaning in, he began with a delicate touch of lips. Trey's breathy moan let Renji know he could explore more. And he did. Taking that delicious mouth in a heart pounding kiss. When he finally pulled away, they were both panting and Trey was writing in Renji's lap. His eyes were nearly black, cheeks flushed. His beauty was enough to take Renji's breath away. Flower indeed.

"Renji," Trey moaned, laying his head against Renji's chest.

"I have you, hana." As careful as he could, Renji picked Trey up and carried him to the stateroom, one of the perks of having a private jet.

"You're going to throw your back out hauling me around like this."

"Hardly." Renji chuckled. "Besides, you feel good in my arms." He placed a tender kiss on Trey's sweaty brow then walked over the threshold to the bedroom and a king size bed. There, he gently placed Trey on the red satin comforter and pillows.

Taking a step back, Renji let his eyes feast. Trey's skin and hair glowed golden against the red of the satin, the robe making his eyes shine like aquamarine gems. His kiss swollen lips were parted, eyelids heavy with arousal. That lithe muscular body was writhing with need, the robe parted to let his erection stand at glorious attention. "You are so beautiful, hana."

"Renji…please." Trey grabbed himself again, back arching as he slowly pumped, those elegant fingers moving up and down. With the drug at full force, Trey's shyness and hesitance was slowly being eroded away.

A low moan escaped Renji at the sight. His own body burning, balls aching and heavy, erection needing desperately to be set free. He wanted more than anything to make love to Trey. But he'd made a promise, he wouldn't take Trey while he was under the drugs influence and he would keep that promise. Even if it cost him his sanity. And with the way Trey was whimpering and writhing on his bed, losing his sanity might just be a guarantee.

Not wanting to be tempted any further, Renji took off everything but his briefs then lay down beside Trey, gathering his warm softness close. Trey went eagerly, hands and lips seemingly everywhere, his hips pumping that hot hardness against Renji's thigh.

"So good…feel so good."

Renji grabbed those wandering hands and pushed Trey onto his back. He had to keep the upper hand, or at least a modicum of sense, or risk doing something he would regret later. Of course, that didn't mean he couldn't explore and satisfy them both in the process.

He looked into Trey's eyes, dark with need. "Trey," he groaned, unable to stop himself from taking those ruby lips and plundering that luscious mouth.

Trey whimpered, clinging to Renji as he tasted every inch of Trey's mouth, their tongue's dueling and lips sliding together. The taste, the unique flavor of Trey, went straight to Renji's balls, a deep moan of his own escaping.

"God, Renji." Trey's head arched back to give Renji better access to kiss and nibble over his chin and neck, lips lingering at the spot where neck and shoulder meet. Renji suckled there, causing Trey to gasp and his hips to grind into Renji's stomach.

He smiled against Trey's warm skin, stowing away the knowledge of a hot spot for later use; then slowly moved his way down, letting go of Trey's hands and parting the robe along the way. Tasting, sipping, and touching all the skin he could reach, he finally came to Trey's weeping cock. Once there he stopped, gently blowing over the swollen and glistening head.

"Mmmm." Those elegant fingers were now tangled in the silk sheets with a white knuckled grip and whimpers of need issuing from kiss swollen lips.

That whimper was fast becoming Renji's favorite sound; it did such wicked things to his body. Though at present, he was more interested in doing wicked things to Trey's body. Like swallowing that beautiful cock like a lollipop. So he did. And Trey's reaction was so worth it. He cried out, back bowing, head thrown back with pleasure. He was simply gorgeous, the taste and feel of Trey in his mouth causing Renji to do a little groaning of his own.

"Renji…can't…God, Renji!" Trey shouted as he came, his salty sweetness sliding down Renji's throat as he took all Trey had to give, stroking his own erection to completion and coming with a heartfelt grunt.

Getting his breath back, Renji moved off the bed and went to his small lavatory to clean up, making sure to bring back a few extra towels and wet wash cloths. He would need them in the next few hours. When he stepped back into the bedroom, Trey was sprawled in a wanton heap, robe nearly off, breathing finally slow but skin still flushed and cock still erect. His golden hair was tousled and slitted aquamarine eyes glassy, lips a deep cherry red and kiss swollen. He was desire personified, a carnal dream brought to realization. Never had Renji wanted anyone more than he wanted Trey. And no matter what he had to do, he was determined that Trey would be his.

Renji went to the bed, laying the towels and cloths on the nightstand and climbed in beside Trey. "You alright, hana?" He asked as he tenderly brushed the gold locks from Trey's sweaty brow.

Trey gave him a throaty chuckle. "That was amazing."

"Glad you liked it." He smiled, entwining the fingers of his left hand with Trey's to bring him closer so they could look at each other face to face on their sides.

"Yeah, I liked it so much that I thought my eyeballs were going to pop out my head."

Renji laughed softly. "Well, I can't have that. I like these gorgeous eyes right where they are." The fingers of his right hand came up to trace golden brows.

Those aqua gems closed as Renji softly moved the pads of his fingers down over flushed cheeks and kissable lips, thoroughly enjoying the feel of Trey's soft, warm skin. "Damn, Renji." He swallowed audibly. "I still…I…"

"Shhh." He put a finger over Trey's lips. "I said I would take care of you, hana. I always keep my promises."

Trey's passion filled eyes opened and he nodded. Then Renji took his lips in another steamy kiss and proceeded to make good on his promise for the next several hours.

****

Renji was jerked out of a light doze by the sound of someone knocking on the bedroom door. *"Hai."* He sat up, putting his feet on the floor just as the door opened.

"We're here, Renjiro-san," said pilot and Interpol agent Garret Bostik as he stepped into the room. He was near Renji's height with a stocky build, curly brown hair, and warm brown eyes.

Rubbing the back of his neck with fatigue, he looked at Garret. "How long?"

"About an hour. Thought I'd let you rest while I took care of the post flight and the paperwork."

"I appreciate it," he replied with a grateful smile as he grabbed his clothes and began to put them on. Without his briefs. He'd had to toss the cum soaked cotton after Trey had finally slipped into an exhausted slumber.

"How's he doing?" Garret's soulful brown eyes showed concern and uncertainty.

"He passed out after the sixth round." Renji chuckled tiredly. "So he should sleep well for a while." Finally slipping his jacket and shoes on, not bothering with his socks or tie.

"That's good." Garret's hand ran through his short brown curls nervously as Renji wrapped Trey in the red satin comforter and gathered him into his arms. "Look, Renjiro-san, I didn't say anything before, but this is highly irregular."

Renji ignored him as he carried Trey through the plane and out the door, about to walk down the stairs when Garret placed a hand on his arm and stopped him.

"This young man –"

"Trey, his name is Trey," Renji growled. He really didn't need this right now. All he wanted was to get Trey and himself home. His exhausted brain just couldn't think much further than that.

"Fine." Garret sighed. "Trey is a witness, Renjiro-san, and when Jonah doesn't deliver him to Inspector Conrad, there's going to be hell to pay."

"I'll deal with the Inspector." He jerked away from Garret, careful not to wake Trey, and walked down the stairs to his waiting car and driver.

"Dammit, Renjiro-san, you don't understand."

He rounded on Garret before his driver opened the back door to the car, his patience at an end. "No, Garret, you don't understand. For three years I have done your dirty work," he said angrily. It had only been a matter of time before all he was feeling was let out, his control snapping with fatigue and the threat of having Trey taken from him. "I have sat beside men so vile and sick there were days when I thought I would never come clean after just being near them. And the children..." He swallowed back angry tears, knowing that once started, they would never stop. "Watching those same men buy children like they were at a meat market. I can still see the faces of the ones I couldn't save. See their tears, the fear in their eyes in my dreams."

"Fuck, Renjiro-san, I...I never realized."

"You didn't want to," he snapped. "All that mattered to any of you was the Intel and the witnesses. I was collateral damage. And I took that damage willingly to see justice served. But the moment I laid eyes on Trey, well..." He looked down on that angelic face, somehow knowing that the man he held in his arms was a part of his soul. The missing part. "I won't give him up, Garret. If the Inspector needs a statement, he can come get it. But Trey stays with me." Then he gave Garret a hard, cold eyed stare. "Understand?"

Garret let out a frustrated sigh, running his hands through his curls again. "Fine, I'll try to explain the situation to the Inspector. But you know how he's going to react to this."

"I'll deal with the Inspector," he reiterated.

"Alright. You should have two, maybe three days before he shows up. It'll take that long to get the Intel from your chip processed. But after that…" He shrugged.

Renji nodded. "Don't worry, I know how to handle the Inspector." And he did. Conrad was an ass that had let the case against Rusk consume him. Renji wasn't about to let Trey or himself be two more stepping stones to further Conrad's obsession with bringing Rusk down. He'd seen enough casualties of the case, he sure as hell didn't want him or Trey added to the list.

"I certainly hope so."

"Mmmm." Trey let out a sleepy moan.

"Get your boy home, Takeda-san." Garret smiled as he started to walk away. "And good luck." He waved then went back to the plane.

"You too, my friend," he whispered, turning to find the back door of the car opened and his driver, who was also his second cousin, Hiroko Takeda, waiting patiently.

"Ah, Hiro, *arigato*." He easily switched to Japanese since Hiro spoke very little English as he carefully maneuvered himself and Trey onto the backseat. The door then closed and Hiro got in the driver's seat, starting the car and getting them on their way.

"It's good to see you home, Renjiro-sama."

"It's good to be home, Hiro."

"Mmmm, Renji, I…I don't feel so good," Trey groaned, his body beginning to tremble, face flushed and eyes glassy. This was nothing like earlier though. Renji had seen these symptoms too many times and knew the difference.

"Shit! Hiro, call Steven, tell him to meet us at the house and get the Med Room ready. It's an emergency," he ordered Hiro as he held Trey's shivering body closer.

"Yes, sir." His phone out and already getting the man on the line.

"Renji," Trey gasped, face pinched with pain. "Hurt."

"Rest easy, hana, I've got you," he soothed.

This just couldn't be happening, not now. Trey hadn't shown any signs that he was having a bad reaction to the drug. Most who did showed symptoms considerably earlier. Some, not at all, sleeping off the exhaustion and effects. But to show signs now, it wasn't good. Not good at all.

"The doctor will have everything ready, Renjiro-sama."

"*Arigato*, Hiro." He sighed with relief. But looking out the window, he could see that they were still a good fifteen minutes away. "Hang in there, baby, please. Just stay with me." He pulled Trey closer to his chest, whispering the words against Trey's sweat soaked brow.

"Ren…Renji," Trey stuttered, his teeth chattering with chills.

"I'm here, hana, I'm here."

"Scared. N…ne…need you."

Renji nearly choked on the lump in his throat. "I need you too, baby. So much."

It was the longest drive of Renji's entire life. All he could do was hold Trey's shaking body, unable to help with the fever or his pain. He had never felt so helpless. Then they were finally home, Hiro pulling up to the front of Renji's traditional Japanese home with modern touches. His close friend and at one time, college roommate, Dr. Steven Kroger was waiting on the porch. His tall frame, medium build, dark hair, and light blue eyes a welcome sight as Renji carefully got out the car with Trey.

"Details, Renji," Steven demanded as he lead Renji and his charge into the house, down a long hallway, and to the Med Room on the left. It was the room they used in case one of Marshall's guys or Renji became sick or needed any kind of medical care.

"Normal progression, nothing unusual. After going six rounds, he finally passed out. He slept for little over an hour before we got to the car," he began as he placed Trey on a regular bed surrounded with medical equipment then stood back to let Steven go to work.

"When did the symptoms start?" He stripped the comforter away, checking Trey over, and then started an IV.

"About twenty minutes ago. It came up fast, Steven, faster than I have ever seen." Renji went to the white overstuffed chair in the corner, his weak knees finally giving out.

"Mmhmm," was all Steven said as he continued to attach the various equipment to Trey and check over it all. Then, "Aha! I had a feeling that was it." He was looking at Trey's inner arm.

"What is it, Steven?" He was almost afraid to ask.

"Bastard double dosed him," Steven growled angrily. "That thought came to mind when you said the symptoms had come on fast."

"Will he be alright?" That lump was back, making it difficult to talk, his eyes unable to leave Trey's pale form on the bed. His breathing was choppy, body covered in a cold sweat as Steven continued to work on him.

"I…" Steven didn't get a chance to finish when one of the monitors began to beep. "Shit! BP is dropping."

"No!"

Through a blur of tears, Renji watched Steven move with swift assurance as he did all in his power to save Trey. Twice Trey's heart monitor flat-lined and twice Steven brought him back while Renji quietly sobbed and prayed, the only two things he could do. He was useless otherwise, hoping his faith in Steven's skills weren't unfounded. They weren't. After what felt like days but was only an hour or so, Steven had Trey stabilized and resting comfortably. But it had been a near thing.

"He's out of the woods, but I still want to keep an eye on him for the next twenty-four hours." He knelt in front of Renji, clearly exhausted, but smiling with triumph.

"*Arigato*, my friend," Renji said with a watery grin, then proceeded to break down, the events of the last day finally catching up to him as he sobbed on Steven's shoulder.

When the tears had finally stopped, Renji pulled back. "*Gomen*, didn't mean to lose it like that."

Steven got up, went to the in-suite bathroom, and came back with a warm wet washcloth, bathing Renji's face with it. "Nothing to be sorry for, *niisan*. It was a long time coming I'm thinking."

Renji laughed softly, knowing he was right. "Yeah." He took the cloth and blew his nose.

"Well, c'mon." He stood and took the cloth back, tossing it into the bathroom. "Kiko probably has the tea ready by now and you could use a cup or three."

Renji took his hand to help him out of the chair and stood also. "Tea sounds good right now, but…" He looked over at Trey, seeing all the monitors and tubes, a frown pulling his lips down.

"Don't worry, he'll be fine. And we won't be gone that long. Besides, the monitors are loud enough to be heard on the other side of the house," he assured Renji.

"Alright, but not long." He gave Trey's still form a last lingering look then followed Steven out the Med Room and to the small sitting room down the hall. Kiko Masaki, his housekeeper, had tea and a light meal prepared.

"Oh, *bocchan*, welcome home." She was small and middle-aged, her long salt and pepper hair done in a tasteful bun, a green and pink kimono gracing her slight form. She was still beautiful in a timeless way. She bowed respectfully as she greeted him in Japanese.

Renji returned the bow then gave the dear woman a hug. "It's good to be home, *obaasan*," He replied in kind since Kiko's English was very limited.

She smiled warmly, her dark eyes shining and quiet personality a balm to Renji's battered nerves. "Come, sit and eat. You both must be starved."

The two did as she bid, pulling out their chairs and sitting while Kiko served them.

"Will the young man be alright, Steven-sama?" She asked as she filled their plates with the light meal and gave them steaming cups of fragrant tea.

Able to speak fluent Japanese, Steven had no trouble responding to her question. "*Hai*, though I will stay the night just to make sure." He took a sip of his tea. "He will need plenty of rest for the next several days. Getting double dosed like that nearly killed him."

Renji growled, his blood boiling with anger. "That bastard."

"Easy, Renji, he's fine now. That's all that matters," Steven soothed.

He took a few deep breaths and a large sip of his tea to calm the rage burning inside. It helped some, but if he ever got his hands on Rusk..."Thanks, Steven, for everything."

"Hey, it's what I do." He waved a hand casually.

Shaking his head with amusement, Renji dug into his meal. Steven was a good friend and the best doctor he had ever encountered. Of course, working in the ER in Hell's Kitchen for nearly three years had not only honed Steven's skills but made them razor sharp. There wasn't much he hadn't seen and Renji thanked what powers that be that he had asked Steven to join the company all those years ago. It was the best decision he had ever made.

"I'll get your room prepared, Steven-sama," Kiko announced.

"*Arigato*, Kiko-san."

After she left, Steven turned to Renji, his light eyes probing. "All right, my friend, out with it."

Renji choked on his tea with laughter at that, accepting a napkin to clean up the small mess. "Didn't take you long."

"I was busy, now spill. And I don't mean the tea."

He did, telling Steven everything from the moment he saw Trey to when he finally laid him down on the bed in the Med Room.

"Wow, five times. I'm impressed." A dark brow rose.

"You're impressed." Renji snorted. "I didn't think I could go past three, but there's just something about him, Steven. I can't explain it, he's…"

"You feel a connection to him."

The statement and Steven's serious expression caught Renji off guard. "I…I…" he stammered.

"Renji, I've known you for over fifteen years now and never have I seen you act like this with any of your past lovers."

He sat back in his chair. "Trey's not like them. He's…different. He's…"

"There's a connection between you."

And Renji realized there was. Even after so short an acquaintance and knowing nothing about him, Renji could feel something between them. It was tenuous and fragile, but there. It made Renji feel a little giddy. He couldn't keep the bright smile from his lips as he faced the truth of that. "Yeah, I do feel a connection to him. Crazy as that may sound after knowing him for only a day."

"Hey, we go where our hearts lead us no matter how short the path might be." Steven winked. "And it's not like Miko and I had a lengthy courtship either you know."

Renji snickered at that. "Yeah, you two waited what, a whole two weeks before you got married?"

"And will be celebrating our eight year anniversary in three months," he pointed out.

"Okay, okay, but there will be some obstacles to overcome." Renji frowned, thinking about Conrad and all that entailed. Then there was Trey himself. Because of the drug, Renji had no idea what Trey's real feelings were. If he too felt a connection to Renji. The thought of what Renji felt being one sided left a sour taste in his mouth.

"Please, American doctor raised in the slums of Boston wanting to marry a relation to the Japanese nobility?" Steven rolled his eyes. "Now that was an obstacle."

"Humph, just be glad she isn't related to the royal house. Then you would have been screwed."

Steven groaned at that. "Don't go there, please. I thank your mother every chance I get that it was her own relation to the royal house that helped us to marry. Otherwise, we would have had to elope."

"Right, and Miko's father would have hunted you down and gutted you like a fish." He laughed.

"He still wants to." Steven grinned. "But he keeps it to himself now that I've provided two strapping grandsons for him to spoil rotten and pass on his Kendo knowledge."

"What a suck-up," Renji tsked, shaking his head.

Steven snorted at that. "You would too if you knew what that man could do with a katana. Kendo isn't just a sport to that man, it's a lifestyle. And I like all my parts where they're supposed to be. Firmly attached and in good working order. Miko wants another child and I can't provide that if I'm gelded."

Renji laughed again and they finished their meal, continuing to catch up until Kiko returned to let Steven know that his room was ready.

"*Arigato*, Kiko-san." Steven rose and bowed.

She returned the bow, also letting Renji know that she had set up a cot beside Trey's bed in the Med Room for him.

"You're too good to me, *obaasan*."

She smiled, placing a small hand over his heart. "Your young man is in here and here." Her fingers lightly touching his temple. "Only right you be where he is."

Renji hugged her. "I love you, *obaasan*."

"I love you too, *bocchan*." She returned the embrace then moved back. "Now shoo, you and Steven-sama are exhausted. You both need a good nap then a good meal. Go on now." She waved them both away.

He and Steven bowed low once more and left, happy smiles wreathing their faces.

"I'll check on Trey then I'm going to call Miko and follow Kiko-san's orders for some sleep," Steven said as they walked back into the Med Room. Steven went directly to Trey's side, his experienced eyes missing nothing. "His color is a lot better, so that's a good sign. And his vitals are much stronger. I'm going to keep the IV in and the monitors on though. He's doing better and I want it to stay that way."

"So he's alright?"

"He's doing well, Renji," Steven assured him. "Though he'll probably feel like shit when he finally wakes. The aftereffects of that cocktail will leave him with quite the hangover. My gentle ministrations will only add to that I'm afraid."

"Better that than the alternative." Renji frowned, heart racing at just how close he had come to really loosing Trey as he gazed at the still form on the bed.

"He's fine, *niisan*." Steven laid a comforting hand on his shoulder. "Aright?"

Renji took a couple of deep calming breaths. "Yeah, just…yeah, thanks."

"Good." He gave that shoulder a pat. "Get some sleep. You could use it." He stopped at the door. "Orgasm man," he snickered.

"I never should have told you." Renji shook his head with a wry grin.

"Hey, I said I was impressed. And as a doctor, even more so." The twinkle in his light eyes belying the serious tone of his voice.

"Go call your wife you *hentai*." Renji waved him away.

Steven went, his laughter echoing down the hall.

Renji let out a snort, smiling as he stripped. Putting his clothes in the corner chair, he went to the bathroom and turned on the light, closing the door to let a sliver of brightness through. He then climbed in the cot and pulled the covers over him, stretching out. After getting comfortable on his side facing Trey, he reached out and took one of Trey's hands in his. Thankfully, the cot was close enough to do so, feeling the warmth and steady beat of Trey's pulse. It was a comfort to Renji as he finally closed his eyes. He fell into the void as the sun went down and bathed the room in velvet darkness.

Chapter 3

It was the splitting headache and the feeling of having been run over by a fully loaded dump truck that finally pushed Trey to wakefulness. And he didn't like it one bit. Even his worst hangover had never felt this bad and that was when he had gone on a bender after his gran had died. That had definitely been a bad one. This was a thousand times worse.

He opened bleary eyes only to groan and close them again as the light from a nearby window shot daggers of pain into his pounding skull.

"Jesus," he croaked, his throat dry as a desert and his tongue three sizes too big for his mouth. He needed a Tylenol the size of Texas, water, and to empty his bladder in the worst way, though not necessarily in that order. At the moment, it was his bladder that needed the most attention though.

After much straining and grunting, Trey finally got to a sitting position with his legs over the side of the bed. His stomach and head did not appreciate the move at all.

"Damn." He rubbed his temples, noticing that there was an IV in his hand. "What the…" He was feeling so bad that anything else beside that just didn't register. But the IV made him take in his surroundings.

The entire room was done in tans and creams with what looked like bamboo mats on the hardwood floors. There was a white overstuffed chair in a corner, two pine colored nightstands on each side of the bed, a set of sliding doors that probably opened to a closet, and another door that he hoped was the bathroom. The only decoration in the room was a potted palm beside the door leading out of the bedroom and a framed kimono the color of deep ebony with bright jewel toned butterflies at the bottom that slowly trickled upward and over the right shoulder, leaving the other bare. It was beautiful, making the room simple yet elegant. Of course, it would have looked that way if not for all the medical equipment. The only one Trey recognized was the IV attached to his hand. Everything else was a mystery. Then one of the machines began to beep quite loudly, causing Trey's already pounding head to feel as if it was going to explode.

"Trey!"

His head whipped around at that to see Renji and another man almost as tall with dark brown hair, a stout build, and light blue eyes walk through the door. And it was a good thing too because the sudden movement nearly toppled Trey over and would have if Renji and the other guy hadn't been quick enough to steady him on the bed.

"Steven?"

"Its fine, Renji, his IV is done," the man, Steven, said as he checked over all the equipment. "I'll take it out now that it's done and he's finally awake."

"Alright." Renji sat on the bed at Trey's hip. "You scared me, hana."

"Uh, Renji, what's going on?" His mind was a little fuzzy about what happened on the plane and since he felt like three kinds of shit, remembering didn't seem all that important at the moment. "And who is this guy?"

The man, Steven, chuckled. "I'm Steven Kroger, a doctor and long time friend of Renji's," he explained as he took out the IV then bandaged the entry site. He then started to take off all the chest monitors that Trey, in his own pain filled world, hadn't noticed until Steven began to remove them.

"Oh, uh, okay."

"How are you feeling?" Steven asked, checking him over, taking his blood pressure, and such.

Trey snorted. "Like I've been beaten with a baseball bat."

"And the head probably doesn't feel much better." He chuckled with sympathy.

"No, it doesn't."

"I can help with that." He reached into his pants pocket and pulled out a white bottle of pills, turning to Renji. "Can you get Trey a glass of water?"

"Sure." Renji carefully got off the bed then went to the bathroom, coming back quickly with a small filled cup.

Steven took two white pills out the bottle and handed them to Trey. "It's only Motrin, but these will help with the headache and soreness."

Renji sat down easy again and gave Trey the cup. "Sip slowly, hana."

Smiling with gratitude, Trey took the pills and sipped the cool water. It felt great going down his parched throat. "Thanks."

"Now that you're up, I'll have Kiko prepare you some tea and soup. You need more on your stomach than just water and Motrin," Steven told him with a warm smile, taking the empty cup and placing it on the nightstand.

"Yeah, I could eat a little. But if it's not too much trouble, I really need to use the bathroom." He felt his cheeks heat because he knew he was going to need help. No way was he making it to the bathroom under his own power. Hell, he wasn't even sure he could stand on his own much less walk.

Not that he had to because Renji gently picked him up and cradled him close. "Go ahead Steven, I'll take care of Trey."

Those light eyes twinkled merrily, causing Trey's face to heat again. "No doubt," he smirked. "And it'll give you two a chance to talk as well." With a wink, he left.

"You don't really have to carry me you know." Though secretly glad he was. Trey felt safe with Renji for some unknown reason and needed the closeness. As it stood, Renji was the only person he knew in a strange and unfamiliar place. It wasn't a feeling Trey was used to. Nor was it one he particularly liked. His fuzzy memories of what happened after being taken to Renji's bed certainly didn't help either.

"Trey." The way Renji said his name made Trey look up and see, really see, Renji. His handsome face was drawn and tight with dark circles under those mesmerizing eyes giving Trey the impression of missed sleep. His jet hair was mussed and his clothes were wrinkled. But it was the haunting look in those black diamond eyes that gave Trey pause.

"What's wrong, Renji?"

"Let me help you with this and I'll explain everything, alright?"

"Sure." A hundred questions raced through Trey's pounding head as Renji put him down in front of the commode. He wobbled a bit, getting a steady hand from Renji, and then did his business, washing his hands after.

All done, Renji picked him up again and took him back to the bed, covering his nakedness that he had just noticed in the bathroom with a tan and cream comforter. He plumped up some pillows behind Trey's head and shoulders so he could sit up comfortably then pulled over the corner chair and sat.

"What is it, Renji?" He asked as Renji took his hand and laced their fingers together. The way Renji was acting had him worried. The familiarity also had him feeling a bit uncomfortable. What the hell had he done on that plane?

"You were sick, Trey. Rusk gave you a double dose of that poison and you had a bad reaction to it. Worse than an overdose. In fact, you nearly died…twice." He saw Renji swallow with difficulty, now knowing why those dark eyes looked so haunted. "If it wasn't for Steven, you would have died."

"Jesus." Trey closed his eyes as he tried to process that news. He couldn't, he just couldn't wrap his mind around the fact that he had almost died. And that was probably a good thing. He was alive and that's what mattered most. Though it did explain why he felt like he's gone several rounds with a prize fighter.

"Trey?"

That softly concerned voice made Trey open his eyes to find Renji looking at him, those black eyes full of worry. It made Trey smile and he squeezed Renji's hand, glad he hadn't pulled away. He needed the life line. "I'm fine, darlin'. Just a little shocked is all."

Renji let out a breath, giving Trey a wan smile in return and brought Trey's hand up to kiss his knuckles. Those warm lips gave Trey a small jolt of surprise. Surprise that he liked it despite this man being basically a stranger. A hot as hell stranger, but one nonetheless. He was also surprised that he didn't want to let Renji's hand go. Yeah, those pills really needed to hurry and take his pain away so he could concentrate on getting his memories back. Or at least, the important parts.

"And it certainly explains why I feel like I got hit by a bus." His attempt to lighten the mood got a lukewarm response. "You alright, Renji?"

"I…" He rose, letting Trey's hand slip from his, and started to pace with angry strides. "I couldn't do anything, hana. I just sat in that chair, scared out my mind, while Steven did everything to save you."

"Hey, hey." Trey stopped him before he could go any further. "Come here." He patted the bed beside his hip. Renji huffed out a breath and came over. Trey placed his hand on Renji's arm as he sat down. "If it wasn't for you bringing me here, I would be dead." That made Trey go cold inside because it was the truth. If Renji hadn't brought him…he let the thought go.

"But –"

"No buts," he interrupted. "I'm alive because of you, Renji, so don't you dare think otherwise."

Trey watched that big body tremble, the black eyes looking haunted. "I just found you, hana, I can't lose you now," he choked.

"Come here, darlin'." Without thinking, he held his arms out and Renji came willingly, his shoulders shaking with apparent emotion. Trey held him close, the feel of that warm body too much. Trey let go, giving vent to his pent up feelings, the tears falling like diamonds into Renji's ebony hair.

Tears finally spent, Trey let out a contented sigh. It felt so good to be held, to feel another's warmth next to his.

With his gran gone these past five years and no lover to speak of, Trey had missed the touch of another, that feeling of closeness. And with Renji, for some unknown reason, he wanted that closeness and more. Odd considering that he barely knew the man, but there was just something about him, something that Trey couldn't name that drew him in and wanted so much to be near. It scared Trey, that connection he felt. But when Renji made to move away, Trey stopped him.

"Stay, please, just a little longer?"

Pulling back, Renji smiled, his eyes now clear as he reached out to wipe away the lingering wetness from Trey's cheeks. "I'm not too heavy?"

Trey took his hand, the warmth and strength in it a comfort to his battered emotions. "No."

"For ever how long you need me, hana." He then wrapped his arms around Trey's waist, laying his head on Trey's chest. "Better?"

"Much, thank-you." His own arms wrapped around Renji's shoulders and held him tight. It felt as if he belonged there, secure and safe in those strong arms. It was a new feeling for Trey. One he really didn't want to examine too closely for the moment. Later. When he wasn't so raw.

"You're more than welcome, hana."

There was that word again, some kind of name that Trey had noticed Renji calling him. "What does that mean? Hana?"

Renji chuckled, the sound vibrating against Trey's naked chest. "It's Japanese for flower."

"Flower?" *Renji had been calling him flower?*

Pulling back a bit, Renji looked at him with a grin and slightly pink cheeks. "Yes, well, with that sunny gold hair, rosy red lips, and petal soft skin, hana—flower—came to mind."

Trey blinked with surprise, feeling his own cheeks heat at such a sweet compliment. "Oh."

"You're not offended are you?" His grin slowly turned to a frown with uncertainty.

"No," he said hastily. "Not at all. It's just that, well, I've never had anyone but my gran call me by an endearment before." He smiled, suddenly feeling kind of shy. "I…I like it."

Renji rose up and gave him a sweet peck on the lips. "I'm glad." Then he lay back down on Trey's chest and snuggled close.

Trey was still wearing a goofy grin when Dr. Steven came back in with a loaded push cart, his own bright smile warm and sunny.

"I see that even after Renji's talk you can still smile." He pushed the cart toward the nightstand and parked it there.

He felt his face heat again at that as he heard a muffled chuckle from Renji. "Uh, yeah." Not getting into that territory yet. "So, what's the soup of the day?"

"Chicken broth, lightly seasoned, with a nice herbal tea containing a good dollop of honey. And if your blanket there would kindly move, I could serve it to you," he laughed.

"Not very subtle, is he?" Renji snorted, but reluctantly moved back to the chair, leaving it close to the bed.

Trey felt the loss of Renji's warmth and comforting weight keenly. He wasn't sure which he disliked more. Not having that comfort or wanting it back. He really needed to get a grip. Despite these two men saving his life, he still didn't know them. He felt kind of bad about not fully trusting them. However, he had been kidnapped, sold off, and nearly murdered. Trust was earned.

"I'm a doctor, we don't do subtle," he retorted, taking a tray from the bottom of the cart and placed it on Trey's lap. He then put a bowl with steaming soup and a cup full of fragrant tea on the tray. "Drink as much of the soup and tea as you can. It'll help to get your strength back," he instructed after handling Trey a spoon. He then turned to Renji. "And when he feels up to it, a good soak would do wonders for the soreness."

Renji nodded. "I'll take him later this evening. It'll relax him enough to help him sleep."

"Good." He prepared cups of tea for himself and Renji as Trey began to sip his soup. It was quite tasty and the tea had a wonderful flavor. "I don't want to put anything stronger than Motrin in his system right now." He handed Renji a full cup. "It's been well over twenty-four hours, so the drug is out of his system. Still, after what he went through, I'd rather not risk it. And soaking the soreness away would be better for him anyhow."

Hearing twenty-four hours got Trey's attention. "I've been here that long?"

"Longer actually," Renji replied. "A little over two days. You were exhausted, so you slept a full day."

Trey put his tea cup down. "Two days." His eyes widened as the ramifications of that sank in. Of how close to death he had really come. And how much these two men must have sacrificed to keep him alive. Now he really felt bad for not trusting them. He closed his eyes with a groan.

"Trey?"

He opened his eyes and looked over at Renji, his handsome face showing worry. Trey now knew why he seemed so haggard, so run down. He tentatively reached out and grabbed Renji's hand. "Thank-you."

Renji's cheeks pinkened, his smile bright as he gave Trey's fingers a gentle squeeze. "Anytime, hana."

Trey couldn't help the happiness, or the heat, that blossomed on his face at hearing Renji call him hana. It made his heart race and joy to fizz in his veins. It felt good, real good. Which was crazy. This kind of chemistry, connection, just wasn't possible. Not after so short an acquaintance. Right?

Finishing his tea and most of the soup, Trey lay back with a replete sigh. He felt better than he had when he first awoke. Much better now that the pounding in his head had stopped.

"All done?" Steven came over and took the tray off Trey's lap.

"Yeah, thanks." A huge yawn overtook him. "For everything, Doctor." With a full stomach and pain free head, his eye lids were getting heavy. He was so tired.

"You're quite welcome."

"Sleepy, hana?"

Trey just nodded, a warm lethargy stealing over his body as he was barely able to keep his eyes open.

"A nap will do him good," he heard Doc Steven say. "And you as well, Renji."

"Yeah, a couple hours sounds good."

The clink of dishes sounded distant to Trey as someone, the Doc probably, moved away from his bedside. "Do I need to bring the cot?"

"I think I'll manage," came Renji's dry reply.

Steven laughed softly. "Alright, I'll wake you in a few hours." Then Trey heard Steven walk away.

"Let's get you more comfortable, hana."

Trey cracked his eyes open to see Renji hovering over him then helping him lay flat, a fat pillow under his head. "Mmm, thanks. Stay." That was all he could get out as his eyes closed again. He wanted, needed, the warmth and safety of Renji close to him. He couldn't explain it and was too sleepy to try at the moment.

"I'm not going anywhere, hana." Renji then climbed in beside Trey and snuggled close, putting his head on Trey's chest.

Lifting a heavy hand, Trey put it on Renji's back, letting out a deep sigh as Renji's warmth and solid comfort followed him into peaceful slumber.

****

Renji came awake slowly to the feel of Trey plastered to his back and Trey's arm securely around his waist, his even breathing blowing small puffs of air against Renji's neck. He had never felt as content as he did at that moment.

He lay there a bit longer then carefully turned to face Trey, not wanting to wake him yet and just stared. Trey was so beautiful. Unable to resist, he ran his fingertips softly over high cheekbones and down to a square jaw where a light dusting of gold stubble was starting. He then traced full red lips and a straight nose, moving his way up to dark gold brows and a smooth forehead.

"Do you know what you do to me, Trey? And I know absolutely nothing about you. Your hometown, education, even a last name."

"I'm from Gastonia, North Carolina, I'm an arts history major, and it's Morrison." Those luminous aquamarine eyes opened and a sweet smile stretched ruby lips as Renji was momentarily shocked. He recovered quickly enough and chuckled.

That explained the delicious accent. Renji knew a couple guys from North Carolina. They didn't have the twang Trey did though. It was cute as hell.

"Didn't mean to wake you." His fingers continued their exploratory journey, making a slow path down Trey's neck, chest, and stomach until he reached a very hard cock.

Trey jerked his hips away, cheeks bright pink. "I...sorry." He kept himself close, but just out of reach of Renji's questing fingers.

Once again, Renji had moved too soon. "No, hana. I'm the one who's sorry." He brought his hand back up, making sure his touch was gentle and non-sexual. "I feel a very strong connection to you. But I keep forgetting we're still getting to know each other. I didn't mean to push."

"I..." Trey let out a deep breath. "It's not one sided, Renji. I feel a connection as well. I just...I just don't understand all this. Why you saved me, brought me here. If what I'm feeling is real. Or because of what happened on the plane," he said softly.

"Ah. You remembered, huh?"

That gold head gave a slight nod, gem bright eyes looking down and cheeks cherry red in obvious embarrassment.

Reaching out, Renji lifted Trey's chin with a finger. "You have nothing to be ashamed of, hana."

"But –"

"Listen to me," he cut Trey off. "You were the victim of a very cruel man. He knew exactly what would happen. I knew as well and tried to make sure the experience was anything but sordid. That any memories you came away with would be good ones."

"They are," Trey replied hastily. "It's just…feeling so out of control like that," he paused, frowning with a shake of his head. "That wasn't me, Renji," he whispered. "That's not the kind of person I am. It's why I'm still a…why I haven't been with a guy yet," he stammered. "I was even having second thoughts about going out with John Ross Carter after he asked me."

Renji couldn't help but smile. His hana was so sweet. "I know that wasn't you, hana," he assured Trey. "And I find it admirable that you don't want to jump in the sack with just anyone."

"You don't think I'm being too picky? Or...or girly?"

"Not at all," he said with conviction. "It just means you value yourself and want your partner to feel the same."

Aquamarine eyes widened in surprise. "How..."

"A lot of guys might not say it, but they feel like you do, Trey." Renji chuckled. "Sex isn't just getting off to some of us. In fact, my first time was with an older man who made me feel like I was giving him a gift. He treated me with respect and showed me that there was more to sex than just an orgasm."

"It's not easy to find someone like that," Trey muttered. "College guys...well," he trailed off.

"I completely understand, hana," Renji said with a smile. "Freedom and hormones is a potent combination."

"Unfortunately," he grimaced. "Still, I'm not ungrateful. You helped me, rescued me. I just…I just want to understand why. Why did you save me?"

Renji knew this question would come. He just didn't think it would be so soon. Letting out a deep sigh, he answered, "Because the moment I laid eyes on you, I felt something."

"You did?" Trey's voice was soft.

"This is new to me as well, Trey," Renji stated. "I've never brought anyone to my private home before. Never felt the need to. But seeing you there." He shook his head, leaving for the moment the details of Trey's appearance at the auction. "I knew if I didn't save you, didn't bring you with me, I would lose something very precious. Something I would never find again." He tentatively touched Trey's cheek with gentle fingers. "I couldn't ignore that. It was too strong. Too right."

Gem bright eyes searched Renji's, seeming to bore down to his very soul. He let Trey look, holding nothing back. He left himself totally open, wanting Trey to see he was truthful and trustworthy.

"You really believe that, don't you," Trey said with wonder.

"With every fiber of my being." He nodded.

A shy smile curved cherry lips. "I…feel something too," Trey whispered. "And it's definitely more than gratitude." His cheeks flushed rose.

"I'm honored, hana." He grinned, joy bubbling through his system. "And we'll go at your pace, alright? I don't want to push. Make you feel pressured."

"Okay," he agreed with a sunny smile. "But…well…" He bit his lip, expression one of uncertainty.

"What is it, hana?"

"Could…could you…kiss me?"

Like he could resist those wide, aqua eyes. That earnest look. Those lush lips.

"Anytime you want, hana." Renji's voice was raspy as he leaned in and gently laid his lips against Trey's.

He made sure the pressure was light, just enough to glide his lips back and forth before putting a bit more pressure down. Trey's eyes slid closed, a breathy moan escaping. Renji caught it, reaching out with his tongue to slide it over Trey's parted lips. He gasped at the contact, giving Renji better access to his mouth. It was all the encouragement Renji needed to deepen the kiss. Trey went pliant against Renji, letting him lead despite wanting to plunder that sweet mouth.

"Jesus," Trey gasped after coming up for air. He was panting a bit, lips slightly swollen. "That was better than I remembered."

"Yeah?" Renji chuckled, arousal gripping him hard.

"Oh, yeah." Trey nodded, his own arousal poking Renji in the stomach.

"Good." Renji leaned in, giving those sweet lips another quick kiss then pulled away. "I have a surprise for you." He got out of bed, going to the bathroom and getting two white bath robes.

"What kind of surprise?" Trey sat up with difficulty, his face showing the strain.

"Here, let me help." He came to Trey's side, giving him a hand as he aided Trey to a sitting position with his feet on the floor. "Well, if I told you, it wouldn't be a surprise, now would it?" He grabbed one of the robes and helped Trey into it, then stripped off his wrinkled clothes and put the other robe on.

Trey snorted at that. "You know, I feel better than I did earlier, but why does everything hurt?"

Renji noticed the wrinkled brow, his eyes beginning to cloud with pain. "Head still hurt?"

"Among other things." A crooked smile lifted the corner of his mouth as he rubbed the back of his neck. The robe tented slightly.

Seeing his discomfort, Renji took two pills from the bottle Steven left and gave them to Trey. He then went back to the bathroom for a fresh cup of water. "Here, the Motrin and my surprise will help. With the soreness at least." He winked.

Trey took the cup, swallowing the pills and water with a grateful smile. "Thanks." He handed the cup back to Renji where he put it beside the pill bottle.

"Come on, hana." He helped Trey to stand then picked him up and cradled him close.

Trey laughed, wrapping an arm around Renji's neck. "I'm not an invalid, you know."

"I know, it's just…" He let out a breath. "I almost lost you, hana, so indulge me, alright?"

He looked down into Trey's aquamarine eyes and knew Trey had to see just how scared he had been. Renji couldn't help it really, he had seen firsthand just how fragile the thread between life and death really was and how quickly it could be cut. That fear made him a wee bit possessive where Trey was concerned, but it wasn't something he could shut off. It felt as if he let Trey out of his sight for more than a minute, then something might happen to him and that was what really scared Renji the most.

"I'm fine, Renji." Trey's other hand came to rest against his chest.

"I know, but I need to do this, hana."

"Alright," Trey sighed. "But if you throw out your back, don't whine to me." Gem bright eyes twinkled with merriment.

Renji just chuckled. "If I do, you can give me a backrub." He then walked out the room and down the hall to a window lined corridor on the way to the east side of the house.

"That sounds fair," Trey smirked. "Though you really don't need to throw your back out for that."

"Hana," Renji groaned as he stepped into a side room with white and green tiled walls, three wooden benches, and four gleaming shower fixtures. "If you were ready and weren't still recovering, I'd do such wicked things to you."

"What kind of wicked things?"

He put Trey down gently on one of the wooden benches. "Things that would keep us in my king size bed for days."

A becoming blush heated Trey's cheeks. "Then I guess I better hurry and get well then, huh?"

"Get well, yes, hurry at it, no." He smiled. "As much as I want you Trey, we both know you aren't ready for more than kissing and touching. Nor am I about to rush this." Trey nodded, letting out a deep breath. "I nearly lost you. I won't risk your recovery because of raging libidos.

Your health is more important. And besides, we have plenty of time."

Trey peered up at Renji and huffed out another breath. "You're right. I'm not ready. And despite what happened on the plane, I would much rather get to know you physically without the drugs." Then a mischievous grin wreathed his face. "But just so you know, blue balls could be a serious possibility if we wait too long." His finger wagging.

"I'm not worried about blue balls, hana." He laughed as he helped Trey out of his robe then went to turn on one of the showers. The kiss they shared let Renji know Trey was truly alright, but now that he thought about it, Renji would have to be extra careful. Despite the fact Trey wasn't ready for anything of a carnal nature, their flirting aside, letting his passions run wild while Trey was recuperating just wasn't an option. It wouldn't do to have Trey suffer a setback because Renji couldn't control himself. He needed to be more vigilant until Trey got his strength back. "Give the water a minute to heat while I get the bath supplies." Trey nodded as he walked over to a large cabinet.

"Thanks, Renji. I feel like I haven't bathed in weeks," Trey said as Renji got out two large fluffy white towels, a loofah, a large washcloth, a bottle of spice scented hair and body wash, and three rubber duckies. He then grabbed a large wooden pail and put everything but the towels in it then closed the cabinet door.

"You were running a high fever and sweat a great deal, so that probably has a lot to do with that feeling," he replied.

"Could be." He watched Trey look around as he put the pail of supplies next to Trey's hip then Renji took off his robe and laid it over Trey's. "This bathroom looks a lot like the one that my gym has back home."

"Does it?" The water had steam coming from it so Renji adjusted it to the right temp.

"Yeah, but this one's nicer. Cleaner too."

Renji smiled at that. "I should hope so considering that this is part of my home." He went to Trey and helped him to stand, making sure he was steady on his feet.

"Well, just as long as you don't have a gym on the other side of those doors." His thumb pointed to the swinging doors on their right side. "I should be fine. Getting on a tread mill would not be a good idea at this moment." He laughed then groaned when Renji carefully walked him under the warm spray. "Damn, that feels so good."

Renji made sure he was balanced, grinning at his response. "Stand there a minute while I get the loofah and soap."

Trey nodded then slowly turned to face the wall, his hands braced against it as he let the water sluice down his head and back. Renji had to choke on a moan at the sight. Creamy pale skin shiny with moisture, sunny hair turning to dark gold, eyes closed and face showing happy pleasure. Renji wanted so much to bury himself between those perfect ass cheeks and feel the water beating down on them both as he made Trey scream with rapture. But no, he couldn't. Trey wasn't ready, was still recovering, and Renji needed to remember that. Unfortunately, his cock didn't seem to understand. It was hard and leaking and his balls ached with tightness.

Quickly turning, he went to the bench and got the soap and loofah, needing a little distance. And a couple deep breaths to center himself. If he didn't, then putting soapy hands all over Trey's delicious body just might drive him mad. But then, seeing Trey face front, the water running down a well formed chest and abs, an Apollo's belt that begged for a tongue, and a beautiful cut cock in its nest of burnished curls, well, maybe he was already mad.

Taking another deep breath and praying for strength, Renji walked over and took Trey into his arms, glad that his hands were full to keep them from roaming but still needing to feel that slick skin next to his. It was a small concession to what he really wanted, but he needed it nonetheless. Otherwise, his mind would crack with lust.

"Do you usually wear a sword to the shower or are you just happy to see me?" Trey chuckled as his arms wrapped around Renji's waist and he put his head on Renji's chest.

Renji could feel his cheeks heat but there was no point in denying what he felt. Hell, Trey could feel it poking him in the stomach. "Hana, I've had this *sword* since the moment I laid eyes on you." It also felt good to hold Trey like this. He fit so perfectly in Renji's arms, like he was made to be there, his head nestled under Renji's chin.

Trey pulled back to look up at Renji, those gorgeous eyes a little troubled. "I…" He stopped then looked down. "Renji, I…"

Whatever was on Trey's mind, Renji could see he was having some difficulty. "What is it, hana?" His stomach knotted a bit with worry.

Trey took a deep breath and let it out. "I…I've never felt like this before, Renji."

The air Renji didn't know he was holding came out slowly, a joyous grin curving his lips. "Like what, hana?"

"I'm not sure because a part of me doesn't believe that this is real and yet another part really wishes that it is." His voice sounded so small, so scared.

"You think this is a side effect of the drug, don't you?" Renji frowned, his joy of a moment before turning to fear.

"No!" Trey quickly looked up, his cheeks flaming. "Lord, no." His head shook in the negative, water droplets flying. "I mean yeah, it brought us together, but the way I feel now, that's natural, not drugs."

"Alright," Renji nodded with confusion. "But something's bothering you and I want to help if I can."

Trey gave him a shy smile. "Let's wash as we talk, otherwise we're going to look like the prune twins."

Renji chuckled softly. "Here, turn around and I'll wash your back." The good thing about this conversation, his erection was finally going down. For the moment, at least.

Trey turned as Renji poured the soap onto the loofah, putting the bottle on the floor within easy reach then began to wash Trey's creamy skin.

"When I was seven, my parents were killed by a drunk driver on their way home from celebrating their sixth wedding anniversary."

The shock of that statement made Renji stop. "Damn, hana, I'm so sorry."

"Thank you." Even though Trey was an adult, Renji could still hear the sadness in Trey's voice. He continued washing. "Because my gran was up in years, she had to share custody with my Uncle Bob, gran's eldest son, or the courts would have put me in the system. He agreed, of course, so I went to live with them."

"You had no other family?" Renji ran the loofah over every dip and plane, wanting Trey to know that he was being taken care of then he had Trey turn so Renji could wash his front.

"Yeah, but according to gran, mom's family didn't approve of my dad, so they refused to keep in touch. I don't think they even came to my parent's funeral." His head was cocked to the side in contemplation. "Anyway, my years with gran and Uncle Bob were great. Then when I was fifteen, Uncle Bob was diagnosed with lung cancer. He died eight months later."

"Hana," Renji sighed with sadness, but Trey didn't seem to hear.

"Three years later, gran had a massive stroke in her sleep. It was quick and painless according to her doctor."

"Oh, Trey…" He was stopped from saying anything else by a hand on his chest and aquamarine eyes swimming with tears.

"Everyone I've ever cared about has died." Those tears spilled over and mingled with the water from the shower. "That's why I've never had a lover or a boyfriend. I've been so afraid to get close to anyone, to care about anyone. Hell, that date with John Ross Carter was just a means to an end. But when I look at you, talk to you, touch you…" He choked back a sob. "I feel that connection and it scares me, Renji. It scares me that if I let you in, something bad will happen and I'll lose you before I even get the chance to know you."

Renji gathered Trey close as he broke down, his heart aching for the sad young boy Trey had been and the lonely young man Trey had grown into. "None of us know what our destinies are, hana, but to live in fear is no way to live."

"I know." His voice was muffled by Renji's chest, his tears finally spent. "And nearly meeting my Maker hasn't exactly helped either."

Renji grimaced at that, not needing the reminder of how close he had come to loosing Trey forever. "I too have fears, hana, but nothing scared me more than almost loosing you."

Trey pulled back with a questioning frown. "Why? We barely know each other."

"That's true, but like I told you earlier, I felt a connection. It was as if something inside me said if I didn't take this chance, I'd never get another one."

Those shining eyes stared straight into Renji's dark ones, his look intense and searching. "Doesn't that scare you, taking a chance like that?"

"Of course it does." He nodded. "But never taking that chance and not knowing what we could have scares me more."

He watched as Trey let that sink in, a myriad of emotions passing across his face until he finally let out a deep breath, eyes steady and gem bright. "If these last few days have taught me anything, it's that your life can change on a dime no matter your circumstances and…"

"And?" Renji waited with baited breath until a shy grin wreathed Trey's face, his cheeks bright pink.

"Some opportunities shouldn't be passed up."

"Do you mean that, Trey?" He cupped Trey's wet cheek tenderly.

Trey nuzzled his palm. "The fear's still there, but, I'm so tired of it, Renji. So tired of being lonely, of being alone."

"You're not alone, hana." He brought Trey closer until their lips were a breath apart. "And while I can't promise that nothing will ever happen to me in the future, I can promise that everyday we're together, you'll never regret taking a chance on us."

"What doesn't kill you makes you stronger." He smiled. "It was my gran's favorite saying."

"And appropriate."

"Yeah."

Renji didn't let him say more as he laid claim to those moist lips, his tongue plunging deep, tasting every inch of Trey's mouth and wanting more.

"Damn, darlin'," Trey panted when Renji finally let them both up for air.

Renji chuckled huskily, knowing exactly how Trey felt. Hell, he was sure Trey could feel it poking him in the stomach again. "Let's finish so I can show you my surprise." *And before I completely lose my sanity.*

Trey nodded as Renji got the bottle of soap. "Turn around and I'll wash your hair."

He did so as Renji poured a good dollop into his palm and started up a rich lather in Trey's hair.

"Mmmm, feels good."

It felt good on Renji's end as well. Trey's hair was like burnished gold now, the wet locks heavy and soft, reaching well past Trey's shoulders. Renji let his fingers wander through the soap saturated strands, massaging Trey's scalp.

"You have such beautiful hair, hana." He finally rinsed the soap away to show shiny dark gold.

"I've been meaning to get it cut. I don't usually wear it so long."

"Absolutely not!" Renji said adamantly. "A trim, yes, but never cut it."

Trey looked over his shoulder at Renji, cheeks pink. "You like it long?"

"Very much so, yes." He placed a quick kiss on Trey's stained cheek. "It suits you."

He turned to face forward in Renji's arms, wiping the water from his face and slicking his hair back. "Alright, but not too long. Don't want to get mistaken for a girl." He gave Renji a flirty wink.

Renji snorted. "Trust me, hana, a girl you are not. Long hair or short."

It was true. Even with the delicate coloring and slight build, Trey couldn't be mistaken for anything other than male. A very beautiful male, but definitely male.

He placed another quick kiss on those tempting lips. "Rest a minute while I finish." He guided Trey back to the bench.

"Take your time, darlin'." He smiled at Renji. "Not often I get to watch a hot guy shower." His golden brows waggled up and down.

Renji shook his head with a grin, getting the soap and loofah and beginning to wash. "Seen many men wash, hana?" Not that he was overly concerned considering that Trey was with him now, but he didn't like the thought that Trey enjoyed watching or even looking at other men. It was a possessive and not very mature feeling. Then again, he'd never felt like this before.

"Hardly." Trey snorted. "Most of the men I've seen were at my local gym and straight. Not very safe or smart to ogle a straight man." He chuckled dryly. "They take offense to such things."

"No doubt." Renji finished with his body then poured more soap for his hair.

"That smells so good." Trey's eyes were closed as he inhaled deeply. "I can't place the scent though." His eyes opened to look at Renji questionly.

"It's called *Sandalwood Spice*. My mother's pet company makes it."

"Pet company?"

Renji smiled. "Yeah, the company was originally an apothecary shop owned and run by my great-grandmother.

When she passed away, she left it to my mother who expanded it to include herbal teas, candles, aromatherapy, and various soaps." He rinsed his hair then turned off the water and went to Trey. "She had the scent developed for me as a birthday present. The same for my two younger brothers and my father."

"That's pretty cool."

"Yeah." He nodded. "You ready for your surprise?"

"Sure." Trey smiled, but Renji could see that he was getting a bit tired. The drooping shoulders and heavy lidded eyes were a dead giveaway.

"We won't stay long, hana." He grabbed the towels and handed them to Trey to hold. "You need to eat and rest." He then picked Trey up and cradled him close.

"So, this surprise, you're not planning on having your wicked way with me, are you?" Trey leered suggestively.

Renji laughed. His hana was such a little flirt. And Renji loved it. "Not this time, no." Trey pouted at that as Renji walked carefully over to the swinging doors. "Don't worry, hana, once you're ready on all counts, I'll have a lot more than my wicked way with you. And you will definitely need your strength."

"However long that will take," he grumbled into Renji's chest.

Renji put his back to the doors. "Now that you're up and about, you'll be getting better daily. You don't have to push yourself so hard, hana."

"I know." He sighed. "It's just frustrating is all. I'm not used to being so weak. Or so tempted." He smiled up at Renji with pinkened cheeks.

Renji placed a tender kiss on those lush lips. "It'll be worth the wait, hana, I promise. Now close your eyes."

"I'll hold you to that," he said as he closed his eyes and laid his head on Renji's chest.

Renji just shook his head and grinned. Who knew his shy hana was such a charmer? It boded well as they continued to learn about the other. It also gave Renji a peek into Trey's sassy personality. Backing carefully through the doors, steam and warmth enveloped them both as soon as the doors closed behind them.

"Wow, we in a sauna? It's kind of hot in here," Trey commented the further Renji walked into the room. He then stopped when he came to a stone bench.

"See for yourself."

He watched those aquamarine eyes open and widen as Trey gasped with surprise. "Holy shit!"

"Like it do you?" Renji chuckled as he put Trey down gently on the bench, continuing to watch as Trey seemed to take in everything at once.

Trey nodded with wonder. "This place is truly amazing, Renji."

"It's been one of my favorite projects." He grinned proudly.

"With all this stone and the plants, it looks like you carved this place right out of a mountain. And that is the biggest Jacuzzi I have ever seen." Trey pointed to the bubbling water.

Renji laughed, absolutely delighted that Trey liked his surprise, but Renji was going to surprise Trey even further. "I definitely wanted that cave feeling, even with the small skylights." He looked up, pointing out five small windows in the ceiling. "And that's not a Jacuzzi; it's a natural hot spring."

Those gem bright eyes widened even further. "Are you serious?"

"Of course." He chuckled. "Japan is riddled with them. And after my father bought this place for me as a college graduation gift, I wanted this room to reflect the hot springs origins."

"You nailed it." Trey's laugh was filled with wonder. "If I didn't know that we were in a house, this room would make me think that we were in some underground cave."

"Exactly." Renji smiled.

"That smell, is that from the water?" Trey's head was up, sniffing the moist air.

Renji nodded. "It's the minerals and will help you recover, so breathe as deeply of the steam as you can." He helped Trey to his feet. "Damn, forgot the duckies."

"I was wondering what those were for," Trey replied as Renji lead him to a handrail at the top of a set of steps that lead down into the bubbling water.

"Can you stand here a second while I go get them?"

"I'll be fine, go ahead."

With a gentle pat to Trey's shoulder, Renji raced from the room and through the swinging doors. He grabbed the duckies and hurried back, chucking them in the water before returning to Trey's side.

"Can't have a good soak without duckies." He grinned as he helped Trey down into the   steamy water.

"Oh man, damn that feels awesome." Trey's eyes closed in bliss as he sank down slowly in the bubbling water to his neck.

Watching Trey's enjoyment had Renji chuckling. Then Trey got to his back and floated, sighing deeply with pleasure. He continued to watch, Trey's lustrous hair floating around his head like a dark gold halo, creamy skin flushed with warmth, a happy smile wreathing his angelic face. He was the most beautiful man Renji had ever seen.

"No one's ever looked at me the way you do, Renji."

Renji blinked, Trey's voice breaking him out of his musings as Trey stood, water sluicing down that lean body causing Renji to groan. "How's that, hana?"

"Like you want to devour me." His smile was shy as he came to stand in front of Renji.

He gently took Trey's face between his hands, bringing them chest to chest. "Devouring you is just one of the many things I will enjoy doing to and with you, hana." He then took those full red lips in a tender kiss that quickly became heated. Trey's arms wrapped around his neck as Renji deepened the kiss, his tongue dueling with Trey's, his hands moving over shoulders and back to cup that perfect ass.

"Mmmm," Trey whimpered.

That whimper caused Renji to moan deeply in response because it not only signaled Trey's surrender, but it also was Renji's cue to stop. He pulled back with great reluctance, heart pounding and body aching. Trey's eyes were closed, lips kiss swollen, and face dreamy. Renji wanted nothing more than to grab Trey and make love to him all night long.

"You want to devour me again."

"More than I want my next breath." His hand traced the contours of Trey's flushed cheeks. "But I won't risk your health, Trey. Or push for more than you're ready for. You're more important to me than a moment's pleasure."

Trey smiled at that. "You're important to me as well, Renji." His hands stayed on Renji's chest, the touch light. "So, well, I know you said no pressure, but…" He bit his lower lip, giving Renji an uncertain expression.

"What is it, hana?"

He took a deep breath. "Would it be okay if I touched you?"

His hana was going to kill him. Of course, what sane man would say no? Holding back a groan, Renji croaked, "More than okay."

Those elegant fingers were trembling slightly as they began a tentative exploration of Renji's chest. The look on Trey's face was one of wonder.

"So soft, yet hard," he whispered, continuing down, his touch getting firmer and bolder. When he reached Renji's waist, he looked up.

In for a penny. Renji nodded, his body on fire and his balls aching.

The moment those hands glided over Renji's hard shaft, he nearly came. A shuddering groan was forced out. Trey was tentative at first, his fingers running over Renji's aching length lightly. His touch then got bolder as those fingers and palm wrapped around Renji's cock and began to pump.

"My memory is a bit fuzzy about a few specific details after we went to your cabin on the plane." Trey came in closer, his breath ghosting over Renji's nipple, causing Renji to gasp and his cock to jump in Trey's hand.

"I still can't believe you remember most of it." He was trying to hold himself in check and not lose it, Trey's little admission giving some respite, but it was a battle he wasn't going to win.

"Most, yes." Trey nodded. "But what stands out so clearly was how gentle you were and how you let me explore. Like you're doing now. I had never touched a man before, was always too scared and unsure. But you made my first time special, Renji. You made me feel special no matter the circumstances of the moment."

Renji was moved by that. "I knew you were inexperienced and I wasn't about to let some drug take away your choices, hana."

"You didn't." His hand tightened, the strokes coming faster. "And if my spotty memory serves, you really liked it when I did this." His other hand reached for Renji's balls and squeezed as the stroking continued. Trey's mouth was so close to his nipple, Renji could actually feel it there with every breath.

The combined sensations had Renji trembling and panting, on the verge of exploding. Then Trey did the unexpected. That little pink tongue came out and gently lapped at Renji's nipple. That was all it took.

"God…Trey…Trey!" Renji grabbed Trey's shoulders and erupted, his shout of completion echoing in the room.

When he finally came to his senses, Renji found Trey looking up at him with a dreamy smile. "That was so hot."

Renji pushed Trey's damp hair back, noting that his eyes were glassy and his cheeks weren't merely flushed but bright red. His afterglow of the moment would have to wait.

"Thank you, hana." He gave those moist lips a quick kiss then guided Trey back to the steps. "Now I think it's time to go. Don't want you to get overheated."

"Alright, I feel too relaxed to protest."

Renji felt the same even though his heart was soaring and the feel of Trey's tender touch lingered on his skin. It was a feeling he hoped to keep for the foreseeable future.

Helping Trey carefully up the steps, Renji picked up a limp Trey into his arms and carried him back to the shower room. He then put Trey on the bench and went to turn on the shower. Lukewarm water soon flowed.

"Come on, hana, let's get you cooled off a bit." He got Trey up and under the spray.

"Oh, kinda chilly." Trey shivered. "But it feels good too."

Renji had Trey stand under the spray for a few minutes while he went back and got the towels. When he returned and saw that most of the redness was gone from Trey's skin, he turned off the water, dried Trey thoroughly, and put him in his robe. Renji then did the same for himself. Then picking Trey up again, he headed back to the Med Room where he found Steven setting up a large card table with dinner and tea.

"About time." Steven rushed over to the bed to pull the covers back so Renji could put Trey under them. "Thought you two might have drowned."

"No, I just wanted to make sure Trey cooled down before I brought him back."

After Renji adjusted the pillows so Trey could sit up and pulled the covers to his waist, Steven looked him over, taking his wrist to check his pulse. "How you feeling, Trey?"

"Totally melted." His smile was dreamy and relaxed.

"I know the feeling well." Steven chuckled as he patted Trey's leg. He then got a tray with food and tea, brought it over, and placed it on Trey's lap. "Thought you might like something a little more solid." He pointed out what was on the tray. "Soba noodles in beef broth with bits of beef, crispy noodles, and jasmine tea with honey. Eat slowly until you feel full and make sure to drink all the tea."

"Thanks." Trey smiled, starting with the tea then moving on to the rest.

Renji took a seat at the small table Steven set up, his stomach grumbling with emptiness. "I'm starved." Now that Trey was on the mend, Renji's appetite had returned with a vengeance. Lifting the lids on the dishes, he filled his plate, not really caring what was served, just needing to fill his belly.

Steven took a seat next to him, filling his own plate. "Almost forgot, here." He handed over Renji's cell phone. "Your mother has called your phone five times and mine twice. I finally answered on number three, but she wants to talk to you."

"Damn," Renji groaned around a mouth full of food, swallowing. "Kiko?"

Steven snorted. "Of course." He then began to eat, stopping long enough to pour them both a tall cup of tea.

Renji let out a deep sigh. He loved Kiko dearly, but the woman had a nasty habit of keeping his mother informed about everything.

"Just like a band-aid my friend. Best to do it quick," Steven advised with a wink.

"Yeah, right." They both knew that with his mother, nothing was ever quick. He hastily ate a few more bites, washing it down with tea, then opened his cell and punched the number for his mother's phone. She picked up on the second ring.

"Finally, Renji-kun."

"*Gomen, okaasa,*" He switched to Japanese because that's what his mother preferred when speaking with family. "I just now got your message."

"Is everything alright? Your guest hasn't gotten worse has he?"

"No, he's fine. Though still weak." He looked over at Trey who gave him a bright smile, making his heart skip with happiness. "Steven recommended taking him to the hot spring for a soak to relieve the soreness and to help his recovery."

"So the young man is doing better?"

Renji heard the underlying question and knew that his mother was just building up to what she really wanted to know. "*Hai*, he is doing much better."

"*Zen, zen*," She replied. "And just who is this young man, Renji-kun? Steven-kun was very vague as to the details of just how he came to be with you."

He looked over at Steven and mouthed, *Thanks*. Steven merely shrugged and kept eating. "And what did Steven tell you?"

"Well, some very bad men attacked him and tried to kidnap him." Her voice sounded concerned and troubled. "But you intervened."

Renji sighed inwardly. His father and the company's security detail were the only ones who knew exactly what Renji was doing for and with Interpol. His mother had no clue and that's the way it would remain. Being a close relation to the royal house of Japan, his mother's early years weren't a picnic and after having a family, her protective instincts were high. If she had even an inkling what Renji was doing, well, it wouldn't be pretty. Still, he didn't like lying to her, though in this particular case, it wasn't lying so much as not telling the whole truth.

"That's basically what happened as well as Trey being drugged. He had a bad reaction, which caused him to be ill."

"Oh, my," She tsked. "But he's doing better now?"

"*Hai.*"

"You weren't hurt were you?"

"No, I'm perfectly fine."

He heard her let out a relieved breath at that. "And this young man, this Trey-kun. Kiko tells me that you might have some… attachment to him. Is this true?"

"It's more than that, *okaasa*." Renji looked over at Trey again. That sweet smile and gem bright eyes went right to his soul.

"How much more?"

"I feel a very deep connection to him, *okaasa*."

"Oh, Renji-kun."

He heard the happy tears in his mother's voice, not able to stop his own eyes from getting a bit misty, or keeping the goofy grin from wreathing his face. "I know how it must sound, but, *okaasa*, the moment I saw him, I knew."

Her watery giggle came over the line. "It was like that with your father and me, my son."

"It was?" A bit shocked by that news. Their marriage hadn't been arranged, but it had been no secret that their parents had voiced a possible match between them.

"Oh, yes." She laughed happily. "One look and we felt it, that connection."

"*Hai*, like…like your soul recognized it's other half." He felt his cheeks heat at the admission, especially since it was his mother he was admitting it to. His family was close, closer than most traditional Japanese family's because of his mother's upbringing and world traveling, but he'd never had such a talk with her before. It felt odd. Good, but odd.

She laughed again. "Oh, Renji-kun, I'm so happy for you."

"*Arigato, okaasa.*"

"So, tell me what your young man looks like and how old he is. What does he do for a living?"

Renji chuckled. "He's twenty-three and still in school. He's an Arts History Major."

"Well, he is young." Renji heard the amusement in her voice. "Maybe I should be calling him Trey-chan."

"*Okassa*!" He felt his entire face flame at his mother's suggestion of using the diminutive for children.

"I'm just teasing, Renji-kun." She giggled. "Is he handsome?"

Looking over at Trey again, Renji was once again struck by his beauty. "He's beautiful, *okaasa*. His hair is golden sunlight with skin like rare pearls. He has eyes the color of fine aquamarines. They light up whenever he's happy and he has this cute little dimple in his right cheek. He's a little less than six foot and built like a swimmer, all lean muscle."

"He sounds so *kawaii*."

"He's that and more." Trey caught him staring and winked, finishing his meal. Renji gave him a smile then got back to his call and the very unusual conversation with his mother. Renji wasn't the only gay man in the family, but there hadn't been that many talks about his lifestyle. Not that his mother, or father for that matter, minded. They were very open about their children and what they wanted out of life. Unusual considering their backgrounds. But talking with her now, he couldn't be more grateful to have such wonderful parents for he knew that his father would be just as happy for him as his mother.

"Hmm."

"What is it, *okaasa*?"

"I was just thinking. Seeing as Trey-kun is a new member of the family and the fact that you brought him home without any luggage, he's going to need clothes and other items. Kiko tells me that the only garments he has to wear are the guest robes."

Renji rolled his eyes and groaned silently. Leave it to his mother to already add Trey to the family despite him and Renji still getting to know each other. "I was going to take him shopping after he felt better."

"Nonsense, it could be days before he's well enough for such a trip," she replied. "And having only a robe to wear just won't do, Renji-kun. Now have him tell me his sizes and I'll have a few things sent over."

"Really, *okaasa*, you don't have to go to the trouble. I can have Steven or Kiko get a few things. And besides, you and *otosaan* are still in Greece, no need to…"

"Absolutely not," she interrupted and Renji knew that tone. "Steven-kun needs to be there to keep an eye on Trey-kun and Kiko wouldn't know what to get for a young man since she has daughters. I know perfectly well what to get, so the sizes, Renji-kun."

Renji let out a long suffering sigh and looked over at Trey. "Trey, my mother will be getting you a few things to wear and needs to know your sizes."

Those gem eyes blinked in surprise but Trey recovered quickly. "Tell your mom I appreciate the thought but she doesn't have to go to the trouble. I can wait 'til I'm feeling better to get them myself."

"Oh, what a polite, well mannered young man," his mother gushed. "And what a darling accent. Is he American?"

"*Hai*, from the Southern states," he told her while still looking at Trey who was shaking his head no even though Renji had replied in Japanese. It didn't matter, once her mind was made, there was nothing and no one to stop her. Not even his father.

"Interesting, Renji-kun. He's quite different from the others, isn't he?" The question was rhetorical considering that he was too shocked to reply and she didn't wait for an answer. "I'll have to get him something special, to welcome him properly to the family."

"*Hai, okaasa.*" Renji put his hand over the bottom of the phone as his mother continued to speak. "I'm sorry, hana. My mother simply wishes to do this as a way to welcome you to the family."

"To the family?" Trey's cheeks flushed a becoming pink. "You told her about us?"

Renji chuckled. "Don't worry, hana, I've never hidden my sexuality from my parents, so they're fine. But this is the first time that I've brought anyone to my home and my mother understands the significance of that. She only wants to welcome you properly."

"Damn, you just had to say something totally sweet, didn't you?" Trey gave him a blinding smile, that cute dimple peeking out.

"It's only the truth, hana."

Steven snorted. "That and the fact that Sango-san isn't about to take no for an answer. She's a wee bit stubborn when it comes to getting her way."

"She only does it because she cares and wants the best for those she considers family." He smiled sheepishly at Trey, hoping he understood.

Trey huffed out a breath. "I'm not going to get out of this, am I?"

"Afraid not, hana."

"Crap," his groan was followed by a grin. "Alright, but tell her nothing expensive. I don't want her going out of her way for me."

"Sure thing, hana." He chuckled as Trey gave him the sizes. "Thank-you."

"And you call him flower, how very sweet." His mother giggled causing Renji's cheeks to heat again. It was embarrassing. He hadn't blushed so much since he was a teen and his mother wasn't even in the room with them.

"Did you hear the sizes or do you need them repeated?" So much for putting his hand over the phone.

"I wrote it all down. And to make sure Trey-kun gets better, I'll send along some of Granny's teas. Those are the perfect restorative." The sound of grumbling could be heard in the background. "Alright dear, I'll put him on speaker."

Renji shook his head, knowing who it was. "Hey, *otosaan*."

"About time you found someone to settle down with. Now you can start running the company like it needs." That was his father, right to the point. Never mind Renji and Trey weren't even that far in their relationship yet.

"Yes, sir."

"*Zen*. I want to meet this young man, Renji-kun. Have Steven-kun let us know when he's up and about." There was more grumbling. "Damn you Pete, how the hell did you do that?"

"I take it *otosaan* and Pete are playing chess again?" He already knew what his mother's answer was going to be. The loud exclamations on his father's part were kind of hard to ignore.

"*Hai*, and with the usual outcome." Her sigh was loud and heartfelt.

Renji couldn't help but laugh. For the seven years that Pete Billings had been with Takeda Security, he and Genji Takeda had found a mutual love of chess. Problem was that Pete was a master player. Genji had only managed to beat Pete a hand full of time over the years, much to Genji's disappointment and consternation. But Genji loved a challenge. Hence the never ending re-matches. Not that Pete minded. Genji was one of only a few that could adequately play Pete at Pete's level. "*Ganbaru, otosaan.*" His father mumbled a reply, letting Renji know that his mind was back on the game.

"We'll be on our way home in a couple of days Renji-kun, so I'm going to get Kaito-kun to help me with Trey-kun's new wardrobe. He'll have a few ideas I might not think of."

That name caused Renji to groan. "Anyone but Kaito, *okaasa*, please."

"And just what is wrong with Kaito-kun? He's always been there when I've needed him to be."

"Nothing, *okaasa*, forget I said anything." He let out a deep sigh and rubbed the back of his neck.

"I don't think so young man. You will tell me this instant." The authority in her voice was clear; Renji was going to have to fess up, something he had been avoiding for a while now.

"It's just…well…there have been some complaints," he hedged.

"Against Kaito-kun?"

"*Hai.*"

"What kind of complaints?"

Renji looked over at Steven, who had been telling him for months that his mother needed to know.

"Tell her, Renji," he said.

Renji nodded, knowing that he was right. "Well, it seems that Kaito has let his flirting get out of hand."

"What do you mean?"

"What he means is your nephew's behavior has bordered on harassment," his father chimed in. "And he has been making a nuisance of himself."

"And just why haven't I been informed of this?"

"*Gomen, okaasa*, but he's your favorite nephew. We didn't want to upset you."

"This upsets me more, Renji-kun. That such unacceptable behavior would be kept from me, and from one of my family." Her voice was tight with anger.

"*Gomen na sai, okaasa.*"

"Something will have to be done, my love. Favorite or not, I won't tolerate such disrespect." His father's tone was soft toward his mother, but Renji could hear the underlying steel.

"And no offense, *okaasa*, but if he were to say anything untoward to Trey, well…" he let that go, not wanting to upset his mother any further.

"I understand completely, Renji-kun and would expect nothing less. Kaito-kun should know better and it bothers me that his behavior has gotten so out of hand. As his aunt, I'm appalled."

There was a moment of silence as Renji let his mother calm down.

"Since your mother and I are away and will be having Kaito-kun help and deliver Trey-kun's new clothes, I want you to deal with this, Renji-kun."

"Sir?"

"Nephew or not, favorite or not, Kaito-kun is still an employee in this company and as such, he needs to be aware that his unacceptable behavior will not be tolerated, especially from family. We are the examples that others go by, not the exceptions. Are we clear, Renjiro-kun?"

"*Hai, otosaan*, I'll take care of it." He didn't exactly look forward to it, but he knew that his father was right. As President of the company, it was Renji's duty to make sure everyone acted in a circumspect manner, family most of all.

"*Zen*. Now Pete, where were we?"

"Check, I believe." Came Pete's gravelly voice.

"Damn." His father sighed.

"Also Renji-kun, let Kaito-kun know that I will be having my own words with him after we have returned home." Her tone was pleasant enough but Renji heard the cold anger. His mother was extremely livid and would no doubt flail Kaito within an inch of his life for such behavior.

"*Hai, okaasa*." He winced a bit in sympathy for what Kaito was going to receive.

"Now, I'll have him pick up everything and deliver it tomorrow afternoon by the latest. That way Marshall-kun, who I know is listening, will be ready when he arrives."

"*Hai*."

"Zen." Her voice once more sounding happy. "It's getting late and I have a few calls to make, but I'll call you before we get home to check on how Trey-kun is doing."

"Alright, you both be careful. I love you."

"We love you too, *akachan. Ja!*"

"*Ja!*" The phone then went dead and he closed it, letting out a deep breath.

"That certainly went better than I thought it would," Steven quipped as he gathered their dirty dishes, starting with Trey's.

"Says the guy who doesn't have to deal with it." Renji snorted, getting up to help and putting his cell on the nightstand beside Trey first.

"Like you haven't wanted to put the little prick in his place for months now," Steven smirked. "Please, I know better. And the little shit deserves it, so don't even try to give me that line."

Renji couldn't help the evil grin he knew he was sporting. "Alright, I will admit that finally putting a boot in that moron's ass will feel good, but I didn't want my mother to find out. She's quite upset about this."

"As well she should be."

"Who's Kaito and why are you going to put a boot in his ass?" Trey asked.

Renji looked up from folding the card table and smiled. "Sorry, hana. Kaito is Kaito Hisagi, my second cousin and my mother's favorite nephew on her side of the family."

"He's also a menace and a jackass that has let his position go to his head," Steven added.

"That too," Renji agreed.

"I take it he's throwing his weight around?" Trey surmised.

"Unfortunately," he replied with a sigh. "And since he's also gay…"

"Flaming gay," Steven interjected.

"Flaming gay," Renji amended with a chuckle. "He's been using his position as my mother's personal assistant to well…push his attentions on others whom he knows are gay as well."

"Those others include some of the members of Takeda Security. Not very wise when the one you're hitting on is ex-military and armed." Steven laughed.

Trey winced at that. "Ouch."

"Yeah, and unfortunately for Kaito, all he got was a warning. Not that it's done much good. I keep hearing complaints here and there, but because of my mother, warnings were all that he was getting. No more. My mother knows now and my father wants this taken care of."

"And none too soon either." Steven took a pointed look at Trey and raised a dark brow.

"What are you getting at, Steven?" Renji hoped Steven wasn't implying what he thought Steven was implying. But Trey voiced just that.

"You don't seriously think that Kaito would hit on me in front of Renji, do you?"

Steven snorted and Renji growled, both agreeing at the same time. "Yes, he would."

"Well, if he's that stupid, then he deserves a boot in the ass."

"Trust me, hana, a boot will be the least of his worries if he crosses that line." His blood began to boil just thinking about it.

"Just make sure you take care of the little shit outside. It's hard to get blood off wood floors and even more so with the bamboo mats. Terrible stains you know." Steven winked as he took the card table from Renji and the cart of dirty dishes. "Be back in a sec." Then he left to take it all to the kitchen.

Renji just shook his head with amusement and went to sit beside Trey. "I'll deal with Kaito the minute he gets here. Better to let him know the rules before the game even begins."

"Sounds like you'll need to." Trey yawned, his beautiful eyes looking heavy.

Glancing at the bedside clock, Renji noticed that it was just after eight. "You should get some sleep, hana." His hand began to pet that golden head, those silky locks tumbling through his fingers. "I've kept you up longer than I should have."

Trey's eyes closed as a sweet smile curved his lips. "It was worth it, darlin'."

Renji laughed softly, continuing to run his hand through Trey's hair, Trey practically purring. Unfortunately, Steven returning and his cell going off broke whatever spell was woven between them, making them both jerk with startlement.

"Lousy timing as always, my friend." Steven laughed as he took a seat in the corner chair.

That earned Steven a glare that only made him laugh again as Renji grabbed his cell, not about to leave Trey's side. Or give up contact as he grabbed Trey's hand and laced their fingers together. A look at the caller ID had him puzzled though. It was Marshall. Renji flipped the phone open immediately.

"What is it, Marsh?"

"Trouble's on the way I'm afraid," came a deeply resonant voice that held aggravation and strength.

That caused Renji to straighten his spine with trepidation. "What kind?"

"Inspector Conrad."

Chapter 4

"Shit!" Renji groaned. "What's the ETA?"

"Eight minutes."

"It takes fifteen from the airport."

"You can blame Jonah for that. He wanted to make sure the good Inspector was well away before he contacted me." Marshall snorted with derision.

"I'll be sure to thank the ass later." He sighed. "Where are you?"

"Right here." His voice came from the doorway as he and his two team members casually strolled in.

Marshall Bennet was 6'6" with a blond buzz cut, nearly black eyes, and the body of a pro wrestler. The build and hair were from his father's Virginia coal miner heritage but the dark eyes and dusky skin were a gift from his Catawba Indian mother. The oozing confidence and military air was all due to his Special Forces training. Although he was retired and in his early forties, that air of command was still there. Of course, the black muscle tee, fatigues, combat boots, and weapons certainly drove that point home. The fact that he could use those weapons wasn't in question either. One look was proof positive of that.

"Be annoyed, he does us all like that," one of his team members drawled with amusement.

That earned a tolerant look from Marshall and a hearty chuckle from Renji who turned to Trey. He was wearing a curious look on that handsome face. His fatigue of earlier disappearing in light of the new guests.

"Trey Morrison, this is Marshall Bennet," he introduced as Marshall quickly came over to shake Trey's hand. "He and his husband own and run Takeda Security. Because my mother is related to the Japanese royal family, a security company has always watched over her. But after marrying and having a family of her own, my father thought it prudent to hire one with a military background. Marshall and his team have been assigned to me for the last eight years. The rest watch over my other family members."

"Ah. Well, it's nice to meet you, Mr. Bennet." Trey smiled as he returned the handshake.

"Call me Marshall, please." His own smile warm. "I'm not much for ceremony."

"Alright…Marshall." He nodded.

When Marshall stepped back, his two team members rushed to take his place, leering grins on their identical faces.

"Hana, these are the Terror Twins, Seth and Luke Allston. They're the newest members of the team."

They were identical from their mop of flame colored curls, leaf green eyes, ivory skin, 6'3" height, and lean muscular builds. They were also ex-SEALs that were experts with a dictionary's worth of weapons, guns and knives being at the top of the list. Terror Twins just wasn't a casual nickname. They had earned it during their time with the SEALs and rightly so. Dangerous enough on their own, they were lethal together.

Trey shook their hands with a bright smile. "How ya doin'?"

One of the twins threw his arm over the others shoulder and clutched his chest. "Another Southern boy, be still my heart."

"Where from?" Trey asked.

"Cherokee, North Carolina. Mom was half but our granddad raised us," the left twin replied.

"Yeah, he's full and on the council, so we lived with him on the Rez 'till we joined the SEALs," the right twin added.

"That's cool." Trey laughed. "I'm from Gastonia."

"Oh man, we'll definitely have to talk."

"Yeah, been a while since we met another Carolina boy."

"I'd like that." Trey nodded happily.

Renji noticed the calculated gleam in the twin's eyes. "And talking is all that will be happening or you two just might find an extra hole in your asses. We clear?"

"We don't poach, Renji, you know that." After hearing that answer, Renji now knew it was Seth. He tended to talk faster than Luke.

"You can't blame us for trying though." Luke winked as he and Seth stepped back toward Marshall, their casual poses belying their readiness.

Trey laughed softly, his fingers squeezing Renji's. "Don't worry darlin', you're not the only who knows how to use a gun."

The twins nodded in acknowledgement even though their leering grins stayed in place.

Renji brought Trey's hand up and kissed his knuckles. "Seems I need to learn more about Carolina boys." Trey's cheeks heated with a rosy flush at the comment and what it implied.

"I'm starting to feel like a voyeur with these two," Steven said merrily.

Renji closed his eyes and slowly counted to ten then kissed Trey's knuckles again, looking up at Marshall. "How much time do we have left?" He heard Steven chuckle at his refusal to take the bait.

Marshall grinned knowingly as he looked at his watch. "He should be here in four minutes." He then looked over at the twins. "Seth?"

"Meet and greet it is." Then he left.

"Something wrong, Renji?" Trey asked with a furrowed brow.

"Unfortunately." He sighed, having hoped that Inspector Conrad would have called first or at the very least, given some notice of his imminent arrival. As usual, the mans blatant disregard for manners was showing. It also didn't help that Trey didn't know he was a witness. With everything happening at warp speed, that important tidbit of information had been forgotten. "An Inspector Conrad of the Federal Police of Belgium is on his way here. He's one of several Inspectors on the case against Rusk and has been from day one. He's also head of operations of the witness program."

"So he's coming here to talk to me?"

Renji let out a deep breath. "Actually, he's coming here to try to take you to an Interpol safe house."

Trey's face drained quickly of color. "What?"

Renji swiftly gathered Trey close. "Easy, hana. I said he was going to try." He pulled back and cupped Trey's cheek. "No one is taking you from me, Trey. No one," he promised.

Trey went back into Renji's arms and snuggled close, his blond head under Renji's chin. "I'll tell him what he needs to know, but I don't want to leave. This is where I'm safe. Where I feel secure."

Renji felt that statement warm him inside and out. He then looked at Marshall, the silent communication between them clear. He and his team would do all they could to keep Trey protected. He gave Marshall a grateful smile and kissed the top of Trey's golden head.

"Go ahead, love." Marshall put a hand to his right ear and looked down a few moments. "Well now, isn't that interesting news." His smile was hard and calculating as he continued to listen to whoever was speaking into his ear piece, though Renji knew it had to be Gary, Marshall's husband. Renji wished that he hadn't forgotten to put his ear piece back in, then he'd know what was being said. "Are you sure, love?" Marshall let out a deep, sad sigh. "Alright, I understand. I'll see you in fifteen to twenty. Marshall out."

"What's the problem, Marsh? Gary wouldn't be coming out if it wasn't something big." He saw anger in those near black eyes at the question.

"I'll explain in detail after the good Inspector arrives."

Renji was saved from asking further by the sound of loud voices at the front of his home slowly making their way back to them.

"You are impeding an ongoing investigation young man. Unless you want to be arrested, I suggest you cease with the stalling tactics and take me to Mr. Takeda and the witness."

"Bring the jackass on, Seth." Marshall's annoyance was clear as he gave Seth the order. Not that Renji or any of the other's were all that overjoyed either.

"This way, Inspector." Came Seth's cheerful voice, then he walked through the door. There was a fake smile on his face and a deadly coldness in those green eyes that were mirrored in Luke's. Whatever info Gary relayed wasn't good.

"About time," the Inspector huffed.

Inspector Alain Conrad was a born and bred Belgian in his mid fifties and it showed clearly in his 5'9" height. He was nearly bald with hair that matched his watery brown eyes, a florid face, and a body that had already turned to fat as evidenced by the large paunch hanging over his belt and threatening to bust the one button on his suit jacket. A jacket that looked as bad as the rest of his suit, as if it had been slept in for the past week. The Inspector himself didn't look much better. He was pale and sweating, wiping his face repeatedly with a rumpled and dirty kerchief. Something was wrong, Renji could feel it.

"Welcome to my home, Inspector." Not that the man was really welcome, but Renji was trying to be nice. The good Inspector didn't even try.

"I should arrest you, Takeda." His Belgian accent was more pronounced with his agitation. "You took a witness in an ongoing investigation without authority and nearly jeopardized this case. But because of your help, I'm willing to forget this little incident." Seth snorted at that. "So, if you would, get the witness ready and we'll be on our way."

"The witness has a name, you know," Trey said angrily. "And considering I didn't even know I was a witness, I would appreciate you using it."

Conrad blinked at that, finally noticing Trey. "My apologies, Mr. Morrison." He recovered quickly though didn't act or look the least bit sorry. "I was ill prepared for such a situation, so please bear with me." The smile on his face was forced as in a blink, Trey was dismissed, Conrad's focus on Renji once again. "If you please, Mr. Takeda, I have a timetable to follow."

"Do you now?"

"I wouldn't go with this asshole into the hall much less anywhere else." Trey's cheeks were flushed with anger and rightly so. The Inspector was being ruder than usual.

"Now, Mr. Morrison." Conrad's tone was placating, as if he was talking to a small child. It set Renji's hackles rising. "You're a valuable witness in an international investigation. There are strict protocols that must be followed. You simply can't stay here and have the security you need to keep you safe. Now I have the safe house ready for you, so I need you to please gather your things, we need to get going."

Before Renji or Trey could respond to that, Steven rose from his seat. "If I may, Inspector?"

"Who are you?" He asked snidely.

"I'm Doctor Steven Kroger, Chief Physician for the Takeda Company and the Takeda family's personal doctor."

"Ah yes, you've assisted us before." Conrad nodded. "We appreciate all you've done for us doctor, but your services are no longer needed."

"You don't understand, Inspector, I'm also Mr. Morrison's doctor and as such I cannot allow you to take him anywhere."

The Inspector spluttered with indignation. "That's ridiculous, the young man looks perfectly fine."

"Looks can be deceiving, I assure you." Steven's mouth was set in a grim line, his color high. Renji could tell he was seriously pissed, no mean feat with the easy going doctor.

Conrad's watery eyes narrowed with suspicion. "I don't know what's going on here, but I will arrest the lot of you if this interference with the witness continues."

Renji gave Trey's fingers a comforting squeeze, feeling a slight tremor as whatever emotion Trey was feeling he was trying hard to control. "Don't worry, hana, you're not going anywhere." He touched Trey's cheek tenderly with his free hand and gave him a reassuring smile.

"I should have known." Conrad sneered with disgust. "All of this is just a clever scheme to keep your new plaything with you."

Renji saw red outline his vision at the insult, Trey's hand in his the only thing holding him back from doing the Inspector serious bodily harm. "I suggest you keep such perverse comments to yourself, Conrad." Dropping the man's title was deliberate. "My hospitality only extends so far." His voice was calm and deadly cold.

Steven spoke again before Conrad could dig himself any deeper. "Contrary to what you might think Inspector, Mr. Morrison, Trey, is still recovering from a double dose of Rusk's drug. If Renji-san hadn't brought him here, Trey would have died, and nearly did so twice after his arrival here."

Renji pat Trey's hand, giving him comfort with Steven's recount of Trey's near demise.

"Trey is still too weak to be moved. In fact, today is the first day he has been able to sit up for any length of time."

"I see." Those rheumy brown orbs were still narrowed as Conrad tapped his chin with thought. "Well, I guess there really is no help for it then." He nodded to himself. "You'll just have to come along doctor and care of Mr. Morrison until he's well enough on his own."

There was a small pause, like everyone just couldn't believe what the man had suggested, then everyone began to talk at once. The volume and anger rose until Marshall let loose with a loud whistle.

"Enough!" He shouted, the room going silent. "I think this farce has gone on long enough. Wouldn't you agree, Inspector?" Those dark eyes bored holes into Conrad.

"I have no idea what you're playing, sir, but I am on official Interpol business." Conrad's spine stiffened with affront, face red and brow sweaty. "The penalty for obstruction is quite severe."

Marshall crossed his arms, face blank. It was a look Renji had seen only when Marshall was holding his temper in check. "I'd be worried about such a charge if you were still with the Federal Police."

It took Renji a moment to let that register, looking at Seth still in the doorway behind Conrad and Luke near Steven in the corner. Both wore looks of disgust, their green eyes practically glowing with rage and letting Renji know just how angry they were. "Is this true?" He aimed the question at Marshall knowing the man would give him a straight answer. Conrad remained silent, florid face set in hard lines.

Marshall nodded. "Seems Conrad here blew a gasket when he found out you took Trey with you. And from what I understand, it's not the first time he's lost it. But this time, he was stupid enough to lose it with his superiors and half the force in ear range as well as several Interpol agents."

"Idiot." Luke snorted with disgust.

"He's been put on indefinite medical leave and suspended without pay for the next couple weeks. He'll be reinstated pending a full psych eval and formal apology. Though from what I understand, even that won't be enough to get his badge back. The higher ups have grown tired of his outbursts."

Renji turned to Conrad who'd been quiet, face impassive, and stance rigid. He didn't seem to be a bit sorry for his actions. "Even knowing you were suspended, you still came into my home with your threats and lies. Came here to basically kidnap Trey to save your worthless career, putting Trey's health and safety in danger." The red was back, slowly filling his vision every second he continued to watch Conrad's uncaring visage.

"I've done all I've had to do to insure that Rusk is taken down." His chin lifted with defiance. "If that means lying and threatening to achieve that goal, then I will."

"Tell him the rest of it, Marsh." Luke's voice held a sad resignation that Renji was unfamiliar with. "He deserves to know."

"Know what?" Renji growled, the rage at a slow boil, only needing a small push for it to explode.

Marshall nodded, those near black gone deadly cold. "They have a mole, and for some time now."

"Christ." Steven slumped into his seat with an angry sigh.

"I just learned of this because of it's need to know basis and we apparently didn't need to know." Never had Renji seen Marshall so angry, his face seemed carved of granite. "Fortunately for us, this fools outburst changed that."

"So Rusk now knows where Trey is," Renji surmised.

"It's more than that, Renji." Marshall turned those cold, dark eyes on Conrad. "Because of the mole, Trey is now the only witness."

It took Renji a moment for that to really sink in, looking at the Twins and seeing the sad truth in their green eyes. "No, they swore to me that those young boys would be protected. Swore to me that they would be safe, be well cared for." Renji then looked at Conrad and saw that not a speck of remorse showed in his demeanor. "You assured me they would be well guarded."

"Their loss is regrettable, but with Mr. Morrison's testimony, the case can proceed as planned." Conrad's tone was indifferent and uncaring of the poor young boys who's lives had ended much too soon. "Of course, Mr. Morrison will need to be moved to a more secure location. Otherwise, being forewarned won't do much good. Rusk will just bring his men here and put a bullet in everyone's head the same as he did the other witnesses."

With Trey's shocked gasp, Renji snapped. He was on Conrad in a blink, getting in several satisfying punches before he was pulled away by Marshall, Steven, and Luke. Even with those three restraining him, it was the feel of a warm hand on his arm and Trey's gentle voice that finally lifted the red haze of fury clouding his vision.

"He's not worth it, Renji."

He turned to see Trey standing there, pale faced and shaky, leaning on Seth for support. "Hana." He reached for Trey and gathered him close. "I'm so sorry."

"He'll pay, darlin', we'll make sure of it." Trey's smile was bright when he pulled back, those gem eyes showing steely determination. It was a moment Renji would remember for the rest of his life. The moment he fell for Trey.

"You have the heart of a samurai, hana." He then kissed those cherry lips gently. "But you still need rest." Picking Trey up, Renji took him back to bed and made sure he was comfortable. The process of seeing to Trey also helped to calm Renji down least he finish what he started and take Conrad's head off.

When he finished seeing to Trey, Renji turned to find everyone had resumed their places and Conrad holding a blood covered towel to his nose. It was definitely broken and already beginning to swell. The sight gave Renji no satisfaction; his sadness for those murdered innocents was too great. But their blood was not on his hands. That tragedy was the responsibility of Rusk and the sorry excuse for a man before him.

"How dare you strike me!" Conrad's angry retort was muffled by the bloody towel. "I came here to see that Mr. Morrison was taken to a secure location, not get attacked by a madman."

"Spare me your false concern for Trey," Renji snapped. "Saving your pathetic ass and badge are the only reason's you're here." He sat down beside Trey and took his hand again, Conrad stiffening his spine with affront. "As for Trey's safety, that's not your concern anymore."

"Surely you don't think you can protect him?" Conrad chuckled with disdain. "A bunch of rent-a-cops are no match for Rusk and his men."

"That's quite an insult to my Special Forces training." Marshall's voice was calm yet icy. "But seeing as we're all trying to be civil, I'll let it pass. For now."

Conrad's eyes widened at that tidbit of information and the not so subtle threat, his face pale.

"Seth, if you would do the honors, I think Mr. Conrad has worn out his welcome." Marshall was still giving Conrad a steely glare as he instructed Seth.

"With pleasure." Seth went to over to grab Conrad's arm when in a blink, Seth had a very large and razor sharp knife at Conrad's throat. "Pull that gun out and I'll make sure you never have to worry about your worthless badge again. Luke, if you please."

Everything happened so fast that Renji was still trying to wrap his mind around what had just went down as Luke relieved Conrad of his gun.

"Nice Glock." Luke looked the gun over with an artist's eye. "Not exactly standard issue. The Sig Sauer handles better though." He smiled as he handed off the gun to Marshall then began to pat Conrad down for further weapons. When he didn't find anymore, he stood beside Seth. "He's clean, stupid, but clean."

"You son of a bitch!" Renji growled, ready to finish beating the man to a pulp, but Trey stopped him.

"I sure hope you were willing to shoot, Mr. Conrad, because nothing less would have convinced me to go with you." Trey's tone was so frigid that Renji was a bit shocked that it was Trey saying such a thing. "But then, I wouldn't have had to worry too much. You would be dead."

"You don't understand, they can't protect you like –"

"Like you protected the other witnesses?" Trey finished for Conrad, his hand starting to shake in Renji's. "Because of your negligence, those poor witnesses were murdered and now your incompetence has put me and

Renji in further danger. Not to mention that you're no longer a cop with those resources as backup. I'm not an idiot nor am I even remotely loose minded enough to put my life in your hands when you care more about your career than my safety. These men I do trust with my safety. I don't like you Mr. Conrad and I sure as hell don't trust you. Not even enough to let you walk me to the door of this bedroom with everyone watching."

"Mr. Morrison, please." Conrad's tone wasn't exactly begging, but it was close. "Be reasonable." His face was sheet white, watery eyes showing slight panic.

"Unlike you, I am being reasonable." Trey snorted. "Now if you'll excuse me, I'm tired. Seth will be more than happy to see you out."

"Overjoyed," Seth replied as he grabbed Conrad's arm once more.

"Wait! You can't stay here, it's not safe!" Conrad began to resist, pushing at Seth.

"Luke." Marshall nodded, giving him permission to help his brother contain the struggling Inspector.

"With pleasure." He grinned evilly and in no time he and his brother had Conrad subdued and on his way out the door. His shouts at Trey echoed down the hall until all was quiet once more.

"What a complete bastard."

At hearing the quaver in Trey's voice with the remark, Renji turned to see him white faced and trembling. Steven's name was no sooner out his mouth than the good doctor was at Trey's side, checking him over.

"What's wrong, Steven?" Renji could feel the tremors from Trey's hand, the clamminess of his skin. He was so pale, even his lips had a whitish caste to them.

"Adrenaline crash," Steven answered as he checked Trey's pulse. "As weak as his system is, it wasn't ready for all the excitement yet."

"More like wanting to rip that asshole a new one." Trey chuckled shakily. "Though someone should have given me a little heads up." He gave Renji a slight frown.

"I know." Renji sighed, squeezing Trey's hand. "I'm sorry, hana. With everything going on, I didn't want to upset you further. And honestly, I thought I'd have more time."

"You still should have said something." Trey let out a harsh, shaky breath.

"No more surprises," he promised.

"I'll hold you to that." He grinned wanly. "Still want to rip that asshole a new one."

"We all do." Steven pat his knee in agreement. "I'll go make some tea. The liquids will help." He moved to the door but was stopped by Marshall.

"Here, doc." He handed Steven what looked like a solid black hearing aid. "The ear pieces got an upgrade. We now have GPS satellite linking to go with the two way mics and tracking chips. Once you're hooked up, we can find you anywhere on the planet with that thing."

"Sweet." Steven took the old ear piece from his pocket, handing it over to Marshall.

"Keep the old one, you'll need it to contact Davis since your new one isn't in the system yet."

"Gotcha." Steven put the new piece in his pocket then put the old one in his ear. "Guess I should have kept this one in." he gave Marshall a sheepish smile. "I'll contact Davis while I'm preparing the tea."

"I'll give ya a hand, doc," Luke said as he came back to the door.

"No problem with Conrad?" Marshall asked.

"Nah, though Seth had to drive." Luke snickered. "Hard to steer when you're unconscious."

"I hope the bastard's head explodes when he wakes up."

That got a laugh from everyone seeing as they all could tell that Trey was still pissed. The Inspector had made an enemy of Trey this night, but regardless of that, Renji was glad that Trey could and would stand up for himself. He might be Renji's hana, but Trey was no shrinking violet.

"As hard as Seth clipped the idiot's jaw, exploding would be an accurate assumption." Luke nodded as Steven herded him out the door.

Marshall shook his head with a grin then came up to Renji, reaching in his pocket and pulling out two more of the ear pieces. "These are for you two." He handed one to Renji then Trey, making sure both put them in. "Davis," he called out.

"Right here, boss." His voice was a bit muffled, but Renji could still here the deep and cheerful tone of Davis through the ear piece.

"Trey and Renji have the new ear pieces in, hook 'em up."

"It'll take about ten minutes for Trey. Got the bio-rhythm scan from doc, but it'll still take that long for the piece to sync."

"Copy that. Just let me know when it's done. Marshall out." He looked over at Renji. "You get any of that?"

"Yeah, but it was muffled."

"Trey?"

"All I could hear was static."

"That's fine. If it wasn't working, you wouldn't be able to hear anything. Davis will set you up in about ten minutes."

"Marshall." Renji heard Gary's voice come over the ear piece. It was a little clearer.

"Go ahead, love."

Trey looked at them both questionly. Renji pointed to his ear piece, letting him know that a call was coming through. Trey nodded in understanding.

"We're seven minutes out. Passed Seth on the way in and he gave us the heads up." There was a sad sigh. *"Tell Renji..."*

"His piece is working, love, you can tell him yourself."

"Oh, I...I'm so sorry, my friend."

Renji caught Marshall's eye and smiled sadly. "So am I."

"You doing okay? Seth told us you lit into Conrad like an avenging angel."

"Yeah, it was the least the bastard deserves." Renji snorted.

"Copy that." Gary laughed. *"Seth also told us your boy has a razor sharp tongue and took a few strips out Conrad as well."*

"Oh yeah." Renji chuckled. "It was a pleasure to watch."

"He doing better?"

"Got a little over excited telling Conrad off, but he's alright." Renji looked at Trey with a grin and patted his shoulder. Trey took his hand and laced their fingers together with a bright smile.

"That's good. I'm happy for you, my friend, truly."

"Thanks, *oniisan.*"

"Cole behave himself on the flight over, love?" Marshall asked as he winked at Renji and Trey with a smile.

"Humph, bayou boy's lucky I like Jake, otherwise I would have ejected his ass."

"Now cher, I apologized for the turbulence." A silky voice with a clear Cajun accent came across the piece.

"The turbulence excuse got old five years ago gator brain," Gary growled.

"Simmer down, love. I'm sure Jake will make it right. Though how he's dealt with the jackass this long is beyond me." Marshall chuckled.

"Exhaustion, pure and simple." Jake's resonant baritone came across the line, deep love for said jackass ringing loud and clear.

"I'll take your word for it," Marshall replied dryly. "I've got Davis working on Trey's ear piece and when you guys get here, I have a few ideas I want to run by you."

"Copy that," Gary replied.

"Everyone's in their usual rooms so put your gear there," Renji told them.

"Roger that," Jake replied. *"I look forward to meeting your new man, Renji."* There was nothing flirtatious about the statement, not that Jake was the type to flirt with

another man's man. It was just one friend genuinely happy for another at his choice of mate.

"Thanks, Jake. Renji out."

"Another team is coming?" Trey asked.

"Yes." Renji nodded. "Gary Evans, he's Marshall's husband, along with Cole Marcell and Jake Runninghorse. They're also married."

"Were they in the military too?"

"Everyone with Takeda Security has a military background," Marshall explained. "Like me, Gary was Special Forces. Cole was a Captain in the Air Force before he left and Jake was a Seal like the twins."

Trey nodded but Renji could see that there was something else on his mind. "What is it, hana?" The question caused his cheeks to pinken, the most color he had in his face for the last few minutes. It was a good sign that he was starting to feel better. That made Renji feel better.

"It's nothing."

Marshall chuckled. "All the team members are gay, if that's what you were wondering."

Trey's face reddened further. "I didn't mean to be nosey."

"Not at all." Marshall grinned. "Most have had to leave the military because of their sexual orientation and others just got tired of hiding it, like Gary and I. When we started this business, Gary and I just wanted those with a military background because those were the ones who know how to deal with violence and what comes with it. But as the years passed our reputation for hiring ex-military and gay got out. Now we have five teams, all gay, with the exception of Yana, she's our only female, but she's happily married to her two male lovers. They watch over Renji's youngest brother, Ranmaru, in the States while he's in college."

"Wow, that's really cool."

Marshall laughed. "We'll be hiring more soon now that Renji here is going to be an uncle and Yana too is pregnant. With this family growing, Gary and I need to start thinking about expanding."

"C'mon doc, just one, please."

Renji looked up to see Steven coming in the room pushing another cart loaded with tea pots, cups, plates, and platters of cookies. He was smacking Luke's hand whenever he reached for a cookie.

"I told you to wait," he admonished with a laugh. "Don't make me shoot you." He smacked Luke's hand again when he reached for another cookie.

Luke rubbed the offended appendage. "I feel sorry for your boys."

"Humph, they know better." Steven parked the cart then poured steaming tea into a large handless cup. He then put a couple cookies on a plate and handed both to Luke. "Here, make yourself useful and give this to Trey. He needs it more than you do." Looking at Trey, he ordered, "Make sure you drink all that tea. It's chamomile and lemon with plenty of honey."

"Thanks, doc." Trey took the cup and plate from Luke, taking a small sip of the tea. "It's good."

"You alright, hon?" Luke's worried eyes looked over Trey carefully, he too noticing the paleness and slight trembling.

Trey reached out and patted his arm. "Conrad really pissed me off, so I'm a little shaky. I'm fine otherwise, promise." He gave Luke a reassuring smile. "Now get over there and have doc fix you a plate of goodies. Can't catch a psycho on an empty stomach."

Luke lingered a moment longer until Trey finally shooed him away, taking more sips of his tea, the color starting to return to his face and the fine trembling beginning to lesson.

"Here, Luke." Steven held out a plate with tea and cookies. Luke came over reluctantly. "He'll be fine." He gave Luke an encouraging smile.

"Thanks, doc." Luke returned to the corner chair, keeping an eye on Trey as he drank his tea and nibbled his cookies.

Renji shook his head and smiled, going over to Steven to help himself as Marshall joined him.

"Black cherry tea and ginger snaps, Marshall. Thought you might like to have your favorites for the big planning session." Steven handed over a filled and steaming cup with a plate of the cookies.

"I could at that. Thanks, doc." His eyes closed in appreciation as he took a healthy swallow of the tea. He then looked at Steven. "I've been thinking, doc. Might be a good idea to get Miko to your father-in-law's 'till this all blows over."

Steven sighed as he poured his own cup of tea. "Yeah, was thinking that myself." He took a sip, light eyes troubled. "Even though I'm not a major player, we don't know yet if the mole has told Rusk about my involvement. Small though it has been, I'm a close friend of Renji's and Trey's doctor. Rusk could use that in a multitude of ways."

"Unfortunately," Marshall agreed.

"Steven…"

"Don't look so worried." He gave Renji's shoulder a comforting squeeze. "The boys are already with their grandfather and Miko will understand once I explain everything. Being the wife of a doctor, she knows how I am."

"I'm sorry, *aniki*." Renji gave him a warm hug, regretting getting his close friend into such a mess. But Steven, ever the optimist, wasn't having it.

"Hey now." He pulled away. "I knew the consequences when I when helped that first boy, so don't go blaming yourself."

"But…"

"No buts. I'm a doctor and we go where we're needed, plain and simple." He gave Renji's shoulder another squeeze. "Besides, this could be just the thing to get the old man to start respecting me more." He smiled and winked.

The three looked at each other for a moment then burst out laughing.

"Yeah, wishful thinking on my part, huh?" Steven chuckled.

"You'll be fine, doc." Marshall nodded.

Steven snorted at that. "I worked for three years in the ER in Hell's Kitchen, this is nothing."

"You'll be careful anyway, right?" Renji knew Steven could take care of himself, but it wouldn't stop him from worrying.

"I'll take every precaution," he assured Renji. "And after I tell the old man, he'll have his own security so far up my ass I'll be tasting shoe leather for weeks." He grimaced.

Marshall laughed at that. "I'll call his head of security and give him a heads up."

"Thanks." Steven gave him a grateful grin then finished his tea. After putting the empty cup back on the cart, he went over to Trey, giving him another check up.

"You're not leaving now, are you?" Trey's color was almost back to normal, the trembling gone.

"I'm afraid so." He nodded. "The sooner I get Miko to safety, the better I'll fell. And since the old man decided to use his country place for a little holiday, we have quite a drive ahead of us."

"Oh, well, thanks Dr. Steven. I don't know how to ever repay you."

"Bah, getting better and keeping that one out of trouble is payment enough." Steven thumbed toward Renji. "So keep drinking plenty of fluids, the tea with honey especially. You can start on the solid foods tomorrow, but not a lot. Eat slowly 'till you get full. No packing your stomach. If you get tired, rest, don't push it," he ordered.

"Yes, sir."

"Good." He smiled. "Renji will keep taking you to the hot spring. The water and minerals will help."

Trey held out his hand but Steven was having none of that and gave Trey a gentle hug. "Keep an eye on him, alright?"

"I will."

Steven pulled away and pat Trey's arm then walked back to Renji. "You make sure he follows my orders. He'll get antsy once his strength starts to return."

Trey let out a frustrated sigh causing everyone to laugh.

"To the letter, *aniki*."

"Good." They embraced once more. "Be careful, my friend."

"You too."

After they pulled apart, Steven reached out and shook Marshall's hand. "Take care of yourselves. I don't want a call about any unnecessary holes, got it?"

"Only for the bad guys, doc." Luke saluted him.

"You just concentrate on keeping your family safe doc, we'll be fine." Marshall gave him a confident smile.

Steven nodded and went to the door, looking at Renji with a mischievous grin. "Make sure you get some rest as well five o, you're going to need it." He winked then was gone.

"Steven!" he called out but only received an echoing laugh in response.

"Uh, five o?" Marshall looked at him with a questioning grin.

Renji felt his cheeks heat as he poured another cup of tea then went to sit beside Trey. "It's nothing."

"Right." Marshall chuckled.

He felt his face get hotter as he sipped his tea, but said nothing, taking Trey's hand in his empty one. Thankfully, he was saved from further embarrassment by Gary.

"Marshall, we're here."

"Copy that. Stow your gear and come ahead. Got the tea ready."

"Black cherry I hope."

"You know it, love."

"Be there in two. Gary out."

"I heard some of that, but it was very faint," Trey said.

"That's great. Davis should be about done then." He picked up an empty cup from the cart and filled it with fragrant tea. He then looked at Trey. "Need a refill?"

"Yes, please."

Renji took his cup, bringing it to Marshall who had the pot ready to pour and filled it. Renji took it back, resuming his seat. "Careful hana, it's still hot."

"Thanks." Trey took a tentative sip. "Good though."

Renji leaned over and gave him a gentle kiss on the brow, then heard the sounds of boots coming down the hall. The situation was too great to have them take off their boots in the house, otherwise, they would have. Looking up, he saw Gary enter first with Cole and Jake behind. Gary went immediately to Marshall who enfolded him in a loving embrace and kissing him deeply.

"Missed you, love."

"Missed you too, baby."

Gary Evans was your typical California beach boy. With his sun streaked brown hair, sky blue eyes, and perpetual tan set off by a 6'4" height and buff body, he was the poster boy for surfing and fun in the sun. But behind the looks and easy going attitude was a sharp mind and ruthless determination to protect those he cared about. It was a deadly combination for those stupid enough to go against him.

"Why is it we get picked on about still acting like honeymooners and these two act that way even after twenty years without anyone saying a word?" Cole sighed like a man greatly put upon.

Jake smiled indulgently and pulled Cole into a backward hug, his front to Cole's back. "I don't mind, baby, 'cause in twenty years, we'll be still be acting the same way."

Cole looked back with a wicked grin. "You know it, mon cour." He then gave Jake a steamy kiss.

Cole Marcell was a born and bred Cajun who grew up working on his family's fishing boats. It was hard work and big business, but Cole wanted to fly. He joined the Air Force after High School. At 6'1", he was stout and strong, the perfect pilot.

Jake Runninghorse was full blooded Lakota Sioux destined to follow in his grandfather's footsteps as the next tribal Shaman. His father discovering that Jake was gay stopped those plans cold as well as being thrown out his family's home. He stayed with his grandfather, who didn't care about such things as homosexuality, until he decided to join the SEALs. There, he was able to use his innate skills and natural instincts to their fullest potential. His 6'4" height and lean muscular build gave him a definite advantage as well.

Renji had to smile as he looked at the two men. They were such complete opposites. Cole was flamboyant and opinionated; Jake was quiet and thoughtful, their personalities balancing out. They were also striking together with Cole's caramel skin, rust colored hair, and amber eyes contrasting nicely with Jake's red bronze skin, dark brown eyes, and long ebony hair. Yet they fit and anyone could see the love they had for the other. Renji could also see something else about the two. Jake's warrior braid had beads of amber braided into it that were the exact color of Cole's eyes. And at the top of Cole's right ear was a silver hoop holding three large onyx beads the same shade of black as Jake's hair.

"Nice accessories." Renji pointed to Jake's braid and Cole's ear. Cole blushed, touching the hoop and beads with a smile. Talking about Jake was the only time the man ever blushed.

"Wedding gifts to each other," Jake replied. "So, slant-eyes, you going to introduce us or we going to stand here all night."

Renji raised a brow. "Maybe you need to go back on your honeymoon, Injun Joe. I don't think your mood has improved."

The two continued to stare at each other, faces blank, eyes dark, then they broke out into large grins and met each other for a bear hug.

"I really hate it when they do that." Luke sighed loudly.

"I am so happy for you, *oniisan*." Renji pounded Jake's back then pulled away. "And the beads are a nice touch." He winked.

Jake chuckled. "Braiding them in was the fun part." Those dark eyes twinkled with the carnal memory. "But enough about us, I want to meet the one who has put a sparkle in your eyes, my brother."

"Glad to." He led Jake over to Trey who had a very perplexed look on his handsome face. "I'll explain in a bit, hana." He took Trey's hand, lacing their fingers together. "Trey Morrison, this is Jake Runninghorse, Cole Marcell, and Gary Evans." He pointed to each one as they came and shook Trey's hand.

"It's nice to meet all of you." Trey smiled.

"His accent sounds familiar, almost like the twins." Gary's head was angled to the side with thought.

"It should be," Luke said. "Trey's a Carolina boy too."

"My condolences, cher." Cole grinned as Luke flipped him off.

"Now children," Marshall admonished.

Trey laughed. "No need to be sorry, Mr. Marcell. I'm proud of where I came from and it's good to know that the twins are around should I ever feel the need to reminisce."

"Well, put in my place with a smile and grace. Flower indeed." He winked. "I'm impressed, cher. And it's Cole, no need to be formal around here."

Trey laughed again, a becoming blush high on his cheeks. "Cole it is then." He nodded then turned those dancing aquamarine eyes on Renji. "You were saying, Mr. Takeda?"

"Oh, he's quick," Gary snickered. "I like him"

"Sorry, hana." Renji kissed his knuckles. "To make a long story short, about a year after Jake joined the team, we were both going through some tough times, feeling sorry for ourselves and got quite drunk."

Jake snorted at that. "More like totally shit faced."

Renji laughed. "Anyway, we talked as the drunk usually do about anything and everything, including stereotypes."

"Ah." Trey nodded in understanding.

"It's become an inside joke between us now." Jake smiled sheepishly. "I'm sorry if we alarmed you."

"Not a problem." Trey waved the apology off. "I get the redneck jokes and Mayberry theme thrown my way on occasion."

"A kindred spirit." Jake grinned.

"We're all different. It's the uneducated and mean-spirited who choose to make it the problem it still is today."

Renji noted the looks of admiration and appreciation as everyone nodded in agreement. His hana was a lot more than just a pretty face.

Jake laid a hand on his shoulder. "You did good, my brother."

"Don't I know it." He squeezed Trey's fingers with pride and admiration. Trey blushed again with the attention.

Jake went back to Cole's side, leading him over to the cart and pouring them both a cup of tea as well as helping themselves to the cookies.

"Marshall," Seth called over the ear piece.

"Go ahead, Seth."

"Coming in."

"Roger that. Marshall out."

Luke got up and went to the cart, pouring himself a refill and pouring a cup for Seth. He was putting a few cookies on a plate when Seth came through the door. He didn't see Seth's face.

"Seth, what the hell!" Gary blurted out causing Luke to look up.

"Seth!" Luke rushed to Seth's side. "What happened?"

There was a large red and purple bruise coming up on Seth's right cheek and a deep cut still oozing blood at the corner of his right, lower lip. Seth did not look happy.

"Bastard was playing opossum," Seth growled with a wince when Luke gently touched the bruise on his cheek. "He elbowed me when I parked the car."

"I hope he looks worse, cher."

Seth snorted, trying not to smile. "He'll need to see a plastic surgeon about the nose Renji already broke and a dentist about the two teeth he's now missing. Oh, and he might have a concussion. I wasn't exactly gentle when I tossed his ass on the plane."

"Just as long as he got on it, I don't care about the how," Marshall quipped then nodded to Luke. "Go get your boy cleaned up."

"The first aid supplies are still in the cabinet above the sink," Renji told them as they went to the bathroom.

Jake caught his eye and nodded toward Trey who was still staring at the closed bathroom door. He sighed inwardly, hoping he would have more time to explain the twins. But from the odd expression on Trey's face, that time was now. He just hoped Trey wouldn't judge them too harshly after he told Trey about their relationship.

"Uh, Trey…"

"They're lovers, aren't they?"

Renji and the others looked at Trey with surprise. "How'd you know?"

Trey smiled sadly. "My uncle Bob and his lover, my uncle Danny, were first cousins."

"Hana." Renji sat down at Trey's side.

"Being Southern isn't exactly a great thing sometimes, but to be gay as well…" He shrugged with a sigh. "They grew up together because they lived so close. Uncle Danny's mom and my gran were sisters, twins in fact, so the two sisters wanted to stay near each other. Uncle Bob and Uncle Danny were hardly ever apart and kept their relationship secret for decades. Until I caught them in Uncle Bob's garage. He has a back room with a large futon in case he happened to be working late on a restoration." Trey paused; those beautiful eyes were full of memories. "Seeing them together was the most beautiful sight I had ever seen. Me and my uncle shared the same the coloring, blond and pale. But Uncle Danny was all browns, hair, eyes, year round tan. Watching that contrast and the obvious love they had for the other, it was wondrous. And life changing."

"How old were you, cher?"

"I had just turned fifteen."

"Oh hana, no."

"Uncle Bob was diagnosed with lung cancer not long after that. He died eight months later. Uncle Danny committed suicide a week after that. Police found his body, laid out in his best suit, next to Uncle Bob's grave. I had him buried beside Uncle Bob and a marriage stone placed over them with some of the money Uncle Danny left me. They couldn't share their love out in the open when they were alive but I made damn sure they could in the afterlife." Tears spilled down his creamy cheeks. He wiped them away with a smile. "I put their names and dates and at the bottom I put three words, 'At last. Forever.'"

Renji pulled Trey into his arms and held him close, his own eyes misty. "You're something special, hana." He pulled back and wiped away the wetness on Trey's cheeks then kissed him tenderly. "Very special."

"No." He gave a watery grin. "I just wanted them to be together like they should have been."

"They are, cher." Cole and the others had tears in their own eyes, moved beyond words by Trey's story. "As for those two, well, the odds were against them from the start, I'm afraid."

"Why is that?"

Jake sighed sadly. "Their mother was half-Cherokee and never knew who the twin's father was because of her drug addiction. She finally od'ed when the twins were just toddlers. Their grandfather took them in, but, it wasn't easy for them on the Rez. Being half is bad enough, but being a quarter and showing no traits of their heritage, well, you can imagine how it must have been." Jake frowned, no doubt knowing exactly what the twins went through.

"All they had was each other." Trey nodded. "They're lucky, some don't even have that much."

"Unfortunately, it was their relationship that got them kicked out of the SEALs." Jake shook his head with sadness. "They were the best to come along in decades, passing on the first try, nearly unheard of, and excelling at everything. But that made enemies of those who weren't half as good. It was one of those assholes that caught them and turned them in. They were discharged without a care."

"Fortunately for me though, I happened to get wind of the whole thing a few months later." Gary grinned. "I still have several contacts that let me know when a potential employee might come along. After reading their service records, I was on a plane in hours. I knew they were the perfect additions to our team."

Marshall chuckled. "Of course, we were told up front about their relationship and that they weren't going to hide it. I told them that as long as they did their jobs and didn't embarrass the company, they could go at it like monkeys for all I cared. They've been with us for almost two years now."

Trey looked at them with luminous eyes. "You gave them a real home."

"For the rest of us as well, cher. Not easy being different and alone." Cole took Jake's hand and held it close. "Marshall, Gary, and the Takeda's changed that, made us family. All of us."

"You too, hana." Renji pulled Trey close again. "Family takes care of its own."

"Family, I like that." He sighed with clear contentment. "Though I never thought I'd have so many big brothers. And such hot ones at that."

Renji chuckled and gave Trey a tender hug as the others laughed. Seth and Luke finally came out the bathroom as the laughter died down.

"'Bout time," Marshall huffed. "Thought maybe you two had drown or something."

By the look on their flushed faces, it was 'or something'.

Trey patted the other side of the bed for Seth to sit down as Luke retrieved their tea and cookies. "Have a seat, darlin' and let me get a look at that shiner." Seth sat and let Trey look him over. "It'll be a nice shade of green and yellow in a couple days. It'll match your eyes better than the purple and red. And the puffy lip look suits you." He touched both places lightly.

"I've had worse." Seth shrugged.

"And I've seen worse but that doesn't mean I like or want seeing it on you," he admonished, Seth's eyes widening. "You'll be careful from now on, ya hear?"

Seth's eyes looked greener as he nodded.

"Good, now drink your tea and eat your cookies. You can't plan a battle strategy without a little something in your stomach."

Seth took the tea and cookies from Luke, about to get up.

"You'll sit right there," Trey commanded.

Seth nodded again, sipping his tea and carefully eating the cookies. Trey patted his shoulder then looked at Luke. "Sit down and eat as well. Make sure you drink all your tea." Luke did so without question as Trey sat back and took Renji's hand in his again.

Renji shook his head and grinned. His hana was one of a kind. And from the appreciative looks the others were sending his way, they knew it too. Plus there was the added bonus that the twins now had a friend, and a protective one at that.

"Alright, gentlemen," Marshall began. "Seeing as we have been with this operation from the beginning, we have plenty of Intel about Rusk and his little army of mercenaries. What we don't know is when and how they'll strike. And since Rusk has made this personal." He nodded to Renji and Trey. "That makes Rusk even more dangerous."

"From what my contact at Interpol could ascertain, the mole has been leaking info for about three, maybe four months," Gary added. "Renji has been to five auctions in that time."

"He was playing with me." Renji's blood went cold with that realization. "I knew something was up this last time, but when I saw Trey, I thought that was it. A new jewel to show and sell off."

"Playing is right," Marshall agreed. "And when he saw your interest in Trey, he upped the ante. But now the mole has no doubt told Rusk that his little plan didn't work and Trey is still alive."

"He wanted you to suffer, cher, and it didn't happen. His reputation and own warped sense of honor will demand he rectify that."

Renji nodded in agreement with Cole. "Alright, so what's the plan?"

"Protect you and Trey and take Rusk down," Marshall stated baldly.

"You're not going to capture him and turn him over to Interpol?" Trey asked.

Marshall shook head. "No offense to Interpol, but a man like Rusk would never stand trial. He knows too much and has too many influential contacts for that to happen."

"Plus, he would never stop coming after you and Renji," Seth added. "Not a psycho like him. Taking him out is the only way, Trey."

Trey sighed. "Yeah, I understand."

"The world would be a safer place without him in it, hana."

"And seeing as Rusk is the sole brain of the operation, getting rid of him would put an end to the trafficking and drugs," Gary said.

Luke snorted. "The bastard's too paranoid to bring in a partner. And if the Intel is correct, no one but Rusk knows the formula to that drug either. The knowledge about that poison can die with him."

"Agreed." Renji nodded. "The trafficking is bad enough, but if that drug ever got to the streets…" He shuddered at the thought.

"We won't let that happen, my brother. With Rusk's paranoia and need to be in charge, he wouldn't give a drug he invented to anyone. Being the sole supplier holds too much power to give up. Even knowing he could die won't change that. He'd rather die than and take the knowledge with him than let another have it," Jake surmised.

Jake was right about that. Rusk was an egomaniac. His need to be in charge at all times bordered on the extreme. Even his small army of mercenaries didn't make a move without his approval.

"Yeah, Rusk loves the power, any power, too much to give it up," Renji agreed.

"All the more reason to take him out now," Gary replied. "The longer he has this power, the more he'll want. Absolute power corrupts."

Everyone agreed to that.

"So here's what we're going to do," Marshall began. "The grounds already have sensors planted, but at first light

Jake, I want you to go over the area and fill in the gaps with your bag of tricks. Do whatever you need to let us know when and where these bastards are coming from."

"I'll throw them in a surprise or two as well."

"Such a devious mind, mon cour," Cole said with a smile.

"When Davis calls back about Trey's ear piece, I want him to put an eagle eye on the house and grounds. Infrared, satellite imaging, the works," Marshall continued.

"That could take some time, hon," Gary said. "Hacking into the right satellite won't be easy."

"I know. That's why Jake will do his thing. Before the eagle eye is set up, Jake's surprises will give us the added security and warning," he explained. "A watch will be set up as well. With six of us, that's three pairs, a pair outside, a pair inside, and one to rest and act as backup. We'll change every five hours."

"You know, we're not sure how many Rusk will bring. His small army of mercenaries numbers about twenty and most are military rejects. While the reject part helps, we don't know who has the better training and who just likes to fight," Gary pointed out. "If he decides to bring them all, the six of us won't be enough, regardless if they're rejects or wannabe's."

"What did you have in mind, love?"

"With Ikakku and Ruki's baby due in a couple weeks, any kind of long distance travel is out. That leaves Davis and the boys with some free time on their hands. And Davis can hack into a satellite just as well here as he can in Tokyo."

Marshall nodded. "Tobias can bring some of his toys as well and get this house wired for sound."

"Nine against twenty morons is better than six against twenty when we own the high ground."

"We also have better training, better toys, and better organization," he added. "I fell in love with a genius." Marshall gave Gary a quick kiss. "Davis."

"Right here, boss. Trey's ear piece should be coming…up…now."

"Hana?"

"Static's gone."

"Ooh, what a very nice voice," Davis cooed.

"No time for that, Davis," Marshall interrupted. "I want you and the boys on a company helicopter and on your way here within the hour."

"What's up, boss?" Davis' tone had changed from flirty to professional in seconds.

"We're taking Rusk down."

"Copy that. Anything special you need us to bring?"

"Have Tobias bring his toys, I want the house wired. There could be some close contact so Joey should be prepared for that. While you're in transit, I need you to find the right satellite to put an eagle eye on the house. I want the works, Davis."

"Roger that. The boys are already in motion. I'll call when we're close. Davis out."

"I know it'll be quite a while before they get here so just have them use their regular room if I'm not up." Renji also needed to let Trey in on the relationship the three had. "Hana, just so you know and won't be surprised, Davis and his team are lovers."

"All three of them?"

Renji nodded. "Davis Jenkins and Joey Carlisle are cousins, like your uncle and his lover. Tobias Durrand is a childhood friend."

"It hasn't been easy for them, that's for sure." Gary shook his head. "They were all raised Mormon but Tobias' family are, well, zealot comes to mind."

"He was excommunicated when they found out he was gay. Davis and Joey's family were threatened with the same if they harbored the boys in any way," Marshall added. "They joined the Marines to get away and be together. But it wasn't as easy as they thought it would be. Then they were deployed to Afghanistan. Joey got shot there and nearly died."

"Their relationship came out after that and they were all discharged. Which was a good thing for us." Gary grinned. "Davis is an IT genius, so when I heard he was no longer in the Marines, I contacted him. Who knew we'd get a whole other team?"

"What do the other two do?" Trey asked Gary.

"Tobias is an electronics wizard and inventor. He does the security on all our homes and buildings. He's the one who also came up the ear pieces."

"Wow, smart guy."

Gary nodded with a grin. "Joey, he's our hand to hand expert. Holds more black belts and degrees of black belts, it's incredible. He also helps Davis and Tobias with whatever they need."

"And one of these days I'm going to pin that guy," Seth growled.

"You can try, cher, you can certainly try." Cole chuckled.

"I almost had him last time," he mumbled into his tea cup.

Trey smiled and patted his shoulder. "It's good to have a goal, darlin'. Nothing like motivation to make you want to achieve that goal. And the challenge will only push you to try harder and be better."

Seth looked at Trey and blinked, that realization just occurring to him from the expression on his face.

"You're never too old to learn something new, Seth. Remember that the next time you and Joey spar. The results might surprise you." Renji winked.

Seth nodded. "Yeah, thanks."

"Alright guys, let's get moving. We've kept Trey up long enough. He needs his rest," Marshall instructed. "Seth and Luke have the first watch. Cole and Jake will relieve you in five hours."

Seth and Luke both rose, taking their cups and plates to the cart. "We'll gear up and get started," Luke said.

"You two will be careful." The warning in Trey's tone was clear.

Luke saluted. "Yes, sir."

Seth merely smiled and nodded, then they were out the door.

"Well, cher, I must say I'm glad you're here." Cole took his and Jake's dishes to the cart as well. "For Renji especially, but for them two as well."

"Welcome to our family, Trey." Jake and Cole bowed low with respect.

Renji could see the tears in Trey's eyes, his face radiant with happiness. "Thank-you." His voice cracking a little.

"Let me take those dishes, hana." Renji took them from Trey and stood. "Rest a bit while I take the cart back to the kitchen. I won't be long." He reached down and gently kissed those ruby lips then moved away to the cart. Gary and Marshall had put their dishes there as well.

"Goodnight, Trey."

"Night."

"Sleep well, cher."

"Sweet dreams."

"Night, guys." Trey waved a hand to them as he snuggled down under the covers.

Renji pushed the cart out the door and to the kitchen, Gary, Marshall, Cole, and Jake following. At the sink, he opened the dishwasher and loaded it but didn't start it. Instead, he stood there, mind troubled as he looked out the kitchen window into the darkness.

"The moment Rusk steps foot on this property, he dies. No hesitation, no question. He gambled with Trey's life and I nearly lost him. It won't happen again." He took a deep breath, body shaking with emotion. "Trey...I can't...I won't...lose him. I won't." He pounded the sink with a fist, trying to keep the tears at bay.

"Easy, my brother." Jake wrapped an arm around his shoulders and put a hand over his fist. "He's safe and we're going to do all we can to keep it that way."

Renji took a few deep breaths. It wasn't very often he let his emotions get the upper hand, but caring for Trey as much as he did and knowing that Rusk had tried to kill him and would try again because of revenge, well, it was enough to rattle him more than was safe. For him and Trey.

"*Gomen.*" He turned in Jakes embrace and gave everyone a half smile. "Didn't mean to lose it like that."

"No need to be sorry, cher. You care for Trey and want him safe. I'd be worried if you didn't lose it." Cole smiled tenderly.

"We all understand what you're feeling," Marshall added. "Worrying about your other half is the price you pay for a lifetime of love and happiness." Gary went into his arms, his smile radiant with love.

"What would I do without you guys?" Renji sighed with a smile.

"Fall to rack and ruin, I'm sure." Gary chuckled.

Renji grinned at that, a huge yawn overtaking him.

"You're exhausted, cher." Cole came up and touched his cheek. "Go to your young man and get some sleep. We'll be here, keeping you both safe."

He reached out and pat Cole's shoulder. "*Arigato*." Then he walked away only to stop. "Almost forgot. Kaito is due to arrive tomorrow afternoon." That caused Cole to growl. "I'll let Marshall explain the good news. *Oisme*." He was halfway back to the bedroom when he heard Coles' shout.

"Hell yeah!"

Renji just shook his head and kept going. When he got to the bedroom, he found Trey with his eyes closed and snug under the covers. Renji took a moment to watch him, then went to the bathroom to wash up and undress. He left the bathroom light on but closed the door part ways to let the light in should Trey need it. He then turned off the room light and climbed in beside Trey.

"Mmm, Renji, waited for you." Came Trey's sleepy voice as Renji gathered him close, spooning behind him.

"I'm here, love, go to sleep." But he was already out, his breathing deep and even. Renji smiled into his golden head, snuggling closer to Trey's warm, soft body, his own breathing evening out as he followed Trey into peaceful oblivion.

Chapter 5

Trey was dreaming. It had to be a dream because there was no way what he was feeling could happen when he was awake. Of course, he did vaguely recall such a feeling on the plane, but that could be a drug induced hallucination.

Those thoughts were stopped suddenly when Trey felt wet warmth engulf his aching shaft, the touch of firm fingers gently squeezing his tight balls. "Mmm." The combined sensation caused Trey to whimper, a feeling of silver lightning to spark through his body. Then the feel of hard suction and a swirling tongue bowed his back, making him cry out. "Oh, God!"

"That's it, baby, come for me."

Trey heard that husky command and looked down to see and feel Renji's mouth wrapped around his cock. Added with the carnal look in his eyes, Trey couldn't hold back. "Renji!" He shouted his release as he emptied himself down Renji's throat.

"Good morning, hana."

His breathing finally back to normal, Trey opened his eyes to find Renji looking down at him, a smile on that handsome face.

"It is now." He reached out and wrapped his arms around Renji's neck, pulling him down for a steamy kiss. He tasted man, warmth, and himself, the flavors caused Trey to moan.

Renji pulled back with a chuckle. "Keep that up and we'll never leave this bed."

"Sounds like a plan to me." Now that he was feeling better, much better, Trey so wanted to explore. Starting at the top of Renji's ebony head and down that strong neck. Making a slight detour at nut colored nipples and a ripped stomach to the rigid shaft and heavy balls on down to well muscled legs and dusky toes. His memory and the little interlude at the hot spring had only whetted Trey's appetite. The very hard cock poking him in the stomach said that Renji was up to a little exploration as well. "You feel so good, Renji." He ran his hands up and down Renji's muscular chest to his back, interspersing wet kisses to a delicious neck.

"God, hana." Renji wrapped him in a tight embrace, taking his lips and kissing the air out of him. "I know I said I wouldn't push. Would wait until you were ready. But I woke up to your erection poking me in the ass and well, I just couldn't help myself. The temptation was too strong."

When Renji pulled away long enough to trail nibbling kisses down Trey's neck and shoulder, Trey had made up his mind. "Make love to me, Renji."

Renji's head popped up like a jack-in-the-box. "Trey?"

"I want to feel you inside me, filling me up." He cupped Renji's cheek. "I want you to make me yours."

"It's too soon, hana." Renji shook his head. "You're still recovering, getting your strength back. And while I said I wouldn't push –"

"Listen to me, Renji." Trey brought his other hand up, using both to cup that dear face. "You told me that neither of us knows what the future holds and that living in fear is no way to live. I believe that, Renji, just like I believe in you. I also believe that we take our chances when we can." His thumb rubbed over a stubbled cheek. "The way things stand, tomorrow might never come for us. I don't want to pass up this chance if it might be our last, Renji."

"We're safe, Trey. I'm not going to let anything happen to you or us, I swear."

"You don't know that, darlin'." He rose up and tenderly kissed those full lips. "We have now, right here, and I don't want to regret not making the most of this chance if the worse should happen."

"Hana —"

"Please, Renji." Trey kissed him again. "Make me yours."

Despite holding Renji to his promise of not pushing, the morning blow job notwithstanding, after everyone left last night with Renji to the kitchen, Trey had done a little thinking. About several things. Yeah, he was terrified that Rusk would find them. Hell, the bastard nearly succeeded in killing him. Twice. And from the sounds of it, still wanted to. Him and Renji both. Conrad wasn't entirely trustworthy either. The asshole. But even before knowing all that, Renji had been there. Been there from the beginning to save him, comfort him, keep him sane even.

Then there was the connection they both felt. Not just attraction, for that was surely there, it was more than that. It was a precursor to a love that Trey could feel developing by the moment. It wasn't love yet. But with enough time, enough nurturing, it would be. Unfortunately, time wasn't exactly on their side. Any day now, Rusk would show. Trey wanted, needed, Renji. Needed his closeness, his warmth, and the caring he saw in those dark eyes. But most of all, Trey wanted the connection they shared to be more than just a feeling. Trey wanted it to be physical too.

Those black diamond eyes seemed to see into Trey's soul, direct and probing until with a great sigh, Renji's shoulders slumped in defeat. "Your first time, it... it's going to hurt a little, hana. I'm sorry."

"I'm sure you'll make it up to me." Trey lay back and brought Renji with him, kissing those tempting lips then nibbling that strong jaw.

"For the rest of my life, Trey, I promise." Renji's dark eyes went even darker with that vow then he swooped in and melted Trey's brain with the hottest kiss he had ever received.

After that, Renji continued with the melting assault. His hands and lips were everywhere, pushing Trey's arousal toward a burning conflagration of need so hot that Trey was begging to be burned by it.

"Renji…please…can't…please." Firm fingers slowly moved down his crack until they reached his hole, rubbing it with wet, slick strokes, then one finger gently entered. "God." Trey moaned.

"So tight, hana, so hot." Renji's hot breath ghosted over his hip. "I'm going to make you soar baby, take us both into the clouds."

When Renji added another finger, it caused a burning and stretching sensation. It wasn't all that unpleasant, but it was different. "Mmm, burns." Trey's arousal was too ramped up to be stopped by a little burn though. In fact, it kind of added to the pleasure, pushing him a notch higher as Renji's fingers went in and out, wiggling inside. Then Renji rubbed over a certain spot that nearly made Trey lose it completely. "Oh, God…Renji…please, now…please." He was so close but he wanted Renji inside when he finally found paradise.

The distant sound of paper tearing caused Trey to look at Renji as he was sheathing himself in a condom, a tube of lube in his hand. "Relax, hana," He crooned, liberally coating his erection then moving between Trey's legs. He got a pillow and put it under Trey's hips to make him higher, then came over Trey, kissing him deeply as something a lot larger than a couple fingers pushed into his body.

"Mmm," Trey whimpered with the burning pain as Renji slowly entered.

"I know, baby, I'm sorry. Just relax and let me in." His voice was tight, but Trey did as he said, trying to relax his anal muscles. "That's it, hana, just a little more."

When he was finally all the way in, Renji stopped.

"God, you're huge, so full of you, Renji," Trey panted as the burning slowly faded.

Renji groaned, his own breathing fast. "You're tight, hana, so tight and hot. You feel perfect."

Taking his lips in another melting kiss, Renji moved a bit, the feeling sending sparks straight to Trey's balls and outward. "Jesus!" He gasped. "Do…do that again." Renji did, keeping the in and out motion slow. "Mmm, good…feels so good."

"Want to make you feel better, baby." Renji's breathing was harsh, that beautiful body moving with such power.

Trey's hands roamed over fluid muscles encased in silky skin, wanting nothing more than to be connected with this man forever. "Renji…" His name came out on a moan as Renji twisted his hips, rubbing over that spot inside that made him see stars. "God, please…need, Renji…need…" The pressure was building, his balls tight with it, body starting to tremble.

"Yes, my hana." Renji picked up the pace, hips moving faster now as he plunged deeper into Trey's body. "We're going to soar so high." He kissed Trey again as a warm hand wrapped around Trey's aching cock.

"Ah!" Trey cried out at the added sensation, his body on overload. "Oh please, Renji…I…I…can't take it…please!"

Both their bodies were sheened with sweat as Renji continued to push Trey toward release. Using his hips, hands, and lips, Renji did all he could to drive Trey insane with pleasure. It was working. Trey was shaking, skin oversensatized, cock throbbing painfully when finally, he could hold back no more.

"That's it, hana, soar with me."

Renji nailed his sweet spot then bit down where neck and shoulder meet. Trey lost it.

"Renji!" Trey screamed as the strongest and longest orgasm of his life stormed through him. A muffled shout let him know that Renji had followed him into the clouds.

The feel of gentle fingers caressing his cheek had Trey blinking open his eyes. Renji was lying beside him, a smile on his face and black diamond eyes shining with happiness. He was the most gorgeous man Trey had ever seen.

"Have a nice nap, sleeping beauty?" His fingers continued to caress Trey's cheek, the heat rising in his face at the question.

"Yeah."

After the brain melting orgasm, Trey vaguely recalled Renji cleaning him up and tucking him in. Sleep sucked him under after that.

"I would have let you sleep longer, but its almost one and Kaito will be here in a few hours." He brushed the hair from Trey's brow, those fingers keeping a steady touch on Trey's skin. "Kiko, my housekeeper, is preparing a late lunch for us, so I thought you might like a shower and a soak before we eat."

Trey couldn't take it anymore. He pulled Renji close, needing to taste those full lips, feel the silk and warmth of his skin. He certainly wasn't hungry for food at that moment. "Mmm, you feel so good." His whole body was tingling, cock aching with renewed fullness as he felt Renji respond.

"I'll never get enough of you, Trey." Renji pulled Trey up and into his lap, wrapping Trey's legs around his waist. There was a very hard cock pointing directly at Trey's hole.

The moved caused Trey to wince as protesting muscles let themselves be known. Including the one with the hard erection poking at it. But as he settled into Renji's embrace, feeling the warmth of the man surround him, Trey slowly relaxed.

"Sore, baby?" Renji's magic hands kneaded his back, lower back, and ass.

Trey felt his face heat. "A little, but it was worth it." He nibbled at Renji's neck, the ache in his body turning to a slow burn. He pulled back and looked Renji in the eye. "Thank you." A world of meaning was conveyed in those two words and he hoped, his deepening feelings as well.

Renji cupped his cheek, eyes bright. "You were made for me, hana." He then crushed Trey against his chest and plundered his mouth, his tongue dueling with Trey's.

Trey whimpered in surrender, clinging to Renji. He writhed against him, wanting to crawl inside the man and never leave. "Renji."

"God, I want you so much, Trey." He kissed and nibbled at Trey's neck and shoulders. "So much."

"Please." He pushed back on Renji's hard length, the soreness in his ass letting Trey know that it hadn't faded with his arousal.

"Easy, baby." He pulled Trey up and moved his erection from under him.

"But…" He settled back down onto Renji's lap, his hard cock sliding against Renji's. He moaned at the feeling.

"You're too sore, hana, but there are other ways." His hand wrapped around both their pricks causing Trey to gasp. "Other ways to make you soar."

He took Trey's mouth again as his hand pumped, but it wasn't enough. A keening whimper escaped as Trey moved closer to Renji's body, his hips pumping up and needing more friction. Renji moved his hand away and slammed their bodies together, both their erections trapped between their stomachs. It was just what Trey needed, feeling his aching cock rub against a muscled abdomen and feeling Renji's hard length rub against his own. They were both trembling and sweaty the closer they came to their peak.

"Oh, God…Renji…oh…oh…" He buried his face in Renji's neck as he cried out, spurting on himself and Renji. More wet warmth and a loud groan signaled Renji had followed Trey over the edge.

Still panting a little, Trey let out a deep sigh, sated and relaxed. Renji kissed his forehead and cheeks. "My beautiful, hana." He kissed Trey's lips, languidly exploring Trey's mouth.

"Mmm." Trey smiled, resting his head on Renji's shoulder. Trey needed to get cleaned up, but he didn't want to give up their closeness just yet. "What was that you said earlier? That I was made for you?"

"Yes." He paused and held Trey tighter. "You are, Trey. In every way. You...you mean the world to me. And...I'm falling for you, Trey. Hard."

Trey blinked, not sure he heard right and pulled away a little. Renji's cheeks were pink, but his eyes were diamond bright. "Oh, Renji."

"I know it seems like it's too soon." Both his hands cupped Trey's face. "But I think I began to fall for you the moment I saw you, Trey." He smiled, thumbs rubbing both cheeks. "You don't have to say anything now, hana, I just wanted you to know how I felt."

He mirrored Renji, taking his face in both hands as well and smiled, tears of joy welling in his eyes. "It may be too soon, but, I care about you too, Renji. How could I not?" A tear spilled and rolled down his cheek, onto Renji's hand. "You make me feel whole, like there was a piece of me I never thought was missing but was suddenly found, right here in your arms."

"Trey." Renji took possession of his mouth again, gentling his assault before finally pulling back, planting kisses over Trey's face. "You've already become such a vital part of my life, hana."

"It's like you've always been here with me." He kissed Renji again then settled into his embrace, his heart full as tears of joy continued to fall.

For the last five years, Trey had been alone. With no family left or friends that he was close to, he had only existed, not really living. Because of his gran's death, he had taken a year to himself before starting college. But once enrolled, he only took a few classes at a time, wanting to prolong the inevitable. After graduation, he knew he would have to move back to his gran's house. That empty house with all the golden memories of his childhood. He got depressed every time he thought about it. But now, now there was Renji. For the first time in Trey's life, he had found love, the real kind. The kind his parent's had, his grandparent's, and his uncle's. Even though he and Renji were being targeted by a madman and could be killed tomorrow, Trey was happy that they had today. It was more than he could have hoped for, to have this man love him.

"As much as I would rather stay like this for the rest of the day, hana, we need to clean up and you need to eat." He pulled away a bit, the stickiness on their stomachs beginning to dry around the edges. It was not a good feeling.

"Cleaning up would be nice." Trey felt the heat rise to his cheeks at the evidence of their love making.

Renji chuckled, wiping away the last of his tears and giving him a quick kiss before he moved away. "We'll shower and soak for a bit. Kiko should have lunch ready by the time we're done." He went to the bathroom and brought back a wet cloth, cleaning himself then Trey, tossing it back when he was finished.

Trey stood and stretched, raising his arms above his head and rising up on his toes. His muscles were still tight, but the soreness was almost gone. He felt loads better than he had the last couple days.

Brushing his hair back, he found Renji looking at him with heat in those dark eyes. "There's that look again, darlin'." He stepped over to Renji, putting his hands on that gorgeous chest.

"What look is that, hana?" Renji remained still while Trey leaned in and up.

"Like I'm a tasty snack." He rose up and gave Renji's lips a quick kiss.

Grinning broadly, Renji took his hands and kissed the tops of both. "More like a feast." He chuckled, Trey's face heating up again. "And when we have more time, I intend to gorge myself."

Trey's heart picked up at the image that promise invoked.

Renji chuckled again, moving to the closet and grabbing two white robes, handing one to Trey. "Better get moving or we'll never leave."

Nodding, Trey put on the robe and tied the sash. He hoped his semi-hard cock went down before they got in the hall. Wouldn't do to accidentally run into the guys sporting a halfie.

"You need me to carry you again?" Renji had his own robe on, standing close.

"No." He smiled. "I feel steadier and the exercise will help."

"Alright, but we'll go slowly." He took Trey's hand and they strolled out the room. "You start to feel tired or weak, let me know. Steven said not to push it."

"Don't worry, I will. I have a feeling doc would have my ass if I didn't." He chuckled as they made there way slowly down the glass hallway.

"Mine as well."

Getting to the shower room, Trey went to a bench and took off his robe. "Want me to get the water started?"

"Please." Renji went to the large cabinet. "I'll get everything we need."

"Don't forget the duckies." Trey grinned as he turned the water on and waited for it to heat. He then adjusted the temp and stepped under the spray. "Mmm." He let the water run down the top of his head and over his body.

"Here, hana." Renji handed him the loofah and soap then went to turn on another shower.

Trey gave him a questioning look but Renji just grinned. Sharing the shower could delay them further.

After they washed and turned off the water, Renji grabbed the duckies along with Trey's hand. "We'll need to cool off after so I'll just leave the towels here."

Trey nodded, following Renji through the swinging doors. Renji had thrown the duckies in the water and made it to the steps when he stopped, his gaze locked to the far corner. Trey moved beside him, wondering why he stopped so suddenly, and looked in the same direction. His eyes widened, a small gasp escaping in the moist laden air. It seems they weren't alone.

Seth and Luke were on the other side on a built in seat, Luke perched on Seth's lap in a loving embrace. They were kissing, being careful of Seth's lip, Luke slowly moving up and down. Seth's hands were on his hips, the steamy water barely covering the tops of Luke's thigh's as it sloshed languidly with his movements. Their skin shone like moonlight under the skylights, flame hair darkened to banked embers in the steam laden air. It was the most erotic sight Trey had ever witnessed, his body responding to the beautiful pair. He couldn't take his eyes off them.

"Quite stunning, aren't they?"

Trey jerked as Renji whispered those words in his ear, his arms wrapping around him from behind. He could feel Renji's hard cock against his lower back. "I…um…"

Renji chuckled darkly. "There's no harm in looking, hana, in watching such love between two beautiful men."

"Oh." Even in the hot moist air, Trey could still feel his cheeks heat.

"Come, they know we're here." He took Trey's hand again and led him into the steamy, bubbling water.

"They won't mind?" He groaned at how good the water felt as it closed over his body. He dunked his head then pushed the wet strands back. "I don't want to disturb them if they'd rather be alone."

"It's fine, hana." He smiled as he pulled Trey into his arms then devoured his mouth.

Trey moaned in surrender, their erections rubbing together as he wrapped his arms around Renji's neck. How this man could make him want, and with the least provocation.

"Every moment I crave more of you, hana." He kissed the side of Trey's neck, lapping at the moisture there. "I'll never get enough. *Zettai*."

He took Trey's lips again in a quick yet thorough kiss then turned Trey around, having him face away. Directly at the twins who were in the same position, looking right at him and Renji.

Renji pulled him in tight, his erection sliding easily between Trey's legs in the mineral laden water. "Oh, Renji." His eyes began to close after Renji wrapped his strong fingers around Trey's aching shaft, pumping it oh so slowly.

"Don't close your eyes, hana." His voice was deep and commanding. "Watch them as they watch us. See how the pleasure builds between them as it builds between us as well."

Trey couldn't have closed his eyes if he wanted to. With the sensual web Renji had woven with voice and hands and the visual of the twins making love, it was all

Trey could do to blink. His breathing was harsh, skin sensitive as Renji continued to stroke his cock with one hand and caress him with the other. When the fingers of that other hand pinched a nipple, Trey cried out.

"Oh, God!"

"I love how responsive you are to me, hana. How your body reacts with every touch." Renji's hard shaft began to thrust between Trey's legs, its tip bumping his balls with every in motion. "The delicious sounds you make as I love on you."

A keening whimper escaped when Renji sped up the stroking of his cock, his other hand going from one sensitive nipple to the other. And all the while he watched the twins, heard their sounds of pleasure.

"Seth, oh God...Seth please!" Luke's cry was one of pure rapture. Of course Seth's response to that plea was to wrap his arms around Luke and pound into him harder. "God...yes!"

Trey gasped at the sight, his balls unbelievably tight, body tingling. He was so close, so close. "Renji, I...need...please..."

Renji pulled him in tighter, his hips snapping, the friction against Trey's balls getting stronger. The faster stroking and nipple pinching was almost more than Trey could stand. Then Renji bit down where neck and shoulder meet and Trey saw stars. His shout of release echoed in the room, Renji's muffled cry not far behind followed by the twins as they too found bliss.

Slumping back in Renji's embrace, Trey closed his eyes and rested his head on Renji's shoulder. The feel of moist lips against his cheek made him smile. "Between you, the twins, and the water, I'm boneless."

"I know exactly how you feel, hana." Renji chuckled, a deep sigh leaving no doubt just how good he felt as well.

They continued to soak for a bit, the steam and bubbles only adding to their sense of contentment. Unfortunately, that contentment had to come to an end.

"Time to go, hana."

Trey groaned but nodded, following Renji out and up the steps. He was a little wobbly at the top, holding the handrail for support.

"You all right, Trey?" Renji held his arm and pulled him away from the water.

"Yeah." He laughed. "A little too relaxed I think. Jelly legs."

Renji grinned, keeping a hold of his arm for added support as he led them to the swinging doors. "A cool shower will help."

They went through, the coolness of the shower room a big difference compared to the hot spring. Seth and Luke were already there, water sluicing over their naked bodies. If Trey weren't so spent and blissed out, he would have appreciated the sight more. Instead, he gave them a languid smile and followed Renji under the water. The coolness hit him immediately.

"Shit! There just went my hot spring high." He shivered a bit even though the water probably wasn't that cool. He was just that hot.

"You'll get it back, hana," Renji told him with a kiss to his cheek, then moved over to the next shower. "Promise."

"I'll hold you to that, darlin'."

Trey stayed under the pray a little longer then turned it off, grabbing a towel and drying off. Renji was still using the shower so Trey took a moment to admire his lover. Renji caught him and winked causing heat to rise to Trey's cheeks as he reached for his robe and put it on. He turned at the sound of footsteps and whispering, continuing to dry his hair.

"Go ahead, Seth." They had their robes on, green for Seth and blue for Luke. Their fingers were interlaced as they held hands, cheeks bright pink. Whatever was on their minds, their expressions said it was serious.

"What's up, guys?" He finished with his hair, brushing it away from his eyes, then put the towel on the bench.

"We, well…" Seth began. Luke nudged his shoulder, giving him an encouraging nod. "We wanted to thank you."

Trey blinked. "For what?"

Both their faces reddened further, Luke putting his hand over Seth's in a show of support and affection.

"For sharing what you and Renji have and for not, well, most people don't understand what me and Luke have, ya know? They see it as unnatural." He shrugged, but Trey could tell that these two had been hurt by such words and probably even more.

He put a hand on each of their shoulders. "I'm the last person to judge anybody, least of all two men who love each other as much you two do. And it doesn't matter to me if you're related either. My uncle had the same relationship with his cousin, a male first cousin." Their eyes widened at that news. "You two are truly gorgeous together and I feel very honored and humbled that you allowed me and Renji to witness just how beautiful and special your love is. Seeing you both together like that was…well, it was one of the most wondrous sights I've ever seen."

Trey watched as two pairs of green eyes filled with tears. He had the feeling that very few people had accepted the love they shared or even understood it. He pulled them in close and hugged them tight, their silent sobs breaking his heart.

"It's alright, I'm here, I'm here." He rubbed their backs as they clung to him, the anguish and hurt of countless years seeming to pour out of them with each shake of their shoulders. "Just let it out."

When the emotional storm ended, Trey grabbed the towel he used and wiped their tears away, careful of Seth's cheek.

"Sorry 'bout that." Seth took the towel and blew his nose on one end, Luke on the other then he threw it on top of the ones they had used.

"None of that now." Trey cupped their cheeks, the blush still high in them. "There's no shame in showing emotion. Means we have compassion. That was one of many lessons my gran made sure to instill in me during the years I was lucky enough to have with her."

They both took deep breaths and nodded, happy smiles wreathing their faces.

"Good." He patted their cheeks. "You two belong together and I'll tell you why."

Twin looks of expectation waited for his answer.

"Many cultures believe that twins are the reborn souls of doomed lovers that were never given the chance to be together." He gave them a bright smile. "So the love you two have, well, it's quite possible that you've always loved each other. Something to think about, huh?"

They looked at each other and grinned, their love so bright and shiny, it near blinded Trey.

"Thanks, Trey."

"Yeah, thanks."

"Anytime, guys." He squeezed their shoulders. "I'm here if you ever need to talk or just need a friend. Us Carolina boys have to stick together, ya know?"

They nodded with wide grins, hands held tight together, then left.

Trey let out a sigh of happiness, glad he could help those two. They might show the world they're tuff, but Trey had seen the sadness and pain they kept hidden. Maybe some of it was gone now, lessened by the understanding of a friend. Trey sure hoped so. Those two deserved to be happy and together just as much as anyone.

"That was very caring, what you did for them."

Renji's voice startled him and he turned. Renji had his robe on, hair still damp as he came to Trey's side and took his hand, interlacing their fingers together.

"They have the right to be happy just as much as anybody else. Being related shouldn't have any bearing on how or why you love someone."

Renji let out a small sigh. "It shouldn't, no, but society has always viewed their type of relationship in an even darker light than being gay. Incest is the ultimate taboo, regardless of how much the two involved love each other. It's something they'll have to deal with for the rest of their lives I'm afraid."

"Yeah." Trey nodded then smiled. "But they have us now and a place where they're accepted."

"That they do, hana." He leaned down and tenderly kissed Trey, his tongue leisurely exploring his mouth. When he pulled away, they were both breathing a bit faster. "You have a good heart, Trey Morrison and I feel damn lucky that you were the one to steal mine."

Trey chuckled, his cheeks feeling warm. "More like a mutual exchange." He gave Renji a quick peck on the lips.

Renji pulled Trey in for a hug but Trey's stomach chose that moment to protest its emptiness. "Come on, hana." He grinned. "Let's get you fed. Man cannot live on love alone."

Trey felt the heat take over his entire face. "Yeah, I could eat." He smiled sheepishly.

Renji grinned again and squeezed his hand, leading him out the shower room and to the right down to the end of the hall then they took a short right and a left that led to a huge room.

"Wow." Trey stepped in further and looked around the wide open space.

"This is a formal Japanese audience room," Renji explained.

The room was simple and beautiful with bamboo mats on the hard wood floors. There were two black lacquer tables at each end of the room with a vase of yellow and white roses placed in their centers. On each side of the door where they entered were two large silk hangings, one with koi in a pond and the other with a stunning peacock. The facing wall wasn't a wall at all but five sets of very large latticed rice paper panels that let in rays of golden sunlight. Renji walked over to one of the panels closest to the wall.

"Each panel can slide or be popped out and slid back to open the room to the courtyard."

"You have a courtyard?" Trey's jaw nearly dropped.

"See for yourself, hana." He smiled as he slid the panel back. As he did so, Trey noticed that the entire panel was encased in glass. "Rice paper isn't very sturdy or energy efficient," he explained when he noticed Trey looking at the glass. "Especially in winter. But I wanted that authentic look so I had these encased in tempered glass. Also good protection for the rice paper from bugs and weather." He tapped the glass over one of the paper squares.

"That's pretty cool." Trey touched the glass himself then followed Renji out and gasped. "Good Lord!"

"Glad you like it, hana." Renji laughed.

But Trey barely heard, his eyes glued to the small slice of paradise in front of him and walked carefully to the edge of the wooden porch.

Where they were located, Trey noticed that the house was L shaped, the majority of the house to his left and the porch looked to wrap around it entirely. There were more of those rice paper panels, so more rooms that also led to the courtyard. And what a courtyard it was. Simple in it's beauty yet massive in scale, the layout was based on concentric circles, a set of three in the center. The center of the circles was a koi pond with a small stone fountain depicting jumping koi. The next ring was a zen garden, its pure white sand sparkling in the sunlight and what looked to be black lava rocks placed near waves made by a nearby wooden rake. The last ring was a flower bed with bright white paving stones leading to the zen garden or out to the rest of the yard that was covered in thick and vibrant green grass. There were small circular beds of flowering shrubs, roses, and tress interspersed throughout the yard.

Trey closed his eyes and inhaled deeply, taking in the scents of growing things and the tranquility of the surroundings into his being. When he opened his eyes, Renji was beside him, giving him a warm smile and love filled gaze.

"If tranquility and peace were a place, this would be it."

"Thank you, hana." He put an arm around Trey's shoulders. "It's a simple design, so I didn't have much trouble with it."

Trey nodded then stopped. "Wait, you designed this?"

"I dabble." He shrugged those broad shoulders.

Looking out over the yard again, Trey shook his head in wonder. "Yeah, dabble."

Renji chuckled. "Being an architect, I love creating new structures, but sometimes you need to recharge or you'll burn out. Doing projects like this and the hot spring room helps me recharge because it's something different. There's the also added benefit that I find it fun to do as well."

"You are a man of many hidden talents, Mr. Takeda." He turned and reached up to wrap his arms around Renji's neck, bringing them close as Renji put his arms around Trey's waist.

"And you, Mr. Morrison, are a man with a very big heart." He leaned down and kissed the tip of Trey's nose.

"We match up pretty well then."

Renji brushed their lips together. "Perfectly." He then claimed Trey's mouth, thrusting his tongue deep.

Trey moaned into Renji's mouth, the taste of him, the feel of him, went to Trey's head. It was as if Renji was a drug and Trey couldn't wait to get his next fix. Rather funny when it was a drug that helped to bring them together.

Being brought out of their mutual haze, Renji jerked back abruptly, the sounds of discreet and not so discreet coughing sounding behind them.

Trey laid his forehead on Renji's chest and groaned, feeling his face flame. "There are people behind us, aren't there?" Soft laughter followed that question, Renji laughing as well.

"I'm afraid so, hana." He pulled back and lifted Trey's chin. "I tend to forget my surroundings with you, not a very wise move given our circumstances."

Letting out a sigh, Trey took Renji's hand. "Just something we'll have to work on 'till this mess is cleaned up."

That earned him a gentle smile. "That we will." He then led Trey over to a very large round table with fat cushions on the floor where seven men and an older

Japanese woman were sitting. Four of the men he did know, three of the men and the older Japanese woman he didn't.

"Trey, I'd like you to meet Kiko Masaki." She was an attractive woman for her age in a beautiful lavender and white kimono, her salt and pepper hair done in a tasteful bun. She was also very small, barely coming to Trey's chest.

She rose from the floor gracefully at Renji's prompting, coming before Trey with a wide smile and bowed. Trey returned the gesture.

"She doesn't know that much English so I'll have to translate." He did so, saying something to Kiko. She smiled and bowed again, her words coming out quick.

"She says that she welcomes you to my home and asks how you are feeling."

"Oh." Trey smiled and returned the bow again. "*Arigato*, Kiko-san, I am feeling much better." Renji and the others looked at him with surprise. "Just because I don't know the language doesn't mean that I don't know a few simple words or the polite way to address someone."

Shaking his head, Renji laughed. "You just keep surprising me, hana, wonderfully so."

Renji translated for Kiko who clapped her hands with a bright smile and beamed, then came up to Trey and Renji, putting a hand over both they're hearts, closing her eyes. After a moment, she opened them and spoke.

"She says that our hearts beat as one, a sure sign of how strong our connection is." Renji's cheeks pinkened.

"Oh, uh, *arigato*." His own cheeks felt warm as well with her words.

She nodded then moved back to the table where another large cart was set up. It contained covered plates, teapots, and cups. She poured a cup and said something to Renji who smiled.

"*Hai, obaasan*." He looked at Trey. "I call her grandmother because she has been with my family since I was born. When I moved here, she decided to come with me because a man my age shouldn't be living in a house this large by myself and no one to take care of me." She then said something else. "And that I need to stop babbling and introduce you to the others before your food gets cold."

Trey laughed along with the others, Kiko smiling as she handed out cups of fragrant, steaming tea. "Hey Marshall, Gary." He nodded to the two, noticing that the twins were already dressed in their gear like everyone else. Black tanks and fatigues. "That was a fast change," he told them as he and Renji sat down on two empty cushions sitting across from them and beside Gary and Marshall.

"Nah, you two just took too long." Seth winked, causing Trey's cheeks to heat a bit. He really hated to blush, made him feel naïve and girly.

"Our room's right over there, Trey." Luke poked Seth in the side then pointed to one of the rice paneled doors.

Trey gave Seth a mock heated glare. Seth just smiled and drank his tea. Shaking his head, Trey grinned. The twins looked relaxed and a lot more at ease. It was good to see.

"As you've no doubt figured out, hana, these three miscreants are team three. They watch over my middle brother and his wife in Tokyo." Renji pointed to the three men sitting near the twins. "On the right is Joseph Carlisle, Joey. In the middle is Davis Jenkins and last but not least is Tobias Durrand."

Reaching over the table, Trey shook their hands. "Nice to meet you."

They were good looking men in that all-American way. All three were blond, Tobias having a darker version than the other two's sunny color, his eyes a light brown while Joey and Davis were blue eyed. There was also a marked resemblance with Joey and Davis, letting anyone who met them know that they were related. It was there in their similar height and stocky build, the set of their shoulders, the shape of their mouths and noses. Tobias was much different. Taller than the other two, even sitting down, he was slim yet muscular, slashes of cheekbones, a blade of nose, his skin a light olive compared to Joey and Davis' peaches and cream complexion. They also loved each other very much. Trey could see it in the way they talked to each other, in their smiles and looks. It shined like a multi-faceted crystal between them.

"When Davis said you sounded kind of like the twins, I thought he must have been hearing things." Joey's blue eyes twinkled with mischief. "Now I'm not so sure."

"I'm from the same state." Trey grinned as Renji handed him a cup of tea.

"Really/"

"I was just as shocked, babe," Davis said, shaking his head.

Seth flipped them both the bird, his grin saying he wasn't taking the bait. Everyone laughed, Luke giving his brother's shoulder a congratulatory pat.

"Alright you two." Tobias looked at Davis and Joey, shaking his head at their antics. "You'll have to excuse them, Trey, I'm afraid the home training didn't quite stick." That earned him a raspberry from Davis and a snort from Joey. "See what I mean?" He sighed deeply like a man greatly put upon.

"Don't worry about it." Trey waved his hand with a grin. "Being family means you take the good with the bad."

Tobias laughed at that. "Too true."

They continued to talk, joke and drink their tea, then Kiko came over and placed several covered plates in front of Renji and Trey along with a tea pot. She then knelt at Trey's side and removed the lids covering the dishes. Everyone groaned.

"Man, knew I should have waited for the late lunch," Davis complained.

The smells coming from the plates was fantastic. The one in front of him had thin slices of beef and what looked like skinny egg rolls. Another plate held steamed veggies with rice shaped into triangles, some kind of red veggie in their centers. There was also a small bowl of soup with noodles and had green onions floating on the top. His stomach grumbled with empty complaint he was so hungry.

Kiko poured him a refill then gestured to the plate with the meat and egg rolls. "*Douzo.*"

Trey looked over at Renji.

"She wants you to try the egg rolls first, hana. She makes them herself and are a special treat."

He picked one up. It was a lot different from the ones he usually ate. This one was longer and skinnier, but the texture was about the same. He took a small bite then closed his eyes on a groan. It was manna from heaven. The crust was flaky and light, the cabbage and meat stuffing so flavorful and tender, it melted in his mouth. He took another bite and it was even better than the first.

Renji chuckled at his response. "Good, hana?"

All he could do was nod and chew as Renji translated for Kiko. Her smile was bright as she said something else.

"She's pleased you like the egg rolls and has ordered us both to clean our plates."

Trey swallowed and washed the rest down with a drink of tea. "*Arigato*, Kiko-san."

She patted his shoulder and beamed, saying something else to Renji, then gracefully got up and went back to her place beside the cart.

"She says you are a very polite and well mannered young man," Renji translated between bites of his own meal.

Trey smiled, cheeks feeling a little warm and continued to eat his meal. The others talked and joked around as they ate.

"How's that satellite looking, Davis?" Marshall asked.

"One sec." Davis turned around and behind him were two laptops hooked up to a variety of equipment. He tapped some keys on one of the laptops and frowned. "Still a couple more hours, boss. Found the best but so is the security. I'm having to cover my tracks, so that's what's taking so long."

Marshall nodded. "That's fine, just as long as it's up by then. Jake's done his magic, but the eagle eye will give us better warning."

Everyone nodded in agreement.

"Oh, Seth, I missed your spar with Joey," Gary spoke up. "How'd you do?"

"Surprisingly well," Joey answered with a laugh. "He was so focused this morning that I thought it might be Luke if it wasn't for the bruised cheek."

They all looked at Seth whose face was bright scarlet.

He shrugged. "Thought I'd use a new tactic is all."

"Well, it worked." Joey grinned then his face got serious. "Out of all the sessions we've had, Seth, that one was by far the best. Your mind and body were in sync and you listened to my instructions. That's what makes a great martial artist." He bowed his head in acknowledgment of Seth's good work.

"Thanks, *sensei*." His face was glowing as he bowed as well. Luke hugged him around the waist with a large, proud grin.

Trey watched the exchange with a smile of his own and felt Renji's arm come around his shoulders.

"Such a wonder." He kissed Trey's temple.

With a smile and warm cheeks, Trey finished his meal. He was relaxed and full when Kiko took his and Renji's plates away.

"I see you're looking better, Trey," Marshall commented. "How ya feelin'?"

"Better, thanks." He smiled. "Caveman here even let me walk to the hot spring. Slowly, of course."

"Of course." Marshall and the others laughed.

"Caveman?" Renji's dark brow raised at that.

"He does have a point, Renji," Gary smirked. "You do have that chest beating, take charge personality about you."

"Stubborn, too," Tobias added.

"Even heard him grunt a time or two." Davis nodded with a wide smile.

"See, cavemen," Gary laughed along with everyone again.

"Very funny." Renji shook his head good naturedly then brought Trey in close. "I'll show you a real caveman later, hana."

That rich voice sent a thrill down Trey's spine. "I'll hold you to that."

Renji gave him a quick peck on the cheek then turned to Kiko who was speaking to him. He nodded a few times, answering whatever she had to say, then she smiled, bowed deeply to him and Trey and left, taking the cart with her.

"Hiro picking her up?" Joey asked.

"She's going to call him now while she gets the rest of her bags together." Renji nodded.

"Kiko's leaving?" Trey looked at Renji with the question.

"With all the trouble headed our way, I thought it would be safer. She's going to stay with my brother Ikakku and his wife while the boys are here. With Miko so close to giving birth, she needs someone other than my nervous wreck of a brother there with her." He chuckled. "Kiko will take care of her and keep my brother calm. She has two daughters of her own."

"The company helicopter is on standby. It'll be ready when she gets there," Marshall told them.

"Marshall."

"Go ahead, Jake."

"Hiro is here."

"Copy that. Have him go to Kiko's room, she'll need help with her bags."

"Roger that. Jake out."

"That was fast." Trey had heard the exchange through his earpiece. He was startled at first because he had entirely forgotten that it was even still in. It was so small and light, it didn't even feel like it was in his ear.

"He lives only a couple blocks from here, hana."

"How's he doing?" Tobias asked Renji.

"Better, but he still has one more operation on his hip then he'll be done."

"That's good."

Watching the exchange, Trey felt a little out of the loop. "Who's Hiro and what's wrong with him?"

"My apologies, hana. His full name is Hirobi Takeda. He's my first cousin on my father's side. His youngest brother's son."

"You have a really big family."

"Don't I know it." Renji grinned ruefully. "Hiro raced motorcycles, was good at it too. He won championships all over the world and was number three in the standings. Then two years ago, he had a bad wreck. He was thrown thirty feet from the crash. Broke a lot of bones and had some serious internal damage. Almost lost him a few times."

Trey winced, knowing coming back after that probably wasn't an option. "He can't race anymore, can he?"

"No." Renji's dark eyes were sad. "His right hip was nearly shattered on impact and the other one didn't fair much better. With all the pins and rods holding them in place, sitting a motorcycle is hard enough, but the vibrations make it nearly impossible."

"That's so sad." Trey shook his head. "But he works for you now?"

"He needed a place to recover and heal after all the surgeries and needed to feel useful. I also needed a driver. It was the perfect solution."

Trey smiled, reaching up to touch his cheek. "You're a good man."

Renji shrugged and took his hand, kissing his knuckles.

"Marshall." Jake's voice came over the earpiece again.

"Go ahead, Jake."

"Hiro and Kiko just pulled out. I called Takashi to let him know to get the chopper off standby."

"Roger that."

"Jake o…shit." He groaned.

"Problem, Jake?"

"Yeah, Kaito just pulled in with another van."

Everyone let out various sounds of disapproval.

"Copy that. We'll be out in two. Marshall out."

Trey looked around the table at the varying expressions of disgust and hostility. "Real popular guy, your cousin Kaito."

"Unfortunately." Renji sighed.

Everyone got up but Davis. "Give me the details later," he told them. "I need to crack into this satellite."

Marshall nodded then looked at the twins. "You two need some sleep." He held up a hand when they started to protest. "You were up most of the night and this morning, you need sleep. I want you both fresh for your watch tonight."

They agreed, albeit reluctantly. "Yes, sir," they said in unison, stepping away to walk to their room.

"And make sure you sleep," Gary added to the amusement of them all.

The twins didn't respond, just kept going and opened a rice panel door not far from them. They entered, closing the door with a snick.

"You think they'll really sleep?" Joey asked to no one in particular.

"Sooner or later." Gary grinned.

"Tobias, I want you and Joey with Jake and Cole. This could be a good opportunity for Rusk and I would rather that not happen," Marshall told them.

Tobias nodded. "We'll grab our gear and let 'em know." He and Joey turned and left as the rest of them went into the house back the way Trey and Renji came earlier.

When they went past the room Trey was staying in, Renji led them to a new part of the house Trey hadn't seen. There was a sitting area and a place to dine formally as well as casually. And the elegance of the place. It was all simple and understated with the old world of Japan meeting seamlessly with the modern age. Seeing all of it and knowing the large amount of money it took to make the place the home it was caused Trey a pang of doubt. Renji was a successful and very wealthy businessman. He traveled all over the world meeting others like himself and doing the whole rich and famous deal. Trey was a nobody as the cliché went. His family was gone, he was just going to school to keep away from an empty home, and the money he did have wouldn't last another three years if he didn't spend it wisely. That is, finishing school sooner rather than later. So what could he possibly give to a man like Renji? A man who could have anyone he wanted and with a better background than the below middle-class one Trey had.

Those thoughts still tumbling in his head, Trey barely noticed as they went through the front door. Its side panels made of stained glass depicting koi and peacocks was an afterthought as they walked out onto the front porch and into the bright sunlight.

"What's wrong, hana?" Renji came to his side, taking his hand. "You've been wearing a frown since we passed the dining room."

Trey sighed, not sure how to voice his thoughts. Especially after all they had shared. It seemed kind of wrong, really, but now that his head was clear, the doubts were rushing in like a dark tide.

"Talk to me, Trey."

"Well, its just…" he huffed out a breath, taking the plunge. "Just feeling a bit inadequate."

"Inadequate?" Renji's expression was clearly confused. "About what?"

Trey felt his cheeks heat. "I'm…I'm not much of a catch, you know? No family or extensive background. Hell, the only reason why I've stayed in school so long is because the mere idea of going back to my gran's empty house alone depresses the shit out of me." He shook his head ruefully. "I don't even have a passport because I've never had the money to travel. And now, walking through your beautiful home, it really dawned on me that I have absolutely nothing to offer you." He hung his head with embarrassment.

Hearing a soft chuckle, Trey looked up to find Renji's dark eyes shining with affection. "I've fallen for you, Trey. The man who has been shaped by his circumstances. A man who is honest and caring, who has a heart bigger than any I have ever met." He then took Trey's mouth in a punishing kiss that left no doubt that Renji was sincere.

Feeling those firm lips, that questing tongue, Trey couldn't help but surrender. This man was all he had ever wanted and to know that he wanted Trey, just the way he was, well, it was almost too good to be true.

When Renji finally pulled back, they were both panting, Trey's heart racing. "Never doubt my intentions, Trey. Having you here with me…it's the one thing in my entire life I'll fight tooth and nail to keep. Nothing else matters as much. Nothing, do you understand?"

Trey's eyes prickled with tears, his arms going around Renji's neck. Looking into those night dark eyes, he could see that Renji was telling the truth. But most of all, he could feel it, clear down to his soul. "You're under my skin, Renji." The tears spilled over as his fears were laid to rest.

"You're mine Trey Morrison and I'm yours, everything else can be worked out." He held Trey tight against his chest as Trey's tears finally stopped. "I could lose all this tomorrow and not give a damn as long as I had you by my side."

Trey nodded into his chest and sighed, letting all the worry and fears go. "Together." He then pulled back, wiping his tears away. "And I like how you belong to me."

Renji grinned. "Body and soul, hana." He reached out and removed the last of the wetness from Trey's cheeks. "Better now?"

"Yeah." He nodded with a deep cleansing breath. "Sorry…"

"Don't be," Renji interrupted before he could say anymore. "A true and loving relationship can't survive without honesty and communication. If there's something you need to talk to me about, then don't be afraid to tell me, hana. We can't find the solution if we don't know what the problem is. Likewise, I'll do the same. We're in this together, alright?"

"Yeah, together."

"I really hate to intrude guys, but Kaito's about done ordering his minions around and will be heading this way."

Trey jerked a bit at the sound of Marshall's voice, forgetting for the moment where they were and why. "Oops." He grinned sheepishly.

"Don't worry, hana." Renji chuckled as he grabbed Trey's hand and led him to the edge of the porch steps. "Your needs will always come first. Besides, Kaito's been given enough rope to hang himself. All I'm going to do is tighten the noose."

"Well try not to hang him too quick, Renji, the little prick needs to squirm a bit first."

"Don't worry, Gary, I fully intend to give him what he deserves."

Trey saw those dark eyes go a little cold and he shivered, seeing in Renji the fierce protector of those he cared for. Poor Kaito was about to get frostbitten.

"Renji-chan!"

At the sound of that happy shout, Trey turned. "Good Lord." He groaned at the sight of Renji's cousin.

When Steven said that Kaito was flaming, he was right. Unfortunately.

A small man, Kaito looked to be about 5'8" or so and slim in build, his coloring about the same as Renji's. But with a twist. Kaito's hair was short in the back with long bangs covering the right side of his face, the ends dyed a neon blue. He was wearing a snow white vest that bared a good deal of his shoulders, one of which had the tattoo of a red and blue dragon, the tail of it wrapping around his forearm. A bright blue silk scarf was around his neck, the ends trailing in the back. He had on black pants that looked to be painted on and were tucked into black knee boots with three inch heels. And he was definitely working the heels, his hips swinging with every step. The closer he got, Trey could also see that his dark eyes were lined with kohl and his lips were shining with gloss. Trey groaned again, seeing in Kaito one of the reasons why gay men got such a hard time. It was bad enough that the majority of society pegged gays as deviants, but when you acted like Kaito, shoving your sexual orientation in someone's face like that, well, it tended to give other less flamboyant gays a bad name. Not that he was against expressing oneself, but there were ways to do it without causing a scene. Trey had the feeling that Kaito liked the stir he created and that was dangerous.

Trey moved a little further behind Renji, unsure of just how the meeting would play out, but Kaito had spotted him and his eyes lit up like a kid with a room full of presents on Christmas morning. He took the steps up the porch faster than they all anticipated and was dragging Trey into his arms in a loose embrace with the blink of an eye.

"Well, hello there angel." His smile was wide, transforming him from merely good looking to stunning. Like Renji, he didn't have much of an accent, his English perfect. "I see my cuz has been holding out on me."

Before Trey could respond or even move, Renji grabbed Kaito by the throat, hauled him bodily into the air, and slammed him down onto the porch. The air whooshed out of Kaito with the impact. Trey made a move to go to Renji but Marshall put a hand on his shoulder, stopping him. He looked back and Marshall put a finger to his lips, shaking his head. He was right, of course, this was something that Renji had to do on his own regardless of how it was done. And from what Trey could glean from the others, Kaito was stubborn. Gran always said you couldn't shout at a stubborn man, you had to show him. Trey nodded and turned around. He would give Renji his support by letting him do what he needed to do.

"Ren…Renji-chan, what are you doing?" Kaito coughed a few times, trying to get up but Renji stopped him by tightening his fingers around Kaito's throat and putting a knee in his chest.

"You will be quiet and listen."

"Now Renji-chan…"

"Silence!" Renji brought him up and slammed him
back down again. Not hard, but enough to get his attention
and put a little fear in his eyes. "Now that I have your
undivided attention, you will listen very carefully to
everything I'm going to tell you. Do you understand?"

"*H…Hai*, Renji-san."

"Good." Renji leaned in a little closer, those black
diamond eyes frosty, face a hard mask, lips pursed with
anger. "First of all, if you ever lay so much as a finger on
Trey again or say anything inappropriate, I will forget you
are my cousin and gladly finish what I have started here.
Trey is mine," He snarled, Kaito's face paling as Renji
tightened his fingers a bit with the threat. "Are we clear?"

"*Hai, hai*, Renji-san."

Trey couldn't help the tingle that raced over his body
or the flash of aroused satisfaction when Renji told Kaito
that Trey was his. The way he said it, the possessive feeling
he got from Renji with the admission was like nothing Trey
had ever felt before. It was primitive and raw and sexy as
hell. He swallowed down the moan threatening to escape at

just how powerful that feeling was and tried to get his body to calm down as well. There was a time and place for such feelings but now wasn't it. So he took a couple calming breaths and continued to support Renji. Albeit silently.

"Secondly, the complaints about you and your behavior are going to end. Starting today, you are on six months probation."

"Ren…" Kaito didn't finish because Renji jerked him up a little and slammed him back down.

"Not one word out of you." Renji's tone was severe and the look on Kaito's face said he was finally starting to realize that he was in deep trouble. His nod was jerky with fear. "Everything I'm going to tell you is non-negotiable. You are not to speak or respond unless I tell you to, understand?"

"*Hai*, Renji-san," he answered with a shaky voice.

"Because of your behavior and blatant disrespect for others, I have been charged by *otosaan* and *okaasa* to see to this matter." That news caused Kaito to pale even more and a fine sheen of sweat to break out on his forehead. "That's right, cuz, they know and are not happy. So here's what you are going to do to redeem yourself. For the first month of your probation, you are to write five formal apologies to me, to *otosaan*, to *okaasa*, the security teams, and the company as a whole. When they are done, you will bring them to me. If I don't find them sincere enough, I will terminate you." A squeak of distress sounded from Kaito at that. "If they do sound sincere, I will call a general meeting and you will read them aloud to everyone. After that, you will be monitored and if I receive so much as half a complaint, I will terminate you. Third, you are to act and dress in a more professional manner from this moment on. How you dress outside of your duties is no concern of mine, but when you are on the clock, you are a representative of the company and will act and dress befitting your position." Renji straightened a little but kept a hand around Kaito's throat and his knee in Kaito's chest. "*Otosaan* and *okaasa* will return from Greece in two days, on the third, you are to call and *okaasa* will have her talk with you. After that you will explain all I have charged you with. When that call is over, you will then call your *otosaan* and explain everything to him as well." Kaito choked, eyes wide. "Make no mistake, Kaito, neither of them will help you in this. Your behavior has become an embarrassment. If it wasn't for the fact that your skills as an aide are superior, you would have been terminated and brought up on charges of sexual harassment. Still might depending on how the next six months go. As a member of this family, you have abused that connection and your position shamefully. It ends now, do you understand?"

"*H…hai*, Renji-san."

Renji moved then dragged Kaito up with him, settling him on his feet and stepped back. Trey could tell that Kaito wanted to rub that soreness away from his neck, but the look in his wild eyes said that he was afraid to move. Even with the scarf, there would be bruises. Trey could see redness where Renji's fingers had been. It was a small price to pay considering his actions of late.

"I want you to know that as the President of this company, I am disgusted and dismayed by the behavior you have shown to your fellow employees. As your cousin, I am shocked and ashamed that a relative of mine could act in a such a manner considering the upbringing you have received." Renji let his displeasure show on his face and in his voice, Kaito bowing his head in shame as tears rolled down his cheeks. "In six months time, if you have not shown any improvement or even a willingness to change, I will terminate you. Any questions?"

"No, Renji-san." His voice was small as he wiped his cheeks and eyes, fingers smudged with the liner.

"Good." Renji nodded. "You can go set up in the back but don't disturb Davis, he's working on something for Marshall."

"*Hai*, Renji-san."

"Get going, then."

"*Hai*, Renji-san." Kaito gave him and everyone a deep bow then quickly left, immediately giving his helpers orders about what was to be done. It was all in Japanese, but from the way the helpers were scurrying around the vans, Trey got the gist of it.

When Trey turned to see how Renji was doing, he gasped at the fire burning in Renji's black diamond eyes. He had that look that said he wanted to devour Trey, the evidence of it showing quite clearly from the tented front of his robe. Trey's response was immediate and acute. Already turned on by Renji's strength and possessive attitude, seeing Renji in such a state pushed Trey from merely aroused to aching with need in seconds.

"I think we'll go keep an eye on Kaito and his minions." Marshall chuckled.

"Uh, yeah, make sure he doesn't disturb Davis." Gary snickered as they walked down the steps and left.

Trey didn't say a word in response. His attention was focused on Renji, heart pounding, blood rushing in his veins. "Renji." His name come out as a moan full of want.

In two strides, Renji grabbed his hand, pulling Trey back through the door and into the house, leading him to his room and into the bathroom. There, he pinned Trey against a wall and took his mouth in a possessive kiss that threatened to buckle his knees. He clung to Renji, whimpering in surrender and swallowing the deep groans that rumbled from Renji's throat.

"I need you, Trey." Warm, wet lips trailed heated kisses over Trey's chin and throat. "I need you so much."

"God, Renji, please."

That was all Renji needed to hear. He turned the shower on, taking a moment to slowly remove Trey's robe, those dark eyes feasting. "You are so beautiful, my hana." His fingers left a trail of fire behind with each pass over Trey's skin.

"Renji…God!" Firm fingers wrapped around Trey's erection, pushing him closer to the edge. "Mmmm." A keening moan was forced out with the expert stroking.

"So responsive to me, baby. Love the sounds, how you surrender to me." He continued to stroke a moment longer then stopped, Trey protesting with a groan. "Don't worry, hana, I'll give you what you need. What we both need."

He reached into the shower and adjusted the temp, then slipped off his robe and ushered Trey inside the stall, the warm spray raining down on them. After that, Renji seemed to lose what little control he had left and took Trey's mouth again, their naked bodies writhing against each other.

"Please…need…so much." It was all Trey was capable of saying. His body was burning as his mind focused on the man stoking the fire with each kiss and caress.

Renji then growled, spinning Trey around in his arms. "Hands on the wall, baby."

He did so without question, Renji's hard shaft slipping through his legs as an arm wrapped around his chest. A hand gripped Trey's aching cock, causing him to throw his head back onto Renji's shoulder. "Dear God."

"You're probably still tender from this morning. But there are other ways. Just like earlier in the hot spring. Seeing you like that made me so hard, hana. Made me want you so very badly." The words were low in Trey's ear, causing an aroused shiver to race down his spine.

"Please, Renji…want…"

Renji was all around him, his warmth and strength pushing Trey ever higher. Then he felt lips where his shoulder and neck met, teeth nibbling. It was an erogenous zone that Renji had been taking advantage of but hadn't left behind any kind mark. Now, Trey wanted nothing more at that moment than for Renji to bite him, to mark him. To leave behind the proof that Trey was his and his alone. He moved his head to the side, hoping Renji would get the message. "Yes, please."

"Mine…mine." He bit down, but not hard, sucking the skin into his mouth and making the spot tingle, the feeling traveling straight to Trey's balls.

With all the combined sensations zinging through his body, Trey let go, crying out his release. "Yours!" A deep groan followed, signaling that Renji too had found bliss, the warm water washing away the evidence of their pleasure.

Slumping back in Renji's arms, Trey let out a satisfied sigh, turning his head into Renji's neck and nuzzling the warm, moist skin there. "Mmm, so yours."

Renji held him tight. "Yours too, Trey." He pulled back and turned Trey to face him. "I didn't hurt you did I? I'm sorry if I was a little rough." His smile was sheepish, cheeks pink. "Seeing Kaito put his hands on you like that, well, it made me a little crazed."

"I was feeling a little crazed myself." Trey chuckled.

Looking at Trey's neck, his smile remained sheepish. "I'm afraid you'll have a rather dark love bite, hana. Sorry but, this urge to mark you came over me and…"

Trey put a finger to his lips. "I wanted it, Renji. After hearing you tell Kaito and everyone I was yours, well, I wanted something to prove it. Something from you on me, you know?" He felt his cheeks heat at the admission.

"Anytime, hana." Renji kissed his lips tenderly. "Later, you can return the favor."

The image that comment conjured in his mind caused Trey to groan. "God, I'm going to be thinking about that for the rest of the day."

"So am I, hana." Renji's grin was full of carnal promise. "Come on, I think we've kept the others waiting long enough."

That made Trey's face flame as Renji turned off the water and they got out. No doubt the others knew exactly why they were waiting too. Renji got them both a towel from the linen closet so they could dry off. Putting his robe back on, Trey could feel the mark on his lower neck tingle with the brush of the robe against it. He touched it, the heat from it causing a smile to curve his lips.

"You keep smiling like that, hana, and we'll never leave this bathroom," He growled in Trey's ear as his arms wrapped around Trey from behind.

"Sounds good to me." Trey would like nothing more than to spend the rest of the day exploring his lover's body and leaving his own marks behind on that dusky skin.

"It does. Unfortunately, this isn't something we can get out of." His sigh was deep and heartfelt.

"And I wouldn't put it past Marshall or Gary to come fetch us either."

Renji snorted. "That too."

His mark covered and their robes securely tied in place, they left the bathroom hand in hand and went back to the courtyard where they found Kaito and his minions. They had taken over a corner of the porch, but were far enough away from Davis so he wouldn't be disturbed. And taken over was not an exaggeration. The corner where they set up was filled to overflowing with two packed mobile clothes racks, four tall stacks of shoe boxes, and two huge plastic totes filled to the rim with what looked like socks in one and underwear in the other.

"Good, God."

Renji chuckled and shook his head. "My mother has never done anything by halves, I'm afraid."

"Halves?" Trey snorted with disbelief. "It looks as if she had your cousin raid a department store."

"More than one probably."

"Jeez." He looked up at Renji. "I can't possibly accept all this, Renji. It wouldn't be right."

Renji smiled and led him over to where Kaito was taking a large garment bag from the rack. "I'm sure not all of this is yours, hana. Nor that all of it will be the right size."

"Renji-san is correct, Trey-san." Kaito bowed. "Some of the items here, because of make and style, may not fit, even if they are your size. Some of the other items are what Sango-san had me purchase for Renji-san."

"Oh, okay." Trey looked around and noticed something missing. A place to change. "Uh, not to be a pain or a prude, but where am I going to change?"

"Good question, hana." Renji laid a hand on his shoulder. "Not that I don't enjoy your charms, I'd rather not have anyone else enjoying them."

"Not a problem, Renji-san." Kaito turned to one of his minions and spoke in rapid fire Japanese. In a flash the young man was gone, returning in minutes with a very long black object.

When the young man set it up, Trey saw that it was a beautiful black lacquer screen with very detailed geisha done in jewel tones on the four panels. All were in various poses depicting the four seasons.

"Wow, that's gorgeous." He walked over and inspected it, noticing the fine workmanship. "I can't believe you would take this out." Trey may have been going to school to keep from going home, but he was learning all he could in his classes and his knowledge so far told him that the screen was a very expensive piece of art work.

"It's alright, Trey-san." Kaito smiled. "The screen is a lot sturdier than it looks." He then held out the garment bag to Trey. "I was going to save this for last, but I have to admit that my curiosity has gotten the better of me."

"What is it?" Trey took the garment bag.

"Something special Sango-san wanted you to have." He walked over to one of the totes and grabbed a piece of black fabric. "You might need this as well."

Trey took it and held it up. It was a pair of silk boxer briefs. "Yeah, thanks." He then went behind the screen.

Once there, Trey hung up the garment bag on one the hooks at the top of the screen and looked around. The screen was situated where he had maximum coverage from the front and only a little bit open from the backside. It wasn't too bad, better than showing his ass and one did not show ones ass when one was a guest. He and Renji cared for each other, but the living arrangements hadn't been talked about, so that still made Trey a guest in Renji's home. Even if they were living together, he still wouldn't bare it all on Renji's back porch. Smiling at that, Trey left his robe on while he put the briefs on. They were soft and fit like a second skin. Reasonably sure he was now covered; he took off the robe and hung it on another hook then opened the garment bag. Inside was a very finely made black suit with a snow white silk dress shirt and a brilliant teal silk tie with matching kerchief in the jacket pocket. A the bottom of the bag were black trouser socks, a black leather belt, and matching black shoes that looked to be made of hand tooled leather. There were no tags or stamps on the shoes to tell who made them or where they came from. Though with all that Renji's mom had bought, it was probably best not to know. He put the socks on first then the shirt. The pants were next, shirt being tucked in and zipping the pants then sliding the belt on, shoes after that. Lifting the collar of the shirt, Trey took the tie out and knotted it, making sure the collar was straight and the buttons all done even though he had no mirror to make sure. The last piece was the jacket. He carefully took it out and was about to put it on when he noticed the tag sewn onto the collar. He nearly swallowed his tongue when he read it. Giorgio Armani. Renji's mom had bought him an Armani suit? He looked at the tag again just to make sure and yes, it said Giorgio Armani. He groaned silently. There was no way he could keep it. Renji's mom's intentions and generosity were appreciated, but Trey, in good conscience, couldn't accept such a costly gift.

With sad resignation, Trey put the jacket on. He buttoned it up and adjusted his cuffs, making sure a little white showed. He then brushed his hair back, took a deep breath, and stepped out.

"Holy shit!"

"Damn!"

"Oh yeah!"

Trey felt his face heat a bit at the whistles and catcalls, but there was only one who's reaction mattered. Renji had been sitting with the guys but after seeing him come out, he got up and slowly walked toward Trey like a stalking panther. His dark eyes feasted on every inch of Trey's body causing his heart to pound and his blood to race south. He had a sneaking suspicion that carnal look would affect him thusly for a very long time.

"Trey." His name came out on a husky breath as Renji ran a finger lightly down Trey's cheek and chest. He then said something in Japanese, those black diamond orbs causing Trey's entire body to flush with heat.

"Do I want to know what you just said?" Trey had to swallow back a moan when Renji stepped into his personal space, their erections bumping each other.

"Not in mixed company, hana." Full lips descended and Trey's world spun on it's axis as Renji plundered his mouth.

"They're as bad as the newlyweds." The comment came to Trey distantly, making him jerk back, face flaming. "Makes me feel like a third wheel."

"You are a third wheel," Marshall quipped.

Trey looked over at the guys, smiles wreathing their handsome faces as Davis playfully flipped Marshall the bird. Trey shook his head, returning his attention to the man making his body tingle.

"You look mouthwatering, hana."

"Thanks, darlin'." His smile quickly turned down. "But Renji, I can't accept this suit."

Renji blinked. "Why ever not?"

"Renji, this is an Armani suit."

"Yes and you look fabulous in it."

Trey sighed deeply. "It's just too expensive a gift for me to accept."

"Trey…"

He held up a hand, stopping whatever Renji was about to say. "Look, I appreciate the gesture, but I couldn't, in good conscience, accept. If I did, I would feel like I was taking advantage and using you."

"Hana, you could never do that."

"And that's why I can't accept. You're a very generous man, Renji, but taking this, well, it wouldn't be right. Please understand."

Rubbing the back of his neck, Renji let out a deep breath. "Alright, hana."

"Renji-san…" Kaito was stopped from saying anything further when Renji said something to him in Japanese with a firm tone. "*Hai*, Renji-san." He nodded and bowed, going back to the rack to get more clothes.

Trey hung his head, feeling like a heel. "I didn't mean to cause any problems."

"You could never cause any problems, hana." Renji put a finger under his chin and raised it, his smile warm and reassuring.

"Here you are, Trey-san." Kaito handed him several hangers of clothes then stepped back.

"Go change, hana. I'm anxious to see how you look in everything." He leered.

Trey couldn't help but smile, his cheek warm. "Alright, be back in a sec." He went back behind the screen with the clothes and hung them up beside the empty garment bag then began to undress.

He really didn't mean to disappoint Renji by not taking the suit, but Trey's upbringing, as well as his own principles, just couldn't do it. He cared about Renji very much, odd considering the short amount of time they've had together, and he wasn't about to jeopardize it by depending on Renji and his family for everything. At the moment, he didn't have much choice, but he wasn't going to take advantage of that fact. Just as soon as the mess with Rusk was taken care of, Trey was going to repay Renji and his family for their kindness and generosity. He was damn lucky to be alive and even more so to find someone like Renji, so he wasn't about to just keep taking and not giving something in return. A relationship was supposed to be an equal partnership. Once he got back on his feet, he would prove that to Renji. He admired and respected the man too much not to.

For the next couple hours, Trey tried on more clothes than he ever had in his twenty three years. There were jeans, trousers, slacks, and dress pants. All were paired with the right tee, polo, and oxford that was also paired with the right socks, belt, and shoes. He never realized just how wide a variety of men's wear there really was. His own wardrobe consisted of jeans, tees, and the occasional polo or button down for special occasions. The one suit he had owned was thrown out after his gran's funeral. He had buried the last of his family in that suit, just looking at it made him sick. But now, he was a bit overwhelmed with the sheer volume of things that fit. And after refusing the Armani, he still felt a little uncomfortable accepting so much. Hell, out of the items that did fit, he had enough clothes for two men. But he didn't want to seem ungrateful. Renji's mom had went to the trouble of purchasing everything, so the least Trey could do was accept graciously. He would. Then after everything was settled with the psycho, he would repay that kindness. It was only right and the only way his conscience would let him accept so much.

"Tired, hana?"

Trey took another stack of clothes and a shoe box from Kaito. "Yeah, a little."

"This is the last of it, Trey-san," Kaito announced.

"Thanks." Trey gave him a grateful smile then plodded back behind the screen and undressed, putting the clothes over the top of the screen for Kaito to retrieve.

Taking the first item from the pile on top of the shoe box, Trey put on white cotton socks, a comfy pair of faded blue jeans, and a soft white tee that he tucked into the jeans. Over the white tee he put on a jewel bright teal v-neck sweater vest. The tag said cashmere and it was soft as down. Putting on the shoes, a pair of white Nike Shox, he was all set and more comfortable in these clothes than most of the others he had tried on that day.

Stepping out from behind the screen, he went to Renji who was wearing a very carnal grin.

"Love how you look in jeans, hana." Renji took his hand then turned him around. "Very nice."

Trey felt his cheeks warm as he turned back to face Renji. "Thanks. I feel a lot more at home wearing this than most of the other stuff."

"It's just what you're used to wearing is all."

"Excuse me, Renji-san."

Trey and Renji looked toward Kaito. He had another pile of clothes and a shoe box in his hands.

"What is it, Kaito?"

"These are for you." He handed the stack over to Renji. "Sango-san wanted you and Trey to have something special. This is it."

Renji took the stack with a questioning frown. "I thought you put all the things my mother sent in my room."

"Everything but this." He nodded to the items in Renji's hands. "Sango-san wanted me to make sure you tried those on before I left."

"Oh."

"Go ahead, Renji." Trey didn't miss the mischief in Kaito's dark eyes. Something was definitely up with those clothes. "After all the clothes I've tried on today, you can try these."

Renji gave him a smile then a peck on the lips. "Alright, hana. Be right back."

Trey watched him go behind the screen then turned to Kaito. His smile was wide, night eyes dancing with humor. Oh yeah, something was up.

"You have got to be joking!" Renji laughed aloud.

"What's wrong?"

He laughed again amid much shuffling. "You'll see, hana."

Waiting along with the others, Trey noticed varying amounts of amusement and curiosity on their faces. He was amused and curious as well. Whatever Renji's mom had sent, it was sure to make a statement.

"Get ready," Renji warned them then stepped out.

There was a pause as everyone looked Renji over, then Trey, then back to Renji.

"Aw, that's so cute."

Everyone erupted into laughter at Gary's comment and just how similar Trey and Renji were dressed. So similar that the only difference was the color. Renji's jeans and sneakers were black and his sweater was a deep, dark ruby red. The perfect compliment of tones to bring out the gold in Renji's dusky skin and the obsidian in his glossy hair. He was breathtaking.

"Leave it to my mother." Renji chuckled.

"Sango-san actually wanted them to be the same color, but teal just isn't a good tone for you, Renji-san, so I compromised."

"Thank-you, Kaito, I think."

"I don't know." Trey went over and ran his hands down Renji's chest, trailing them around his torso as he slowly walked around and checked out that fine ass encased in snug black denim. "Red and black look really good on you, darlin'." He came back around and touched that broad chest again, liking how the soft cashmere molded to it.

"I know what looks even better." Renji grabbed him around the waist and pulled him closer.

"Ahem."

Trey stiffened in Renji's arms, his growing erection dying quickly as his face heated.

"Save that thought, hana." Renji gave him a sweet kiss then stepped back but kept Trey's hand in his. "Have the vans been loaded, Kaito?"

"*Hai*, Renji-san." He nodded as one of his minions took the screen down and folded it, taking it away. "The screen was the last of it. The tea Sango-san sent has been put in the pantry. If there's anything else, just call." He bowed lowed to everyone, then Trey and Renji. "It was a pleasure meeting you, Trey-san."

"Nice to meet you as well, Kaito." Trey returned the bow.

"Don't' forget, Kaito."

"No, Renji-san, I won't." He bowed low again then was gone.

Trey and Renji had gotten comfy at the table again when Jake's voice came over the ear piece.

"Marshall."

"Go ahead, Jake."

"Kaito and crew have moved out."

"Roger that. Marshall out."

"Well, that went better than I expected it to." Gary grinned.

"And I have the feeling that Kaito's attitude will change greatly," Marshall added.

"We'll see." From Renji's tone, he would wait and reserve judgment. Although if Kaito knew what was good for him, he'd follow through with Renji's instructions or he could find himself out of a job. Or worse.

"Yeah, baby!"

"Davis?"

"We're in, boss."

"Excellent." Marshall and Gary moved behind Davis. "Let's see what you got."

Davis tapped furiously on one of the laptop's keys, his smile wide with triumph. "Here ya go, boss."

Trey watched as a grin spread Marshall's mouth. "Make the search parameters larger to encompass the entire house and grounds."

"Not a problem." Davis tapped some more keys. "How's that?"

"Perfect." Marshall gave Davis a pat on the shoulder. "Good work."

"Thanks, boss." He grinned then looked over at Trey and Renji. "Want to see the fruits of my labor?"

"Sure." Trey nodded as Renji grabbed his hand. They stood beside Gary and Marshall, careful not to step on the equipment on the floor. "What are we looking at?"

There were two large laptops on the table and one in Davis' lap with cables running from them to two very large boxes with blinking lights on the floor. The left laptop on the table showed a bird's eye view of the house and grounds in full color. The right one showed the same view but in shades of grey and bright green.

"The right screen is a normal view and the left is the infrared." His fingers flew over the keyboard in his lap then the infrared showed the house and grounds in sections of four. "The bright greens you see are life signs. The brighter, the bigger. Though if I want more detail, I can always zoom in. But this is fine for now."

Looking at the screen, Trey could see where everyone was. Cole and Jake were at the edge of the courtyard with Tobias and Joey at the opposite end near a stand of tress. But something was off. At the front of the house he could see a flicker of bright green. At first, he thought it could be an animal, but the longer he looked at it when compared to the others, Trey knew that the flicker was man sized.

"Uh, Davis, could you pan in to the front of the house?" That seemed to get everyone's attention fast.

"What is it, hana?"

"Not sure, but I keep seeing this blinking and it doesn't seem to be an animal."

Davis did his thing, the spot Trey pointed to coming into focus.

"Shit! Jake, Cole, front porch! We have a breach!" Marshall called out over the ear piece.

"Copy that. On our way," Jake replied.

They all watched as Jake and Cole made their way to the front porch, creeping stealthily to the front steps. Their weapons were drawn as they searched for the intruder. On the other screen, Tobias and Joey took Jake and Cole's place at the edge of the courtyard, both had weapons drawn as well, their heads swiveling around as they looked for further trouble.

"Guys, I think he may be under the house, repeat, under the house," Davis told them, his fingers continuing to fly over his keyboard.

Jake and Cole didn't respond verbally but made their way to the side of the house near the front steps and a little ways down. There, Jake and Cole crouched down low, the infrared showing them carefully opening a small door at the base of the house and going in, slowly closing in on their target. Then Jake's voice came across the ear piece, low and deadly.

"One wrong move and you die here, do you understand?" Jake's gun was raised and pointed at the target. *"Cole."*

Cole moved slowly to the target, his brightness merging a bit in the cramped quarters with whoever he was patting down. *"He's carrying a gun and a knife. I'll pat him down better once we're out of here."*

"Roger that. We'll be waiting. Marshall out. Tobias."

"Go ahead."

"Keep watch. This could be a trap."

"Roger that. Tobias out."

They watched further as Jake and Cole come out with the intruder, Cole checking him over for anymore weapons, then not finding any, secured him like any cop would a criminal, with handcuffs. Satisfied the intruder was ready, they began to walk toward the courtyard. Tobias and Joey nodded as they approached, but otherwise didn't move from their posts.

"Once they're past the trees on the corner of the house, I'll be able to zoom in with the color so we can see who the idiot is." Davis tapped his keys, both cameras' following Jake and Cole. When they were clear of the trees, everyone gasped.

"Son of a bitch!"

"Tell me that is not Conrad," Renji growled in an angry voice.

Sure enough, it was. He was wearing the same suit, though now it was filthy as well as wrinkled. And he definitely looked the worse for wear. There was something else about him as well. It was there in his posture, the slump of his shoulders, and head down, feet dragging. He looked totally defeated and Trey didn't think it was just about getting caught under Renji's house.

Since that first meeting, something had been nagging Trey about Mr. Conrad. Other than the fact that the man was an ass, there just seemed to be something off about him. Maybe it was his disregard for another's feelings or his pushy attitude. But then, how many cops would go to such lengths to secure a witness? All the movies and TV dramas aside, what real cop is going to risk their badge and career after they've been blasted by their boss and ultimately risk going to jail themselves for basically taking the law into their own hands? It was simple really, they wouldn't. Then there was Conrad himself. The man was the biggest asshole Trey had ever met. Besides being callous and rude, the man had the character of a slug. Not very trustworthy in Trey's book. Which was the point really. Interpol was a huge organization and internationally respected, so to have a man like Conrad on the force was disappointing. Of course, Conrad wasn't on the force anymore was he? His behavior had clinched that, making his superiors suspend him. Then it all clicked in Trey's mind.

"He's the mole, isn't he?"

Everyone looked at Trey with a mixture of surprise and respect.

"He was a suspect, but considering his actions, it's more than likely he's the leak," Marshall agreed with a nod.

"How'd you figure it out, hana?"

"Cops won't go out of their way like this just to get a witness." Trey then snorted with derision. "Plus the man is just shifty, ya know?"

Renji chuckled. "Can't argue with that assessment, hana."

"Well, depending on what excuse he has for hiding under Renji's house," Gary spoke up as Jake and Cole turned into the courtyard with Conrad in tow. "We can add quite a few other names to the growing list of Mr. Conrad's character."

"Is dumbass on that list?" Davis snickered.

Marshall and Gary walked over to the top of the steps as Jake and Cole steered Conrad closer. "I believe its number four," Marshall quipped, then he and Gary looked down at Conrad as Jake and Cole parked him in front of the steps. "Well, Mr. Conrad, you seem to have gotten yourself in quite the predicament."

From where Trey was standing beside Renji, he could clearly see just how bad a shape Conrad was in. The left side of his face was bruised, the left eye swollen nearly shut. There was a cut on his upper lip that was crusted over with dried blood and swelled a dark purple. With his mouth shut, Trey couldn't tell about the missing teeth, but that didn't mean they were missing in the front. He had various cuts and scrapes on his face, neck, and hands, and a long deep scratch on the top of his head where the hair was thinnest along with a rather large bump on his forehead. His clothes were a mess. The tie was long gone with several buttons missing on his shirt and a pocket nearly torn off his jacket. The trousers looked just as bad with dirt encrusted at the knees and caked on his shoes. He didn't look or even act like the same man from the night before. He just stood there, hands cuffed in front and eyes down.

"You going to give us some crazy excuse for your presence under Mr. Takeda's house or the truth?" Marshall's stance seemed casual but the underlying tone of his voice was blade sharp.

Conrad hunched his shoulders. "I can't." He choked the two words out.

"Can't huh?" Marshall's eyes went cold at that. "Gary, why don't you enlighten Mr. Conrad on what we've learned since this morning."

"Be glad to." The anger in his voice was clear to everyone. "Made a few calls this morning, Mr. Conrad and what I learned was deeply disturbing. For the last six months you slowly and personally had all the witnesses moved to different safe houses under the guise of making them more secure. You also minimized their security with the excuse that it would be in the witnesses' best interest to blend in with their new home without the officers around. Then you covered up their murders, telling your superiors that they were doing fine and doing well. But you got sloppy when Mr. Morrison wasn't where he was supposed to be, acting out and loosing control in a room full of your fellow officers. With all the vague reports on the witnesses, well, your actions were suspect. And then there are the autopsy reports on the witnesses. Do you know what they found, Mr. Conrad?" Gary paused and Trey could see that he was trying to control himself. Of course, Conrad's silence didn't help. "Shall I tell you? Oh, but you already know, don't you. All of them were murdered execution style."

Trey felt his blood go cold at that, his stomach queasy as he shivered. To know that those poor souls were dead was bad enough, to hear it in detail was enough to make him sick. And all because of the lowlife in front of him. Renji wrapped an arm around his shoulders, hugging him close. Trey snuggled into his side, needing his strength and support.

"I had no choice." Conrad's tone was flat, the sound of a defeated man.

"Really?" Marshall sneered. "And what does Rusk have that it would push you to let innocents be murdered."

"He has…information, personal information…about me," Conrad hedged.

"What kind of personal information?"

Conrad's face reddened and his shoulders hunched even more. "It's…it's a private matter."

Marshall stalked down the steps and grabbed Conrad's chin, squeezing it in a tight grip. "I don't give a damn how private it is, you will tell me why Rusk is blackmailing you." He growled low.

Watery brown eyes widened with fear. "I…I like to…to play rough. With…with young men. There's a…a club…in Paris. It caters to…to men like me," He stuttered.

Snorting with disgust, Marshall let go of Conrad's chin. "A wannabe Dom." He shook his head then went back to stand beside Gary. "The BDSM community must be hard up if they're letting men like you join."

"So Rusk threatened to let out your…proclivities?" Gary asked.

"Yes. If my superiors ever found out, it would ruin my career and my reputation."

Trey couldn't believe what he was hearing. This man, this officer of the law, let six innocent young men be slain just so he could save his own skin? To save his job? The more he thought about it, the more his blood began to boil.

"You're a real piece of work, Conrad," Gary said with disgust. "How much does Rusk know?"

Conrad bowed his head, looking at the ground in silence.

"No need to be shy now." Marshall barked out a humorless laugh. "You have the blood of six witnesses on your hands and have probably been in constant contact with Rusk. Might as well tell us how much you've passed on."

They all heard a mumbled reply.

"Say again, didn't quite catch that."

"As much as I could," He choked out.

"And when can we expect Rusk and his men?"

"He…he gave me a few days to bring Mr. Morrison in when he found out he had survived the drug overdose. If I don't call by tomorrow afternoon, he'll know I've been compromised. I haven't talked to him since yesterday morning when he sent me here."

"So he doesn't know who we really are."

Conrad shook his head. "Like the rest of us, we all thought you were a bunch of high tech rent-a-cops hired to protect Mr. Takeda and his family."

"Good to know our image is intact," Davis sneered.

"Which can only work to our advantage considering all that Rusk does know," Gary added.

Marshall nodded then frowned. "Still, Rusk is the unknown element here. Even with all the info he has, why wait for Conrad? Why not come and take Trey himself?"

"That ones easy enough to guess," Renji spoke up. "Ego, plain and simple."

He and Trey stepped over to where Gary and Marshall were standing.

"Yeah, I can see where he would get off on pulling the strings on an Inspector working with Interpol." Marshall smirked. "Holding that info over Conrad's head must have been a real high."

"And this idiot played right into his hands." Gary snorted. "Easy pickings."

"I…I don't understand." Conrad's face was pale and sweaty.

"You don't? Well, let me spell it out for you." Marshall crossed his arms. "Rusk had no intentions of making good on his deal with you. In fact, he probably would have killed you along with Trey."

"Or better yet, letting you live and leaking your exploits to every news agency in the free world," Gary added.

"That sounds more like what the man would do," Renji agreed. "He'd get more out of your humiliation than your death."

Conrad looked sickly with that news. "But…he promised." His voice was shaky. "He promised to return everything if I delivered Mr. Morrison."

"Fool that you are, you believed him." Gary shook his head with clear disgust.

"No, he…he wouldn't do that." Conrad was shaking his head in denial. "He promised me that after all the witnesses were dead, I would be safe. He would return all the evidence." He was getting agitated, voice rising with panic. "He swore I had nothing to worry about, my reputation would still be good. He swore!"

"Shut up!" Trey screamed at Conrad, causing him to quit griping and everyone to look at him with startlement. He couldn't take it anymore, hearing this selfish bastard whine about betrayal when he was responsible for six deaths and the attempt of Trey's. "Shut up you piece of shit." Trey walked down the steps and stood toe to toe with the wide eyed man. Then, because he couldn't have stopped himself if he tried, slapped Conrad as hard as he could, letting all his anger go and rocking the man back on his heels. "Six people are dead because you put your reputation, your precious career, above their lives and would have handed me over without a qualm knowing I would have been killed as well. And now, all our lives are in danger because of your selfishness." He got into Conrad's personal space; his face was sheet white and rheumy eyes round with fear. Trey's hand print showed bright red on his left cheek. "You sicken me and I hope you get everything you deserve."

Trey stepped back on shaky legs, wanting to get away before he really lost his temper and beat the man to a bloody pulp. Strong arms wrapped around him from behind, stopping him and giving him the comfort he desperately needed.

"Easy, hana, I got you."

"Renji." Trey turned in his arms, seeking shelter and warmth as he clung to Renji's solid body. He couldn't look at Conrad, the sight of the man made him ill. "Renji," A whimper came out as those strong arms held him tighter.

"I think we've learned all we need to know." Gary sighed. "Put our guest in the storage shed, guys. I'll give my contact at Interpol a heads up."

"You get everything, Davis?"

"Loud and clear and in living color, boss," he said merrily as Jake and Cole took a silent Conrad away.

"Tobias," Marshall called out.

"Go ahead," he answered.

"You get all that?"

"Unfortunately." His sigh was deep. *"According to Conrad, Rusk will move if he doesn't hear from Conrad by tomorrow evening. But we can't rely on that info. For all we know, Rusk could be on his way now."*

"My thoughts as well." Trey looked up at Marshall's grim face and shivered. "Luke, Seth."

There was a pause, then, *"You rang?"* He couldn't be certain, but Trey believed it sounded like Seth.

"Sorry to cut your nap time short but I need the Terror Twins to gear up."

"Roger that. Be out in two. Seth out."

At the sound of approaching footsteps, Trey looked over his shoulder to see Jake and Cole returning.

"Our guest is secure but I doubt very much if he'll be comfortable." Jake smirked.

"My heart bleeds." Gary's tone was dripping with sarcasm.

"Where you want us?" The twins came up to Marshall and Gary wearing their black and each carrying a long black case.

"On the roof. One in front and one in back. Now that Davis has the eagle eye set up, we'll see Rusk's crew before they realize they've been spotted so keep the comm open."

"Has Rusk made his move already?" Luke asked as he gave Trey a concerned look. Trey smiled wanly in return while Marshall brought them up to speed. "You alright, Trey?" Luke and Seth had identical expressions of worry.

"Yeah, just lost my temper." A first really. Trey had always considered himself pretty even tempered, but hearing that bastard admit to his crimes, well, he just snapped. He was still feeling shaky, but being in Renji's arms helped. He snuggled closer, soaking up Renji's warmth.

"He'll be fine after he rest's a bit," Renji told them.

The twins visibly relaxed and nodded, then started to walk off.

"Be careful you two," Trey called out.

"Of course." Luke winked and Seth saluted, his smile wide. Then they were gone.

"You need to lie down, hana. I know you're exhausted. I can still feel you trembling."

Trey looked up into those night dark eyes so filled with affection and caring. "Yeah, a nap sounds good."

"Are you steady enough to walk or do you need me to carry you?"

"I…" His face heated as his heart began to race at just the thought of letting Renji go. He had become Trey's lifeline the past few minutes and he felt like he needed that connection or he'd fly apart. He buried his face in Renji's chest. "I'm afraid if I let you go, I'll lose it, Renji. I…"

"Shh, love, I'm here and I won't let you go." He picked Trey up easily and held him close. "I won't ever let you go."

Trey felt the prickle of tears behind his eyes, a sob stuck in his throat. He tried to hold it back, but he felt so out of control that he couldn't stop a small whimper from emerging.

"Hang on, baby."

Trey felt him move, but didn't see where they were going and didn't really care just as long as Renji kept holding him. Kept giving him the comfort he was craving.

"Marshall."

"Go ahead, Renji. I'll give you an update later. Take care of Trey."

With that, they were off, Trey continuing to cling to Renji until he set Trey down. But the room they were in wasn't the one he had been staying in. This one was done in the same style and colors, but the bed was huge and covered in a black and red satin comforter. The night stands were black lacquer as well as a table against a wall holding a set of jade dragons under a framed midnight blue kimono with colorful fall leaves scattered on it. The last piece of furniture was a black and red stripped chair in the left corner.

"Uh, Renji?"

"I couldn't stand not having you in my bed another night, hana. I hope you don't mind." Renji sat beside him and took his hand, his expression wary.

"Your room?"

"Well, I would like it to be our room."

Trey continued to look around the room, seeing Renji everywhere. It was so comforting that the dam on his emotions began to break, the tears sliding down his cheeks.

"Oh, Renji." He flew into Renji's arms, the anger, the fear, the uncertainty pouring out of him as he sobbed into Renji's chest. There was no way to stop it, it had been building for too long.

When the emotional storm had passed, Renji pulled back and wiped his tears away with gentle fingers. "Better now, hana?"

"Yeah, sorry. I'm not usually such an emotional wreck. I haven't cried this much since gran died," he sniffled. "Beginning to think my hormones may be out a whack or something."

He gave Trey a small smile. "It's not your hormones, hana. Just a lot of difficult situations being thrown at you. Situations you're not used to. So I think you're entitled to get a little emotional under the circumstances." He pulled Trey back into his arms and Trey went willingly, snuggling close.

"And seeing Conrad didn't help." He sighed. "Just hearing him confess like that, with no remorse for those poor people…" He shivered.

"I know, love. I wanted to do a lot more than slap him, believe me." He chuckled darkly.

"Beating the man to a bloody pulp did come to mind."

"That too." He kissed the top of Trey's head. "You should rest, hana." His hands were stroking and kneading the tense muscles of Trey's back. His warm breath ghosted over Trey's cheek, causing him to shiver for a different reason.

"Mmm." Trey groaned as those magic fingers went lower.

"Feel good, hana?" The words were raspy in Trey's ear, Renji's warm lips leaving butterfly kisses on Trey's chin and neck.

Giving the only response he was able, Trey took his lips, craving his taste as he plunged his tongue deep into Renji's mouth. Renji groaned, his tongue dueling with Trey's but letting him lead the kiss. That knowledge caused

Trey to become bolder, deepening the kiss until he was dizzy, his body aching for Renji.

Finally coming up for air, their breathing was harsh, cheeks flushed. Trey wanted nothing more than for Renji to take him, to fill him up and make him forget, for a little while, just what they were up against. He wanted, needed to have that connection with Renji. More than anything else, he wanted to feel that closeness when their bodies merged, making them one. It was like their hearts and souls merged, sending them flying. He needed to feel that right now. He needed to feel it desperately.

"It's too soon, hana."

Trey felt his cheeks warm; unaware that he'd said all that out loud. "It'll be fine, Renji." He laid a finger on Renji's lips to stop his protest. "I need you, Renji. With all that's happened the last couple days, you're caring and support is the only reason I've stayed sane, that I haven't totally lost it. Please."

Trey didn't think Renji's eyes could get any darker, but they did. Then with a growl, he pounced, their clothes disappearing in a blink and the feel of skin on skin going to Trey's head as Renji took his mouth and devoured it. Trey whimpered at the power of Renji's passion, at the aggression of it. And he wanted more. He wanted Renji to totally take him over, he was burning with it.

"Want you, Renji. Want you so much." He was aching, his balls tight and his shaft felt as if it would go with just one touch.

Not expecting it, Renji flipped him to his stomach and covered his back, the feel of a very hot body and rock hard erection poked Trey in the small of his back.

"Mmm." He couldn't help the moan that escaped at the vulnerable position he was in.

"Put your head down and leave your ass up, hana," The command was growled in Trey's ear sending a shiver of pleasure straight to Trey's balls.

Trey readily complied, the anticipation of what Renji was going to do making his breath come fast and harsh.

"Just like that, hana. So beautiful you are." His hands were warm on Trey's back, the firm fingers leaving trails of heat on Trey's sensitive skin where ever they touched. "Close your eyes, hana. Soon, I'll make you fly, then we'll soar together."

With that promise heating Trey's blood even more, Renji proceeded to lick, kiss, stroke, and nibble Trey's neck, back, and ass. But Renji didn't stop there. Feeling his ass cheeks being spread open, Trey's lust hazed mind never expected the trail of sensual fire Renji's tongue ignited as he licked a path from the top of Trey's crack to the outside of his anus, that agile tongue licking at the sensitive nerves there. Then with slow deliberation, that tongue entered Trey's hole.

"God!" It was too much and not enough. Renji alternated between slow languid licks and deep probes of his talented tongue. "Oh, God…Renji…oh…" Never in his wildest fantasies did Trey think this was possible or that he would be brought to the edge of release because of it. But now that he was experiencing such pleasure, he was glad he had waited so long. He knew in his heart he wouldn't have found this kind of connection with anyone else.

The pressure was building with every lick and stab of Renji's tongue. Trey's legs were trembling, his breath coming out in raspy pants. It was like he was standing at the edge of a cliff, just waiting for that slight nudge that would push him over.

"Oh, Renji…God…please…please…"

That push finally came when Renji wrapped a firm hand around Trey's leaking cock and plunged a finger deep into his ass. Trey screamed Renji's name into his arm as he emptied his balls into Renji's hand.

Before he could fully recover, Trey dimly heard the rip of foil and felt a very hard, insistent rod at his hole and begin to slowly enter. As relaxed as he was, the burn was minimal but the pressure inside and against his sweet spot roused him again.

"Mmm," the whimper came out as Renji pulled him up and back against Renji's chest, his legs wrapping backward around his waist. It was a very intimate and exposed position. It also caused Renji to go deeper inside him. "Oh, God."

"The feel of you, the taste of you, Trey." Renji pumped into him slowly, his voice like the darkest dream in Trey's ear. "I crave you, hana, your touch, your smile, your heat. You're like water in the desert and I'm dying of thirst." That last word came out as a groan when Renji buried his face in Trey's neck, tightened his hold around

Trey's body, and began to plunge deeply into Trey harder and faster.

"Renji!" Trey gasped out his name, locking an arm around Renji's neck and hanging on. "God…please…oh, please…"

"My Trey. My hana." He grabbed Trey's aching shaft then bit down in the same place where he was marked earlier. That was all it took.

"Renji!" The orgasm raced through him, intense and so powerful it caused black spots to dance before his eyes. Before they closed in, he dimly heard Renji's shout of completion then let the velvet darkness take him.

Chapter 6

After cleaning himself and Trey, Renji put an exhausted Trey to bed. He roused long enough to say good night then was out. Renji smiled, brushing gold silk away from Trey's closed eyes.

"Only sweet dreams, hana." He lingered a moment longer then went to the corner chair and sat, watching Trey as he slept. "Marshall," he said it low enough so as not to disturb his hana.

"I'm here, Renji. Everything all right?"

That made Renji smile. "Yeah, Trey's sleeping finally."

"Sounds like you could use a couple hours yourself."

"Yeah." He chuckled softly. "I will after you give me an update."

"Roger that." Marshall's own deep chuckle was warm with understanding. *"The twins are in sniper positions on the roof. Jake and Cole are patrolling the back and have a few surprises set up. Tobias and Joey have the front and*

Gary and I are inside. Davis is playing maestro with the eagle eye."

"Gary get in touch with his contact at Interpol?"

"Yeah. A team will be sent here in the morning to take Conrad into custody. They've contacted local law enforcement about what's going on so the airport and roads are being watched."

"I doubt Rusk would be stupid enough to fly in."

"That was my thoughts as well, but it doesn't hurt to be careful and have the extra eyes. And since we both know this will come down to a fire fight, our asses are covered as well."

"That's good but I'd hoped the local PD wouldn't have to be involved. The last thing we need are dead cops."

"I know." Marshall sighed deeply. *"The locals have been informed not to engage but act as back-up only. Though you know as well as I do how that will play out."*

Renji snorted with derision. "Unfortunately." Some trigger happy local getting killed wanting to play hero.

"The upside is that all the major roads and the airport are fifteen to twenty minutes away. And we both know that Rusk would never allow a local to catch him, so that should keep them out of the way. With Davis' eagle eye up, we'll be ready before the locals even know what's going on."

"Still, I feel uneasy having them involved."

"I'm not exactly happy about it either, but at least this way we won't have to worry about them showing up and shooting at us then asking questions later."

"Mmph."

"There's something else, Renji."

That didn't sound good. "What is it?"

"I'm sure you noticed that Conrad was hiding something?"

"More like lying." Mention of the man made his blood boil. "Though I couldn't put my finger on just what. But that story seemed way too pat. And if he's a gay wannabe Dom, I'm straight."

"It's more like his story was rehearsed."

Renji sat up straighter. "For what reason and why?"

"After you and Trey left, something about that story of his just didn't sit well, you know? So I took a stroll and questioned the man myself. The naughty pictures was just to be a smoke screen should Conrad ever get caught. Not to say that moron isn't into a little slap and tickle with the right female partner, but the real reason Rusk got to him is money."

"Figures."

"Oh, not like you think, not a payoff. Conrad has a gambling problem, a big one. Owes a quarter mil to the Russian mafia."

"Whose two main players happen to be regular guests at the auctions."

"Yep."

"Christ."

"It gets worse, I'm afraid."

"Of course it does." He rubbed the back of his neck.

"Seems Rusk instructed Conrad to keep tabs on you and Trey and to report back hourly. That whole production last night was just a ruse so he could find out what security measures you had in place and how well Trey was doing."

"Son of a bitch," he growled softly.

"After Conrad told me that, I had Joey and Tobias check under the house. They found a SAT phone near where Conrad was hiding."

"How long had he been there?"

"Fortunately, not long enough to learn anything that useful. Still, he's given Rusk a rudimentary layout of the place, that I'm ex Special Forces, and your relationship with Trey. Even with all that, Rusk was more interested in your relationship with Trey than anything else."

"He would be." Renji sighed deeply and sat back.

"This has gone beyond personal for him, Renji. And that will make him even more dangerous."

Renji rubbed a hand down his face, knowing that Marshall was right, in more ways than one.

"If I didn't know better, I'd think the man was jealous."

"Hardly." Renji huffed. "You have to have a heart to feel such an emotion and Rusk lost his long ago. No, it's more like someone took what he thought belonged to him and he wants it back."

"Being possessive fits the egomaniac profile, but surely you don't think he feels he owns you and Trey?"

"That's exactly how he feels." During the three years he'd come to know Rusk, there were hints of such behavior towards a few of Rusk's acquaintances. Renji had become one of them. "I didn't really recognize the signs because, well, to be honest, I didn't think the man capable of such attachments. But the more auctions I went to and the more I got to know the man, in as far as I was able, I could see a sort of attraction there. I ignored it, of course. The thought alone made me sick."

"You were a challenge, the one he couldn't own, the one he couldn't have. Then when he found out about your duplicity and saw how much you wanted Trey and not what he could offer you..."

"Yeah, I just pushed the knife deeper."

"Shit."

"I'm sorry, *aniki*, I really didn't think it would matter. The man's so aloof and cold that I didn't catch onto the signs and when I did, I just figured I was another conquest. It didn't dawn on me that he would take my own aloof behavior as a challenge. I just thought he'd move on to easier prey."

Marshall let out a gusty breath. *"It's alright, niichan, we all know how unstable the man is. There was no way you could have known how he would react. But now that we have this info, we'll need to be more vigilant. Vengeance is a very strong motivation."*

Renji remained silent a moment, his mind awhirl with a myriad of thoughts. But the one that was first and foremost was keeping Trey safe. Above all, Trey's safety was his number one priority. He looked at Trey, his sleeping angel.

"It ends here, Marshall. No matter what, it ends here. I won't have Rusk be a shadow over our life together. And I meant what I said last night, no matter who sees him first, he dies. No hesitation, no second thoughts."

"Don't worry, the boys have their instructions."

"Good." That made him feel a little better.

"Gary will be preparing dinner in a couple hours, why don't you get some rest? I'll wake you and Trey when it's ready."

Renji couldn't help grinning at Marshall's caring. "Alright, but only a couple hours. Trey needs food as well as rest to recover completely."

"Roger that." The smile in his voice could be heard as well. *"In two hours. Marshall out."*

Shaking his head, Renji got up and stretched, his muscles pleasantly tight and body nicely sated. *For the time being anyway.* That thought caused warmth to steal over him as he looked at Trey's sleeping form. Never had Renji imagined he would fall so hard or so fast, but with Trey, it was as easy as breathing. Like a part of his soul had recognized the part that was missing. He couldn't lose that now, not after having finally found it. He and Trey belonged together and Renji would do everything in his power to see that they stayed that way.

With that thought firmly in mind, Renji climbed in beside Trey and pulled him close, spooning behind his warm body. Trey let out a sleepy sigh, making Renji smile. He kissed the back of Trey's neck and closed his eyes. It wasn't long before he fell into a peaceful sleep.

After being awoke two hours later, Renji and Trey had a pleasant meal with Gary and Marshall. There wasn't much to be updated about, but Renji could feel the tension. It was like a taut wire, just waiting to snap. Trey, thankfully, was still too exhausted to notice. The small nap did little to alleviate his tiredness and after getting a full stomach, Renji could see his eyes beginning to droop. Gary and Marshall noticed as well, both smiling with understanding as Renji took Trey into his arms and picked him up. Trey gave very little protest, letting Renji know just how wore out he really was. Before leaving, Marshall promised to contact him should anything come up and that he had put Renji's revolver under his pillow. Renji had been meaning to get the hand gun himself, but taking care of Trey had come first. Smiling his thanks, Renji left, glad that Marshall had thought to leave it for him. Who knows, he might need it.

Once back in their room, Renji stripped them both, put Trey under the covers first, then checked under his pillow for the revolver. He pulled it out, making sure it was loaded, the safety off, then put it back. Letting out a breath of satisfaction, Renji climbed in beside Trey and pulled him in his arms, Trey's head on his chest.

"Mmm, love you." Trey snuggled close and was deeply asleep in moments.

That sweet admission rocked Renji to his core. Of course, being basically asleep, Renji couldn't rely on it. And well, he knew he was already in love with Trey. It was too soon to say the words, they'd only been together a handful of days. Still, it warmed his heart to know that Trey, even in his subconscious, loved Renji. It was enough for the now.

He grinned, kissing the top of Trey's golden head. "*Aishetero*, hana," he whispered and wrapped his arms around Trey. Closing his eyes, the sound of Trey's even breathing lulled him into the void.

****

It was the sound of shouting and the loud popping of gunfire that jolted Renji out of a dead sleep. His hand went under the pillow for his gun, but it wasn't there. Neither was Trey beside him.

"About time. I thought Morpheous was going to keep you a while longer."

Renji jerked toward the sound of that hated voice to see his worst nightmare. Rusk was by the door, his arm around a naked and white faced Trey. An old school .38 with a wooden grip pointed at his golden head. Rusk was smiling brightly, like he had just won a great prize. But the brown eyes were cold as death. Renji's heart nearly stopped at the sight, but he had to be strong and do whatever it took to save Trey. He would find out later how the madman had gotten past the guys. Trey was priority.

"I must say, Renjiro. May I call you, Renjiro?" The question was rhetorical. "Your welcoming committee leaves much to be desired."

"My apologies." He bowed his head, knowing that he needed to let Marshall in on what was going on. His ear piece was silent, letting Renji know that the others had been unable to call. Otherwise, that would have been enough to wake him. "Marshall…well, he's not very sociable to strangers."

"Indeed."

"Renji! Thank Christ! Are you alright?" Marshall sounded winded, but his voice was strong. *"Answer me!"*

"Seems the rest of your men are of the same mind." Rusk smirked without humor.

"You can't be too careful these days."

"Shit! Try to stall, we're almost done taking care of these guys. And keep the comm open."

"No." Rusk's voice held a dark chill. "I guess not. But then, I never expected them to be so…experienced. Quite a surprise when I was informed they were merely, how did the good Inspector put it? Oh yes, rent-a-cops, was it?" The smile died on his face, a mask of calm rage replacing it. "I detest being made a fool of." His hand tightened on the gun at Trey's head as the sound of more shots and shouts rang out.

Renji's earpiece was alive with the sound of the team, but he ignored it, his focus trained on Rusk and a shaking Trey whose face had paled even more, those gem colored eyes wide with fear. Regardless of what Marshall instructed, this had to end. Renji couldn't gamble with Trey's life and stalling Rusk was just that, a gamble. As unstable as Rusk was, Renji and Trey could be dead before the team ever got to them. No, Renji needed to end this, now.

Making up his mind, Renji lifted his chin and gave Rusk a penetrating stare. "What do you want, Rusk?"

"There he is." In a blink, that bright smile was back. "There's the man I've been dealing with the last few years. Although I must say, I do like your lack of attire." His cold, dark eyes roamed, giving Renji a dirty feeling. "Do stand up. I want to see what I have been denied."

Teeth set, Renji did as he was bid and stood beside the bed. His eyes never left Trey's.

"Well, well, what a lucky young man you are, Joshua. Is he as good as he looks?" Rusk pulled Trey closer, but Trey was too scared to answer. "Come now, my beauty, no need to be shy, you can tell me."

Renji gave Trey an encouraging smile, letting him know it was alright.

"Y…yes, sir." His voice was shaky with fear.

Rusk let out a deep sigh. "I thought as much." His hot gaze roamed over Renji's nakedness again. "The pleasure we could have found, you and I. Such a waste." He shook his head with disappointment.

"What do you want, Rusk?"

"Why, payback, of course." His tone was matter of fact, but those frigid, dark eyes held eagerness and cruelty. "Payback for your deception and lies. For abusing my trust, my generosity. For your blatant betrayal." His cheeks suffused with color at that though his voice was calm. "I offered you what very few have ever been offered…myself. But instead of finding satisfaction with each other, I find out you're a plant sent by Interpol, bent on destroying me. Needless to say, it was a very painful discovery."

"I never led you on and I did what I had to do." There really wasn't much use in lying now and maybe if he kept Rusk talking, he could find an opening. Possibly even have the team come to their rescue.

"Oh yes, Ishida, was it?" Rusk grinned. "Hero's have a tendency to die young."

"The bad guys don't exactly live to be old men either."

"Touché." He nodded slightly. "Although I hardly consider myself the bad guy. I'm an entrepreneur, a businessman like yourself."

"Trafficking in innocents and drugs is not a business nor are we in any way alike."

That smile of his turned cruel. "Oh, I beg to differ. One look at fair Joshua and you did all you could to posses him." Rusk let go of Trey's arm to reach up and stroke his golden hair making Trey cringe. "By your own admission, you take what you want. Seems like we have more in common than you would care to admit."

"No." Renji shook his head, his anger at a slow boil to see Rusk petting Trey in a such a way. "While I did nothing to hide my attraction, I would have never used it against Trey or kept him here against his will. He is a person, a human being, and deserves to be treated as such."

Rusk chuckled darkly. "Such noble sentimentality. But the world is a very harsh place and only the strong survive. Those that are weak deserve what they get." His face became an unreadable mask. "We live in tough times, Renjiro and those like your precious, you called him Trey? Well, ones like Trey will always be prey. It's a fact of nature that the strong live and the weak die. And who am I to go against nature?"

"Or make a profit from the sufferings of others?" Renji couldn't keep the sarcasm from his voice.

"The strongest also means being the wealthiest." He shrugged. "And in today's world, wealth also means power. I..."

Silence. Rusk raised his head, cocking it a bit to the side as he stared at Renji. Even Renji's ear piece had gone quiet. Although that was most likely due to waiting for Rusk to make his move. Thanks to Renji keeping the comm open, the team could hear everything he and Rusk said.

"Well, seems like the social niceties are over." He grabbed Trey's upper arm in a tight grip causing Trey to wince. "We're going to play a game, Renjiro. It's a new game, one I invented. I call it Scavenger Roulette."

Renji felt his face drain of color and his stomach hollow out. "Rusk…"

But Rusk wasn't listening. "The rules are simple. In this room I have hidden your gun. If you can find it and shoot me before I put a bullet in your lovers head, you win. If not, you lose. Well." He gave Renji an evil grin. "You both lose."

"How…" Renji's mouth was dry though he was sweating with sheer terror. "How do I know that gun only has one bullet?"

"You don't." He pulled the hammer back. "Best get to searching. This .38 carries six rounds, five of which are empty." He pulled the trigger and it clicked, making Trey jump, a terrified squeak escaping. "Down to four."

Renji jumped into action, starting with the bed. He flipped the mattress over and then the box springs, finding nothing. When he moved to one of the nightstands, he heard another click and looked over to see Trey with tears streaming down his white cheeks and shaking uncontrollably.

"Three left."

The nightstand and it's contents went flying as did the other one, but no gun was in either. He growled in frustration, feeling helpless.

Click.

Renji whirled around at the sound. Trey was sobbing, a fist stuck in his mouth, probably to keep from screaming as Rusk watched Renji with smug satisfaction.

"Two empty." He tsked dispassionately then pulled the trigger again. "Oops, make that one." His dark eyes glowed with evil triumph. "Better hurry."

Tearing the cushion from the chair, Renji tossed it aside, jabbing his hands down the inside and quickly moving them up and back. His hands were shaking so badly that he nearly missed the feel of cold steel as his right hand swept over it. His brain was in such a panic that it didn't fully register that he'd found his gun until he pulled it out.

Renji jumped up and pointed the gun just as he heard the hammer of Rusk's gun snick back. He had the gun pointed directly at Rusk's head, a deadly calm settling over him as he prepared to fire.

"Congratulations." Rusk nodded at Renji in a mock bow. "But it seems we may have to alter the game a bit."

"No, no more games." As close as Rusk was to Trey, Renji couldn't risk shooting Rusk for fear that he would shoot Trey. That gun was cocked and ready, the barrel at Trey's temple. One wrong move would be all it took. "If you want out of here alive, you'll put the gun down and move away from Trey." He just hoped Rusk's sense of self preservation was greater than his need for revenge.

"We both know I won't be leaving here alive, Renjiro, so please don't insult me." His tone was that of a parent talking to a small child.

"No insult, Rusk." Renji's heart was in his throat even though his hand was steady as he pointed the gun. "I promise that if you let Trey go, you'll walk out of here."

Rusk smiled sadly and shook his head. "You never struck me as being naive, Renjiro."

"It's not naiveté to know that my team will follow my orders. If I tell them to let you walk, you'll walk."

They stared at each other, Rusk's face impassive, dark eyes unreadable. Renji didn't look at Trey, he couldn't. He had the uncanny feeling that if he took his eyes off Rusk, Trey would die. Renji would hold Rusk's gaze forever if it meant keeping Trey alive. But he knew their staring match wouldn't last. Help was on the way and they both knew it. Unfortunately, Rusk would pull the trigger before he could be taken out. And getting that gun from him would end in the same result, Trey dead. A fact the others had figured out as well if the angry arguing over his ear piece was any indication. Renji tuned it all out. His focus needed to be on the madman in front of him and how to save Trey.

"I'm rather curious, Renjiro, was it his looks or his passionate response that made you want him so?"

The question was unexpected, but that was probably what Rusk was going for. "What do you mean?"

"Come now, no need to be coy. Your lover here is certainly beautiful, but surely that wasn't what made you want him so. Under the drug, he was so responsive to my touch. Was that what drew you?"

Out of the corner of his eyes, he saw Trey stiffen in Rusk's hold. Renji silently cursed.

"Well, seems your little beauty doesn't know the details of his time with me. Such a shame." His grin was malicious.

"He had no memory of that incident and after all he had been through, I didn't want to make him feel worse. It wasn't like you had sex or anything remotely like it." He hoped Trey would understand and forgive him for not telling him everything.

Rusk laughed harshly. "No, of course not. But giving him a hand job in front of potential buyers as they watched him come was still a sight to behold."

Trey gasped.

Not taking his eyes of Rusk, "I'm sorry, Trey. I know that's probably not enough, but I never meant to keep the truth from you. There just didn't seem the right time to tell you. Truly, hana, I'm sorry."

Renji could see Trey's tears out of the corner of his eye and it broke his heart to know that he was partly responsible for them. Then Trey wiped them away, a tentative smile curving his lips. Renji swore then and there that he would spend the rest of his life making Trey the happiest man in the world. To have Trey's forgiveness and love was more than he could ask for.

"Let me ask you something, Renjiro." Rusk seemed nonchalant and at ease even after witnessing the exchange between Trey and Renji, but Renji knew the man had to be feeling the heat. "I can clearly see you care for your lover here. Unusual considering that you paid a great deal of money for him. And the way he looks at you, well, the feeling is definitely mutual, your little omission notwithstanding. So, for curiosities sake, do you care enough for your lover to die in his place?"

"Yes." Renji didn't even have to think about it. Trey was his heart, his soul. Before Trey had come into his life, Renji now knew that he didn't really have much of a life and if Trey were to be taken from him, he knew, without a doubt, his life would end. So he would gladly give his life if it meant Trey would live on. "Yes."

"Renji," Trey whispered brokenly.

"Oh, Renjiro, I was so hoping you would say that."

For one long, drawn out moment in time, Renji's heart stopped as sheer terror washed through him. Rusk smiled brightly, obsidian eyes cold as the grave as he his finger began to pull back on the trigger.

"No!" He shouted.

"Goddammit!"

"Wait!"

Everything happened at once. The door was kicked in and Rusk's attention was sent that way. Renji took his chance and yelled at Trey to drop. When he did, Renji put two bullets in Rusk. One in the head and one in the heart followed by several other shots that Renji paid no mind to. Not that it really mattered; the man was dead before he hit the floor.

Wasting no time, Renji ran to Trey, scooping him up and taking him to the other side of the room away from Rusk's body, making sure to lay his gun down beside him. Trey was shaking and crying, clinging to Renji like a limpet as he sat in Renji's lap.

"Renji." He sobbed into Renji's chest.

"I got you, baby, I got you." He held Trey close, shedding quite a few tears himself.

"Clear!"

"Clear!"

The shouts made Trey jump.

"Shh, it's just the twins securing the room, love."

That relaxed Trey a bit but he didn't let go of Renji and Renji sure as hell wasn't about to let go of him.

"Renji! Goddammit, Renji, answer me!" Marshall's voice sounded frantic over the ear piece.

"Better answer before he has to shoot one of the locals to get in here and check for himself that you're okay," Seth said.

Luke snorted. "He wasn't that far from it before now."

Everything had happened so fast that Renji didn't notice the twins, nor had he wanted to. All his focus had been on saving Trey, on getting Trey. But now that Trey was safe and in his arms, he saw that the twins had been in a serious fight and hadn't come out unscathed.

"Dear God! Seth, Luke!" The sound of his voice must have convinced Trey that something was up and looked at the twins.

He sucked in a breath. "Oh no!"

He hurried to the twin's side, smiles on their bruised and bloodied faces.

"Hey, now, it's not as bad as it looks." Seth's face paled, the bruise on his cheek standing out as he took off his shoulder harness, the bandage over his right shoulder soaked with blood, the arm not moving much. "It's just a flesh wound," he joked, but Renji could see he was on the verge of collapse.

"Jesus!" Trey helped Seth to sit, his back against the wall for support. He then looked over at Luke. "Luke."

"I'm fine, just need to rest a bit." He gave Trey and Renji a wan and painful smile as he slid down the wall to sit beside Seth.

"Renji! For Gods sake! Answer me!" Marshall sounded desperate.

"Go ahead, Renji," Luke told him. His left arm was in a makeshift sling. It was clearly broken, the wrist at an unnatural angle and a very large bump in the middle of the arm. There was also a deep slash still oozing blood near his collarbone, though it didn't look broken. "You know how he gets when he's worried." His grin was as pain racked as his brother's.

Renji nodded as Trey fussed over them, glad that they were alright. "Go ahead, Marshall."

"Thank God!" There was a pause then Renji could hear Marshall breathe deep and let it out. *"Are…are you and Trey okay?"* His uncertainty made Renji smile.

"We're fine, *aniki*." There was laughter and whoops of joy from the others through the ear piece. Renji looked over at Trey. There were still tears in his eyes, his face pale, but he smiled at Renji. It was a good sign. "Although you may need to come get your boys. They don't look so hot."

"Those jackasses." Marshall growled affectionately. *"Just keep 'em still. The ambulance will be here soon and the doc will meet us at the hospital."*

"Damn idiots." Trey wiped his eyes as he came back to Renji and sat in his lap again. "Told you two to be careful."

"We tried." Seth's eyes were closed; a fine sheen of sweat covered his face.

"Sorry, Trey." Luke laid his head back, pain and exhaustion lining his features.

Trey sniffed, smiling through his tears. "Just don't let it happen again."

The twins didn't say anything, just grinned. Trey shook his head then laid it on Renji's chest and snuggled close, letting out a deep sigh.

"Hana, I'm so sorry."

Trey looked up, the tears were finally gone but the smile remained. "It's alright, Renji. I don't blame you for not telling me. The past few days have been crazy. And, well, after the shock wore off, I knew what he was trying to do."

"Still, I should have said something. Told you in the limo, on the plane, after you started to feel better. To hear it from that…"

He laid a finger over Renji's lips. "You saved me and made sure I survived despite what that bastard did, Renji. There's nothing to be sorry for. Besides, it's not like I remember, so that's a blessing in itself. Don't beat yourself up over it."

Renji couldn't help but shake his head. "Oh, hana, you are such a wonder." He leaned down and tenderly kissed those lips. "My beautiful hana."

"I love you, Renji." Those beautiful eyes were bright. "I know I should have told you sooner –"

"Shh. You're telling me now. That's all that matters." He wrapped his arms around Trey and held him tight. "And I love you too, Trey. So much, hana, so damn much."

Later that evening, an exhausted Trey sleeping deeply in his arms, Renji got the details of the fight from Marshall in his and Trey's hospital room. Steven wanted to keep Trey overnight for observation and Renji wasn't about to be separated from him.

"Rusk brought seventeen men and split them into two groups. The first was to draw us out. He used the second as a shield. Even with the eagle eye, Davis couldn't pinpoint the bastard in all the bodies running around." After getting cleaned up and his minor wounds seen to, Marshall looked wrung out. But any attempt to get him to rest before he gave Renji his report fell on deaf ears. It was something he said he needed to do first. "We didn't find out where he had gotten to until the fight was nearly over." He rubbed the back of his neck, not looking Renji in the eye. "I'm sorry Renji, he slipped through our fingers."

"Look at me, Marshall." He waited until Marshall finally looked up at him, dark eyes filled with remorse. "You did good, *aniki. Arigato.*" He held Marshall's gaze, conveying without words just how grateful he was to have Marshall and the others there. All alive and well.

"*Itashimashite.*" Marshall bowed his head then took a deep breath, letting it out. "As it stands, of the seventeen Rusk brought, thirteen are dead including Rusk. One is in critical condition and probably won't make it. The agencies in charge of the case took the others along with Conrad who just happened to get out of all this without a scratch. Well, other than the ones he already had," he smirked.

"Humph." Renji wished the man could have gotten roughed up a little, it was the least he deserved after all the lives he ruined. "Our guys?" With all that had happened, Renji hadn't been able to get a clear report.

"Seth came out of surgery just fine. Doc had to repair the damage in his shoulder. Although if that blade had gone just a millimeter deeper…" Neither of them wanted to think about it. "Luke's got twenty-five stitches on his collarbone and his arm is broken in three places. Doc will be putting some pins in it in the morning. After falling through the skylight, he's lucky he only got the stitches and a broken arm out of it."

Lucky was right. The man he was grappling with pushed Luke and they both fell when Luke grabbed on to the guy to save himself. Thankfully for Luke, he landed on the bad guy. Unfortunately, he got cut from the glass and his arm hit one of the stone benches. The gentleman he fell on was the one in ICU with massive head trauma. Steven said he probably wouldn't last the night.

"Gary's finally sleeping. Doc said the leg was fine. It was a thru and thru in his left calf, so he could go home in a couple days if there's no infection. The same for Cole, but he won't be getting much sleep, I'm afraid." Marshall grimaced in sympathy. "He has a grade three concussion and twenty stitches in the back of his head from a rifle butt."

"Ouch." Renji grimaced as well, knowing Cole had to have the mother of all headaches. "Any complications?"

"No, thank God." Marshall shook his head. "The swelling is minor but he lost consciousness for nearly five minutes so Doc wants him to stay for a while. Jake has the dubious honor of waking him every hour."

"Don't know who to feel the sorriest for, Jake or Cole."

Marshall smiled wryly. "Well, considering that Jake has four bruised ribs, a severely twisted knee, twelve stitches on his right side, and has to wake Cole every hour, I'd say he got the short straw."

Renji had to agree. "He should be resting and letting the nurses do that."

"He should, but Cole loosing consciousness like that scared the hell out of him."

"I can understand that." Renji sifted his hand through gold silk, his own refusal to leave Trey's side was probably still echoing down the halls. "How about you? Shouldn't you be resting with Gary?"

"I should." He sighed then frowned with pain, holding his left side. "Gary told me to quit hovering and get in here to give you the report. When I was done, I was to come straight back to bed."

"Bossy of him." Renji grinned.

"He is that." Marshall's smile was bright with love.

"Are the ribs and jaw the only wounds?" There was a dark purple bruise covering the side of his jaw. "And don't give me the glossed over version either," he interjected before Marshall opened his mouth.

"No." The frown returned though Renji knew it was because Marshall hated the fact that he had to tell Renji how hurt he really was. "I've got two broken fingers and a sprained wrist, though not really sure how I got either." He held up his left hand to show that the first two fingers were taped and splinted and his arm was covered in a removable splint. "The ribs and jaw came from one of those bastards tackling me. We fell off the porch onto my right hip which is also bruised. Plus, I have fourteen stitches on my chest from the knife he pulled."

"See, telling me wasn't so bad, was it?"

"Humph."

Renji chuckled softly, careful not to wake Trey. "How's the Triad?"

"Tobias has a broken foot and a dislocated shoulder. The asshole who stabbed Seth decided to use Tobias as a landing pad when he jumped from the roof."

"Damn."

"He's luckier than the moron who jumped on him. That guy got a broken neck and was probably dead before he hit the ground."

"Better him than Tobias."

"Damn straight," Marshall agreed. "Joey got the worst of it I'm afraid. I think some of those bastards noticed how skilled Joey was and just decided to rush him with more than two opponents. His right hand is broken in several places, like it had been stomped on, and he has a fractured wrist. His liver and kidneys are bruised and he has a few cracked ribs. There's a cut over his right eye that needed ten stitches along with a few other scraps and bruises. If it wasn't for Seth and Davis, Joey would have been beaten to death."

"Seth?"

Marshall chuckled. "Hard to keep a good man down. He also gave Davis cover so he could get Tobias and Joey to safety. Unfortunately for Davis, he took one in the upper arm as he was getting Joey secure. Doc took the bullet out, so he'll be fine. He's got a cot set up in Tobias and Joey's room since those two will be staying for a few days."

Laying his head back with a deep sigh, Renji felt the prickle of tears. This was all his fault. If he hadn't gone undercover, none of this would have happened. "I'm sorry, Marshall, so sorry." He tried to hold them back, but the tears spilled down his cheeks unheeded.

"Hey now, you have nothing to be sorry for." Marshall took Renji's hand and squeezed it with his good one, clearly confused with Renji's tears.

"But if I hadn't accepted going undercover, none of you would be hurt. You'd all be safe, be well."

"And you never would have met Trey either."

That made Renji pause as he looked down at his sleeping angel, the tears continuing to stream down his face.

"We all make choices that we're sorry for in hindsight, but Renji, this shouldn't be one of them."

"Marshall –"

"Listen to me, *niichan*." Marshall stopped him before he could say anything else. "All of us have been where you are now, feeling guilty for making the tough decisions. But regardless of those feelings, you made the right call. And yeah, we got banged up a little, but it was worth it considering our wounds are a small sacrifice to keep one more soulless monster off the streets." Marshall squeezed his hand again. "Don't make light of that sacrifice by regretting your actions. It's not fair to the team and cheapens their effort."

He was right, of course. Taking Rusk and his operation down had been the right thing to do despite his feelings now that the dust had settled. Yes, his team was hurt and yes, they could have died, but they were all highly intelligent and well trained men who never would have let Renji make such a decision if they thought it wrong or ill planned out. He was just feeling guilty and scared that the team would blame him for putting them in such danger. But looking at Marshall, he noticed that beneath the fatigue and pain was triumph. He and the team had conquered their foes. They were victorious and the gleam in Marshall's dark eyes showed it clearly for all to see.

Keeping Marshall's hand in his, Renji couldn't hold back any longer. All the pain, the terror, and guilt he'd kept bottled up since the battle ended washed away in a flood of tears. Marshall didn't say a word, just held tightly to his hand, a warm and solid presence at his side.

"Better?" Marshall asked when the tears finally stopped.

Renji nodded, taking a tissue from Marshall and wiping his eyes and nose. "Much, thanks." He let out a deep breath, feeling like a weight had been lifted from his shoulders.

"Were you able to talk to your parents?"

"Briefly." He wiped away the last of the wetness. "*Otosaan* understood but *okaasa* was a bit put out with me."

"I'll bet."

"I'm surprised my ear wasn't bleeding after she finally got done." They shared knowing smiles. "But *otosaan* will explain everything during their flight home. She can't wait to meet Trey."

"I have the feeling he's going to need the mothering too."

Renji stroked Trey's golden head and agreed. "I'm also hoping that the distractions will give him enough time to cope. After I rang off with *okaasa*, I stepped into the bathroom to wash up and no sooner do I get done then Trey's screaming. When I ran back into the room, I f...found him curled..." Renji took a breath. "He was curled into a ball in the middle of the bed, shaking like a leaf and crying." He had to swallow the lump in his throat, remembering how his heart nearly broke at the sight. "I held him and told him that he was safe, but he couldn't stop shaking. Steven finally had to give him a sedative so he could rest."

Marshall gave Renji's hand a comforting pat. "Don't be surprised if he has bad days like that because he will. This was a very traumatic experience and it will take some time to deal with it. And you too for that matter. All of us have been where you're at so if you need to talk, we're here. Sometimes it helps to have an understanding ear when the one you're talking to completely gets what's wrong."

"Thanks, *aniki*."

"And if I might make another suggestion, after all the excitement dies down, take yourselves somewhere quiet for a few days. It'll help to give you two a chance to be alone with each other."

"Some place quiet sounds great." Renji nodded. "*Otosaan* told me not to worry about the house, he'd make some calls, get everything organized. Not that I want to take Trey back too soon. And going to the condo in Tokyo, well, quiet would be the last thing either of us would get there." He smiled wryly. "But the beach house in Okinawa should suit."

"The sun and sea air, the sound of the waves." Marshall nodded with agreement. "The perfect place to recuperate and recharge."

"I'll have to call Minoro, have him get the house ready. Although with you and the twins down, I feel bad making plans to take off without you three."

"Don't you worry about us." He waved his good hand. "We'll be fine. Besides, once the press gets wind of this, they'll be here in droves. We've been able to keep a lid on things so far, but it won't last. We need to get you and Trey out of here before that happens."

With everything that happened, Renji had totally forgotten about the press. Like vultures on a carcass, they would descend on the hospital once wind of the attack got out. With his mother's royal relations and his father's multi-million dollar company, being in the news was a regular event for the Takeda clan. Renji did not want to subject Trey to that yet.

"Damn, I guess after *okaasa* and *otosaan* get here, we'll make our escape. What about you and the team?"

"Steven's already informed the staff and administrators about keeping quiet. The chief of police contacted me saying that Genji-sama had a word with him about the situation."

Renji snickered at that. "Knowing *otosaan*, it was more than one."

"Yeah." Marshall grinned. "At any rate, we've got the locals keeping an eye out and everyone here knows what to do. We'll be fine."

Renji nodded, both of them lapsing into a companionable silence. Then Marshall spoke up.

"Gary and I have been tossing around an idea for a few months and I'd like your take on it."

"Sure."

"With the family growing." Marshall nodded to Trey with a smile. "Gary and I thought having teams of four instead of three would make our jobs a little easier by giving the family better and more security."

"Hmm." Renji knew that Marshall was right. Since the family was growing, they would need more personnel and more security measures in place. "With Yana soon to go on maternity leave with the boys, that hole will need to be filled for Ranmaru to have the security he needs while away at school."

"We have plenty of applications and a few viable candidates, but I didn't want Gary and I to make any kind of decisions like this without first running it by you or Genji-sama first."

Renji gave him a warm smile. "Marshall, the security company may have the Takeda name, but it's still yours and Gary's. If you think adding more personnel is needed, then add them. You know we all trust you and Gary to take care of us."

"I know." He patted Renji's hand again. "But taking care of the family means letting everyone know when and if there will be new personnel. It also means making sure those new personnel clicks with the family."

"*Wakata*." Renji smiled with understanding. "I'm all for it and I know *otosaan* will too."

"Thanks. A few variables and shifting will need to be taken care of, but Gary and I will get things worked out."

"You and the twins will still be mine and Trey's team, right?"

"Like the twin's would allow me to separate them from Trey." He snorted. "They damn near killed themselves trying to run to the rescue."

"I'm glad the three of them could become friends." Renji smiled down at Trey then looked over at Marshall. "And having Gary with you will be good too. I know the separation hasn't been easy on either of you these last few years."

Marshall shrugged, then winced with the movement. "After the company got bigger, we knew it would be a possibility and no, it hasn't been easy, but we've adapted as best we could. Gary leading the back-up team has also helped."

"Well, once you two get everything squared away with the teams." He tried to stifle a yawn, his eyes feeling heavy. "You two will be together again."

"Speaking of together, it's late and we both need some shut eye." He slowly got to his feet, handsome face creased with pain. "Whew, now I know why I couldn't remember how badly bruised ribs felt."

"You alright?"

"Yeah." An arm was around his waist as he gave Renji a pained smile. "Just gonna be a little slow for the next few days." He slowly made his way to the door. "I'm gonna go check on the guys then hug up to my man and get some sleep. You get some too."

"I will. *Oyasuminasai.*"

"*Oyasuminasai.*" Then left, his plodding footsteps slowly receding down the hall.

Trying not to jostle Trey or wake him, Renji inched lower under the covers until he was flat on his back and Trey was lying on his chest. He let out a tired sigh, muscles finally relaxing. Trey was a warm weight, his presence soothing after all that had happened. He hugged Trey closer and kissed the top of his golden head.

"I love you, hana." He closed his eyes. "Everything will be alright." Then let the velvet warmth take him.

****

But everything wasn't alright. They weren't at the beach house a full two days before Trey woke up in the night screaming, his body shaking and sweat covered. It was hours before Renji got him calm enough to sleep again, though it was fitful at best. Then there were the nights when he would toss and turn, unable to fight off the nightmare as he mumbled, "Please, no. Stop. Please stop!" Those nights were the hardest for Renji to witness, his heart weeping at the pain Trey was going through. Of course, Trey wasn't alone with his interrupted sleep. Renji too was having his own nightmares and in each one, he failed to reach Trey in time. He would jolt awake as the gun at Trey's head went off, his breathing harsh, body covered in a cold sweat. He would spend the rest of the night watching Trey, his mind and heart needing the reassurance that his love was safe and nearby.

After a week and a half of sleepless nights and failed rest, Renji could see that the situation wasn't improving. In fact, it seemed to be getting worse. His parents coming by to welcome Trey to the family didn't help either. And Renji's mother knew something was terribly wrong from the minute she met Trey. His hana wasn't the young man Renji had described to her. Not that she or his father was disappointed. No, they were just really worried. About

Renji too. Both of them weren't themselves. Trey was losing weight, the nightmares affecting his appetite. Even his personality had changed. Gone was the cheerful young man with the sunny smile, replaced with a quiet and listless young man who hadn't cracked a smile since arriving at the beach house. Something had to be done. So Renji called Steven with the hope that if he couldn't help then he could recommend someone who could. Steven wanted to see them immediately at the hospital. The administration had hired him on as a consultant for the staff, so he had an office there as well as several of his own patients. Renji explained everything to Trey and they left, Renji's heart lighter for the first time in days.

When they arrived at the hospital, Renji and Trey saw two familiar faces coming out as they were going in. A very happy Tobias was being wheeled by an equally happy Davis. They all shook hands and exchanged greetings.

"The infection in your foot finally get cleared up?" Renji asked.

"Clean as a whistle but this cast is a pain in the ass," Tobias replied with a glare at the offending cover on his foot and calf, it's bright neon green shinning in the sun.

"You guys here to see the doc?" Davis put the wheelchair's brakes on.

"What makes you say that?"

Tobias crossed his arms and snorted. "Seriously, Renji, you two look like warmed over vomit. I'd be surprised if you weren't here to see him."

Warmed over vomit was a bit extreme, but there was no denying that they both looked bad. Trey had lost a lot of weight and it showed, his clothes baggy. His beautiful eyes were haunted and large in his pale face, lines of exhaustion showing clearly. Renji knew he didn't look much better. He certainly didn't feel all that well either. Worry and fatigue were definitely starting to take its toll.

"That's a disgusting description, but yes, we're here to see Steven." Renji took Trey's hand and gave him a reassuring smile. Trey laid his head on Renji's shoulder in response. "I called earlier and he told us to come right away."

"Mmhmm." Tobias looked up at Davis, a silent message being communicated between them as Davis nodded. Tobias looked back at Renji, brown eyes filled with understanding. "Let me guess, nightmares?"

Renji blinked, feeling Trey jerk a little with his own surprise at Tobias' correct assumption. "How…how did you know?"

Davis laid a hand on Tobias' shoulder and Tobias took it, lacing their fingers together. "I've seen that same face and eyes look back at me in the mirror enough times to recognize it on someone else when I see it," Tobias explained.

Having been a soldier on the front lines at one time, Renji could well believe it. That kind of action left a lasting impression on a person and Renji could see the knowledge of it in Tobias and Davis' eyes.

"*Hai.*" He wrapped an arm around Trey's shoulder, pulling him close. "I called Steven hoping he could recommend someone."

"No offense to the doc, but do you really want some stranger rattling around in your head, telling you its Post Traumatic Stress Syndrome and prescribing some drugs? That's not very helpful or healthy."

"I don't have much choice, Tobias." He was getting a bit aggravated with Tobias' attitude. "Trey can't keep going like this."

"Or you."

"I'm fine."

"Bullshit!" Tobias snapped. "You're strong, Renji, but I can see how your own nightmares are affecting you."

"Is that true, Renji?" Trey laid a hand on Renji's chest. "Are you having them too?"

"I didn't want to worry you, hana." He cupped Trey's pale cheek. "You've had enough to deal with."

"I know." He sighed, taking Renji's hand. "I'm sorry, darlin'. I haven't been much of a boyfriend, have I?"

"Hey, no need to be sorry." He pulled Trey into his arms again. "We'll get past this, I promise." He kissed the top of Trey's golden head, feeling Trey's arms wrap around his waist and hold on tight.

"Sorry to get so short with you, Renji."

"Don't worry about it, Tobias." Renji was too tired to stay upset and he knew that Tobias meant well.

"Toby." Davis nudged Tobias' shoulder, both exchanging another look.

Tobias pat his hand then looked at Renji. "Look, I can help you both, if you'll let me."

"You can? How?"

"Don't sound so shocked." Tobias grinned. "Davis and I, well, we've been in your shoes, so we know what you're going through and how to help. Of course, the psychology degree helps as well." He gave them a wink.

"He really can help, Renji." Davis' blue eyes were sincere, his tone earnest.

Renji wasn't sure, but they had raised a good point. Knowing what he and Trey were going through, they were in a better position to help than a complete stranger. Even a shrink with plenty of experience dealing with their problem just didn't appeal. Still, this was Tobias. The man was prickly, pushy, and mouthy on the best of days. But if there was a way he could help, the least Renji could do was hear the man out. Although knowing he had a psychology degree was a shock, it felt good to have a friend help.

"Alright, Tobias, where do you want to meet?"

"No need for that." He waved a hand. "We can do it here."

Renji looked around. "This is a parking lot."

"He has a point, Toby." Davis chuckled.

"Fine." Tobias huffed. "There's a picnic area over there." He pointed toward a group of wooden tables with shady trees around them. "Let's go, Davis."

Doing as ordered, Davis released the brake on his wheelchair and they all trooped to the picnic area. Once there, Davis parked Tobias beside a table, put the brake back on, and sat on the bench beside Tobias chair. Renji and Trey continued to stand, Renji holding Trey's hand.

"I'll start with you, Renji." Tobias crossed his arms. "You feel guilty because even though you saved Trey, you couldn't keep him completely safe. Your dreams are probably reliving the scene of Trey being held but not getting to him in time. Am I right?"

Renji's jaw nearly hung open at Tobias' correct diagnosis. "How…?" He couldn't even ask the rest of his question he was so stunned.

"Davis and I went through the same thing when Joey got shot six years ago." He grinned, but there was a haunting sadness at the memory of that time that Renji could clearly see in his and Davis' eyes. "Guilt isn't exactly a rational emotion during war time."

"It's not a luxury you can afford to have either," Davis added. "But because Joey got shot, we felt responsible for not protecting him better."

"You three were near the front lines, Davis. Everyone was at risk."

"Yeah, they were." Davis nodded. "But we thought that with our training and skill, we could protect each other better."

"It was quite a blow to discover we were wrong," Tobias said softly. "All the training and skill in the world didn't prepare us for almost losing Joey."

"The nightmares didn't help either." Davis rubbed the back of his neck. "That first week home with Joey was the worst. The nights were we'd wake up, covered in sweat, and unable to go back to sleep, watching Joey breathe because we were scared if we did sleep, something would happen to him."

"We didn't even leave the house, too scared to let him out of our sight."

Renji nodded in complete understanding. "Too scared if you did for more than a moment, the nightmare would come true." He looked down at Trey, at that dear face. "It would be all your fault again."

"Oh, Renji." Trey went into his arms and held him close. "It wasn't your fault."

"I should have protected you better, hana. I should have made sure you were safe, like I promised." Without warning, the tears started to flow as he buried his face in Trey's neck. "I'm sorry, hana, so sorry."

He held onto Trey like a lifeline, sobbing out his grief at not protecting him better, the guilt like acid in his gut.

"Shh, it wasn't your fault," Trey soothed. "You did all you could and more."

"But it wasn't enough. It wasn't enough." The confession felt torn from his soul, knowing he had failed to protect Trey, his precious hana.

"Don't be a fucktard, Renji." Tobias' tone was biting, causing Renji to glance up, the tears still streaming down his face. "A full battalion of Marines couldn't have been as prepared as you and the rest of us were."

"He's right, Renji. If anyone needs to feel guilty, it's the team. We were charged with keeping you both safe," Davis pointed out.

"But —"

"Listen to me, Renji," Tobias interrupted. "No one is to blame here. We all did the best we could. And while we may not have come out of this ordeal unscathed, we're alive and that's what matters most. Got it?"

Letting out a deep and cleansing breath, Renji nodded, hugging Trey closer. Some of the guilt was still there, but he did feel lighter for having talked it out.

"Good. Now Trey, tell me about your dreams."

Trey stiffened in Renji's arms, his eyes going wide. "I…uh…"

"It's alright, hana. You're safe here." Renji rubbed his back with soothing strokes.

"That's right, hon." Davis smiled encouragingly. "The suns out and your among friends. Nothing can hurt you here."

"I…well, there are two of them." His body was beginning to tremble.

"Go ahead, sweetheart." Tobias' tone was soft, surprising Renji. The man was always so gruff and abrupt.

"I see Renji running to help me and right before he takes my hand, R…Rusk is there and a shot goes off. Then I wake up screaming."

"Easy, hana, shh." Renji held him tighter, his slight frame starting to shake more, his breathing getting harsh.

"What's the other, sweetheart?"

Trey swallowed audibly, arms snug around Renji's waist. "He's there, holding me, laughing, and I can see the gun barrel out of the corner of my eye, p…pointed at my

head. It…it keeps clicking. It w…won't stop clicking."
Those wide gem eyes looked up at Renji, tears starting to
fall. "Why won't it stop, Renji?"

"Trey." He hugged Trey to his chest, wrapping his
arms securely around that shaking body, Trey's silent sobs
breaking his heart. "Shh, I'm here baby, I'm here."

His hana, his sweet Trey had been through so much.
Now to find out that his dreams were being terrorized by
that madman made Renji want to shoot him all over again.

"Trey, come here, sweetheart."

Renji looked over at Tobias, his hand out and eyes full
of understanding. Renji pulled back and wiped the tears
from Trey's cheeks then kissed the tip of his nose. "It's
alright, hana."

Trey nodded and took a deep breath, then went to
Tobias, taking his hand.

"Sit right here, sweetheart." Tobias pat his lap.

"Oh, I…uh…I…" Trey was looking at Renji with
uncertainty, unsure what to do.

"It's fine, hana. Not like he's going to try anything." He gave Trey a reassuring smile.

"Yeah, Davis would gut me." He winked at Trey then pulled him down onto his lap.

"He's not the only one." That got a snicker from Davis.

Tobias just grinned then turned his full attention on Trey. "Okay sweetheart, I want you to listen very carefully." Trey nodded. "First of all, the reason Rusk did all that to you and Renji was to make you suffer. He was a sadistic bastard who enjoyed tormenting those who didn't follow him, who opposed him."

"It was a mind game, plain and simple, that he used on you two," Davis added.

"And the more you think about him, what he did, dream about it, then he wins."

"That's why he dragged it out, Trey. He wanted you and Renji to remember even if he was no longer around."

"So the longer you and Renji agonize over what he did to you both, then that just reinforces his hold and he wins. He succeeds in making you suffer."

Tobias was right, of course. Rusk's actions were those of a manipulative and twisted mind. Anyone else would have just shot them both and been done with the whole deal. Not Rusk. Rusk had used him and Trey in a very sick game and their minds couldn't stop playing it. Rusk won every time they thought or dreamed. It had to stop. Some way, somehow, they both had to come to terms with the nightmares. Hopefully, talking all this out would help. It certainly made Renji feel better. He just hoped it did the same for Trey.

"Do you understand, Trey?" Tobias touched his shoulder. "Replaying what he did only reinforces the pain and fear."

"I know." Trey's voice was soft and small. "But it's hard. It's like my mind doesn't want to let it go."

Tobias cupped his cheek tenderly, though Renji knew it wasn't in a sexual way. "It's okay, sweetheart. You've been through a hellish experience, so the next bit of information I'm going to tell you is critical." He then held Trey's face in both hands, making Trey look directly into his eyes. "This is important so I want you to listen and pay close attention to every word I say."

"Al...alright." Trey was beginning to tremble again.

"Rusk is dead, sweetheart."

"I know," Trey whispered.

"No, listen to me," Tobias reiterated. "Rusk is dead. I read the autopsy report and saw the autopsy photos. He was shot three times in the head and four in the chest, exploding his heart. The man was dead long before he ever hit the floor. He's gone, sweetheart, and he'll never hurt you or Renji again. Ever."

Trey blinked several times, those beautiful eyes bright. "He...he's dead?"

"That's right, sweetheart." Tobias' smile was gentle. "Rusk is dead."

Trey's expression was one of wonderment. "He's dead." Then a sob caught in his throat and those aquamarine gems filled with tears. "He...he's dead."

"Yeah, sweetheart."

Trey broke down then, great heaving sobs shaking his entire frame as he let everything out in Tobias' arms. Renji put a hand over his mouth, trying to keep silent, but grief and pain have a way of getting out no matter how hard you try to keep it in. And he couldn't. A choked moan got through as fat tears rolled down his cheeks once more.

"Come here, Renji."

The moment Tobias said his name, Trey's head popped up. He looked at Renji with his tear ravaged face then jumped out of Tobias' lap and ran right into Renji's waiting arms. Renji held him tight, both comforting the other through the pain and wracking grief.

"I love you so much, Renji," Trey sobbed.

"I love you too, Trey." He hugged Trey closer. "More than life itself." He placed a kiss atop that golden head and felt better than he had in weeks, the last of his tears melting in Trey's silky tresses.

Both finally calmer, Renji glanced over at Tobias to thank him but found Davis in his lap. They were having their own moment with tears and loving smiles. Renji let them have it, more than content to hold Trey as long as they both needed it.

"Are you two okay?" Davis wiped away the wetness from his cheeks, looking at home in Tobias' lap, Tobias' arms latched firmly around his waist.

Renji gazed down at Trey. "Better, hana?"

Beautiful eyes looked up, clear for the first time in weeks. "Yeah." He nodded, releasing a deep, cleansing breath as he laid his head on Renji's chest.

"Come over here and have a seat. You both seem a little shaky." Tobias motioned them over.

With his first step, Renji realized that Tobias was right. He and Trey were a little shaky. His knees were weak and Trey seemed to have the same affliction. But they supported each other until they got to the picnic table. Renji then sat down, pulling Trey onto his lap. Trey went eagerly, wrapping himself around Renji. He briefly closed his eyes, arms hugging Trey's warm body close and breathed deeply. When he opened his eyes, Tobias and Davis were smiling at him and Trey.

"*Arigato*, my friends, *arigato*."

"You're welcome." Davis grinned.

"Don't mention it." Tobias reached over and patted his shoulder.

"Really guys, thanks." Trey's voice was soft and warm. "I feel...lighter."

"This isn't a cure all, you'll both still have your bad days. And you'll still need to talk to a professional on a regular basis for a while. But getting to the root of the problem is always the hardest."

Davis nodded. "And now that you've worked that out and the underlying cause of the nightmares, dealing with them will be easier."

"And if I may make a suggestion?"

"Sure." Renji nodded.

Tobias smiled. "Take your boy home and make love 'till the wee hours of the morning."

Renji chuckled. "The wee hours, huh?"

"Tobias!" Trey's face was bright red, but there was a sweet smile covering those luscious lips. It was a beautiful sight, that smile, and thanks to Tobias and Davis, he was able to see it again after its absence of the past couple weeks.

"Hey, you listen to Uncle Toby, young man," He pointed a finger at Trey. "Nothing like the loving of your man to make everything right with the world."

"Uncle Toby?" Renji smirked, trying to hold back a laugh.

Tobias shrugged. "I'm older than he is." Like that was explanation enough.

Renji chuckled and just shook his head.

"Well, I like it. In fact…" Trey got off Renji's lap and he could see a bit of mischief in those aquamarine orbs as Trey went over to Tobias. He then leaned down, kissed his cheek, and gave him a big hug. "Thank you, Uncle Toby." When he stood back up, Tobias' face was beet red.

"What am I, chop liver?" Davis whined, still sitting in Tobias' lap.

Trey giggled, giving Davis the same treatment. "Thank you, Uncle Davis."

"Oooh, Uncle Davis, I like that." He leered suggestively.

Tobias popped him in the back of the head. "Quit being a perv."

"Ow!" He rubbed the offended spot. "Says the man who had Trey in his lap." That earned him another pop. "Ow! Stop that."

Trey was laughing at the two's antics, his eyes bright and cheeks pink. He was luminous and Renji couldn't help going to him and picking him up, twirling them both around in sheer joy.

"Renji!" Trey threw his arms out and laughed more, the sound the sweetest music Renji ever heard.

Elation bubbled up from inside Renji and he laughed as well, his heart full to near bursting. It felt so good to just let go, to see his hana glowing with happiness once more. He felt like shouting from the rooftops.

Slowly coming to a stop, he let Trey slither down his front. Their breathing was fast from the exertion, but Renji had never felt better or seen Trey so radiant.

He leaned down and planted a sweet kiss on tempting lips. "I love you, hana."

Trey cupped his cheek, a thumb ghosting over his bottom lip. "I love you, too."

"Hey," Tobias called out. "My suggestion was to go home and do that."

Renji winked at Trey with a grin then turned to Tobias and bowed. "*Hai*, Uncle Toby."

That earned him a glare as Tobias' cheeks reddened. "Brat." A smile peeked through but he said nothing more.

Davis held up a hand before Renji could say a word. "Please, having you call me Uncle Davis would be wrong on so many levels." He got off Tobias' lap as Renji chuckled, then went to unlock the wheelchair brakes and stand behind it. "You're both very welcome. Now shoo, we all have better things to do than hang around here."

"Amen, baby," came Tobias' heartfelt reply.

"Call us should you need to, alright?"

Trey and Renji walked over, both giving more hugs of thanks.

"We will," Renji promised as Trey nodded in agreement.

"Good." Tobias gave them both a penetrating stare. "Remember, both of you, the threat is gone and you have each other. Nothings more important than that."

Renji held out his hand and Tobias shook it, his grip firm and strong. "*Wakata.*"

Tobias nodded and let go, then Davis patted his shoulder and they left.

Taking Trey's hand, Renji and Trey left as well. Once on the road, Renji called his pilot, instructing him to get the chopper ready for the flight back to Okinawa. He then called Steven and explained everything. Steven had a couple shrinks in mind and would send their info for them to look over. He was also relieved and glad that Tobias and Davis were able to help, instructing Renji to call them or himself should he or Trey needed it before a psychiatrist was found. Renji promised that he would then rang off.

After they got back to the beach house, it was late, but Trey went into his arms, his eyes going dark with passion.

"Make love to me, Renji." His hands rubbed over Renji's chest. "I need to feel you inside me, filling me up, making me complete."

Renji went from aroused to aching in seconds, taking Trey's mouth in a punishing kiss, a low groan erupting from his chest.

"God, Trey." His breathing was harsh as he divested them both quickly of their clothes. "I want you so much. Sometimes I feel like I can't breathe without you." He picked Trey up, Trey's legs wrapping around his waist as he strode to their bedroom.

"You're all I'll ever need," Trey replied as Renji laid him down gently in the middle of their bed, Renji's big body covering Trey's smaller one. "You're everything I've ever wanted."

"*Aishetero*, hana." His fingers reverently touched Trey's face.

"I love you, too."

For the next hour, Trey and Renji reacquainted themselves with each other. Sharing and trading kisses, loving touches, licks and sips of overly sensitive skin, they pushed each other until neither could take it any longer.

"Please, Renji...I need." Trey was writhing under Renji, eyes dark and body flushed with desire. He was passion incarnate and Renji needed to be inside him like he needed his next breath.

Getting the lube from under the pillow, Renji slicked two fingers, gently inserting one, then the other into Trey's tight hole.

"God, yes!"

Trey's husky moan nearly caused Renji to lose it, but he breathed deeply, using all his control. Then he inserted a third finger, curling them up and finding Trey's prostate.

"Ah!" His back bowed with pleasure. "Renji...please, please...need you."

Renji needed as well, slicking his aching shaft and pushing Trey's legs up. Once he had himself poised at Trey's hole, he leaned down and kissed Trey tenderly. "Got the test's back, baby."

"Test's?"

He pushed in a little. "*Hai*," He grunted. "Clean, no more condoms." Then he sank the rest of the way in.

"Oh, God," Trey moaned.

After a few moments adjustment and needing to taste Trey's mouth again, Renji started to move. "Oh, hana…Trey…you feel so good, baby." Trey's heat and tightness had Renji's head spinning now that he could really feel it without the latex barrier.

Never had Renji not used a condom with any of his lovers, but then, Trey wasn't just his lover. Trey was his love, Renji's only love and going bareback was the ultimate commitment, the proof of his fidelity. Feeling Trey's heated passage, how it welcomed him with every thrust, the wait had been more than worth it.

"Oh…oh, God…Renji…"

Renji pumped his hips faster, palming Trey's leaking cock. "Yes, baby, come for me."

"Ren…Renji!" His head was thrown back with a scream as thick jets of cream spurted across his stomach and chest.

If the sight and smell of Trey's release wasn't enough, feeling Trey's anal walls squeeze around his shaft was what really sent him over the edge. He came with a ragged shout, emptying himself into Trey's welcoming body.

They stayed joined, letting their breathing and hearts calm, both content and sharing kisses.

"You're really inside me now." Trey's smile was radiant.

Renji cupped his cheek. "Always, hana." He tenderly kissed Trey again then reached under his pillow.

For the last week, he'd hidden the little black box, waiting for the right time or a more formal setting. But no setting could have been any more perfect than the one they were sharing now, their bodies still joined, hearts beating in time with each other.

He pulled Trey onto his lap, keeping himself inside Trey's body. "I love you, Trey Morrison. Would you do me the honor of becoming my partner, my mate, my husband?" He pulled both rings out, showing the smaller one to Trey.

"Oh, Renji." Trey's eyes filled with tears, his smile bright enough to light up the world.

"Does that smile mean yes?"

"Yes, yes!"

Renji's heart exploded with joy as he put the ring on Trey's finger.

"It's beautiful, Renji." He wiped the tears away with his free hand, admiring the ring on his other. "What are the stones?"

"Black diamonds and aquamarines."

Trey gave him a startled look then grinned, his expression saying he knew why Renji chose the stones.

Renji held up his matching ring, the waning light from the windows making all the stones around the band twinkle. "The stones are set in a platinum band and on the inside is an inscription"

Trey took the ring and read aloud. "'My heart, my soul. Forever'. Oh, Renji," He breathed.

"I had the Japanese Kanji character for forever inscribed as well," Renji pointed to it, then looked up at Trey luminous face.

"I love you, Renjiro Takeda. My heart, my soul. Forever." He picked up Renji's hand and placed the ring on his finger then kissed it.

"Forever, hana," He sealed that vow with a breath stealing kiss.

They made love again, slowly and tenderly until their release washed over them like a gentle wave. And when sleep finally claimed them, there were no nightmares, only peaceful dreams as they held each other, safe in the knowledge that they had faced danger and come through it together. Because what doesn't kill you, makes you stronger.

The End

Read on for an exclusive short about the Terror Twins, Luke and Seth. This is for the fans, who wanted a little more. Enjoy!

A familiar warm body at his back brought a lazy smile to Seth's lips as he slowly awoke. The huff of breath at his neck and being held in Luke's strong arms made Seth feel content. Soul deep.

"Love you," Luke told him, voice raspy with sleep as he placed a tender kiss below Seth's ear.

"Mmm, love you, too." He shivered in response.

"Time?" Those lips trailed wet kisses down Seth's neck to the back of his shoulder.

A quick glance at the bedside table showed it was almost seven in the morning.

"We have plenty," Seth replied before quickly turning and pinning Luke to the bed with his body.

Leaning down, Seth took those soft lips, their morning wood rubbing together and painting each other's stomachs with sticky wetness.

"Seth." Luke softly gasped after they came up for air.

Looking down into the identical face of his twin, Seth felt his heart overflow with love. And it wasn't just because they were brothers. Their bond, it was more than being siblings. More than being lovers. He was in love with Luke and always had been. The same that Luke was in love with him. Taboo though their relationship might be, Seth didn't give a fuck. They'd fought all their lives to reach this moment. Seth would gladly do it again if it meant having his twin in his bed and life for all the rest of their days.

Reaching up, Luke cupped Seth's cheek. Love and adoration shone brightly in his leaf green eyes. "Yours." He smiled, wrapping his legs around Seth's waist.

"Always." Seth kissed his palm then went for the lube under his pillow.

Because of the recovery from the attack at Renji's home a little over four months ago, their love making had been put on hold. Except for the occasional blow or hand job the past couple weeks that is. With all the pain and drugs swimming in their systems, getting it up was a no go. Not that Seth wanted to rush. They had been lucky. Damn lucky. And they had plenty of time to heal. Trey definitely made sure of that.

Tracing the red puckered scar on Luke's left collarbone, Seth was grateful. More grateful than he could express. Luke did the same to the raised scar on Seth's right shoulder. Yeah, grateful didn't even cover it.

"I'm fine, Seth," Luke assured. "We're both almost at full strength. Doc said we can resume our regular workouts next week. Now I have a different ache." His desire heavy eyes full of meaning.

"Yeah?" Seth ground down a little, the friction delicious against his hardness.

"Yeah," Luke groaned, grinding back. "Don't tease. Need you, Seth."

"You have me," he promised as he flipped the cap on the bottle. "Always."

Upending the bottle, Seth poured a generous dollop of the slick on his fingers then put it within easy reach beside Luke. With familiar ease, Seth rubbed around Luke's tight pucker, gently sliding a finger past the guardian muscle. Luke's gasp turned to a throaty moan as Seth slowly worked his finger in and out.

"Been too long," Luke croaked, pupils blown with arousal. "Ache for you."

"Shh," Seth crooned as he added another finger. "Not going anywhere."

A twist of his wrist found Luke's gland. Seth rubbed it with firm pressure.

"Seth," Luke cried out, head thrown back, neck and chest flushed with passion. "More."

A third finger eased in, flexing and turning to stretch the tight anal walls. When Seth felt Luke was almost ready, he grabbed the lube with his empty hand. Flipping open the cap, he poured a good bit over his painfully throbbing cock. Satisfied there was enough, he tossed the bottle but was careful not to touch himself too much. He was primed, watching Luke writhe and undulate on his fingers. And his sounds. Christ.

"Now…Seth, now," Luke demanded.

In seconds, Seth had his fingers out and his dick in. It was the most glorious sensation he'd ever felt in his life.

"Oh God, yes." Seth groaned before leaning down and taking Luke's mouth in a heated kiss.

Pulling back just enough to share the same breath, Seth began to move. His hips created a languid undulation, in, out, in, out. The slow drag against his sensitive dick was heaven. The tight heat of Luke's channel was euphoric. He was home.

"Fuuuck…Seth."

There was nothing like that growl when Seth pegged Luke's gland. The first time he'd heard it, Seth nearly blew his load. Even now, it still sent shivers to his balls, making them tighten more toward climax.

"So goddamn sexy, baby," Seth grunted as he picked up the pace a bit.

"Need more…harder." Luke licked at Seth's lips, his hips meeting Seth's, thrust for thrust.

"Know what you need." He nipped Luke's bottom lip.

"You…always," Luke panted then took Seth's mouth in a blistering kiss.

With the way Luke was eating at his mouth, clinging to him as breathy mewls poured out his throat, Seth could hold back no longer. He built up his rhythm until he was pounding into Luke, nailing his gland with each inward thrust. Luke hung on, clawing at his back, expression one of pure bliss and keening sounds of more tearing past kiss swollen lips.

"Seth…close…fuck!" He tossed his head back, eyes squeezed shut.

Oh, no, that wouldn't do. Seth wanted, had to see those beautiful eyes. See the love there as they both succumbed to the passion between them.

"Look at me!"

Luke's eyes popped open at the command, that leaf green almost black with desire as he stared into Seth's no doubt identical gaze.

"Love you. Always," Seth panted, feeling his impending orgasm rushing up his balls.

"Love you, too. Always!"

A keening wail and Luke stiffening under Seth announced Luke's orgasm. That was quickly followed by hot wetness on their stomachs and Seth's dick being strangled in Luke's ass. Seconds later, Seth followed Luke over the edge with a shout, pumping his hips to give his twin every drop of juice.

"Jesus," Luke breathed heavily, his hands wandering over Seth's sweat slick back.

"Yeah," Seth agreed, giving Luke a tender kiss. No doubt he'd feel the scratches later. Worth it though. When he pulled back a bit, Luke stopped him with panic stricken features. "Shh. I know, baby. I know."

Relaxing once again, Luke lay there while Seth reached into the nightstand drawer for the plug. With practiced ease, Seth replaced his softening dick with the plug, making sure it was secure.

"Better?"

"Mmm," Luke replied with a sated smile.

It wasn't often Luke needed the security of having Seth's spunk kept inside him. But the attack at Renji's had been brutal. They'd come real close to losing each other that day. Too damn close. Luke needed the added assurance of having a part of Seth inside him for a while. And Seth needed it as well. It would be several weeks before that fear was tempered enough to put the plug away.

Lying on his back, Seth pulled Luke against his chest, cuddling his brother close. The muscle in his healed shoulder was a little tight from the exercise, but nothing some rest wouldn't fix.

"How's your arm?" Seth kissed Luke's forehead.

Luke languidly stretched the appendage out, flexing his fingers. "It's good. The stiffness is finally going away." He laid the arm back on Seth's chest, snuggling close again. "Glad Doc didn't have to put in the pins and rods. Too long to heal that shit."

They'd definitely got lucky there. After Doc took another look at the X-rays, he had a very experienced orthopedic surgeon come in and set the breaks in Luke's arm. They were clean with no fragments or jagged edges. It meant more time in the cast to keep it immobile, but that was better than several surgeries to put in a few pins and rods to keep the bones together. It also meant the arm would be a weakness Luke couldn't afford if he'd had all that metal implanted. As it was, the breaks were healing well and it wouldn't be long before Luke regained full strength in the arm.

They drifted in a haze of sated satisfaction for a while until a small knock rapped at their door. Luke chuckled. They both knew who it was.

"Come on in, Trey," Seth called out.

The door opened and Trey slipped inside, closing the door behind him. He was in black boxer briefs, color high and sporting a couple fresh love bites on his collarbones.

"Looks like we're not the only ones who got lucky this morning," Luke snickered as he pulled away from Seth.

"You should see Gary." Trey snorted as he walked over to the bed and sat down at Seth's hip. "Both his wrists are red, his bottom lip is swollen, and I swear he's floating around the kitchen."

"That's because he probably is." Seth chuckled. "The kinky bastard."

Trey blushed as they all laughed.

Seth and Luke sat up, backs against the headboard. Seth patted the space between him and Luke. Trey bounded over with a sweet smile, snuggling in the middle of them.

"How you feeling, hon?" Luke asked as he wrapped an arm around Trey's shoulders.

"Better." He let out a deep sigh, laying his head on Luke's arm. "I'm glad all of us are here. "Gran… she really would have loved you guys."

For the past three weeks, the six of them had been staying at Trey's grandmother's house in Gastonia, North Carolina. They came for several reasons. To check on the place and the classic cars and motorcycles stored in the large building out back. To rest and recharge after the attack. And to accept the summons from Horace Rutherford, Trey's grandfather. That had been a mistake from the moment they stepped foot in the mausoleum of a house a week ago. As the man's only grandson, old Horace had certain expectations of Trey despite the fact that was the first time they'd ever met. And being from old Southern money that could be traced back to before the Civil War, old Horace thought his will would be heeded. He was so wrong. Delightfully so. The bastard.

"Yeah." Trey nodded absently, those aquamarine eyes looking a bit haunted. "I still can't believe he's been having me watched all my life. That he didn't even try to save me when I was kidnapped. Then, to give me that ultimatum. Leave Renji or be disowned. I thought I was going to throw up."

"He's lucky Renji didn't gut him and toss his worthless carcass out for the buzzards," Luke stated with amusement.

"He's lucky Sango-san didn't fly out and gut him," Seth amended with a chuckle. "You don't mess with her family. Doesn't matter who you are."

"Now I can understand why my mom ran off with my dad." Trey smiled wanly.

"Hey," Seth said as he took Trey's chin in a firm grip. "We're your family now. The ones who love you and care about you and want you to be happy with the love of your life. That old bastard just wishes he had the same. So no more thinking about that waste of space. He had his chance and pissed it away. You belong to us now. Got it?"

"Seth." Trey's voice wobbled, gem bright eyes welling with tears.

"You're our little brother, Trey." Luke leaned in, hugging Trey from behind. "Our brother of the heart. That kind of bond is unbreakable."

"Luke." Trey turned and buried his face in Luke's neck, shoulders shaking.

"That's it, hon. Let it out," Luke crooned as he and Seth comforted the young man.

Seth pet those golden curls as Trey finally calmed. Too bad the old goat was all the way in Georgia. Seth would love to pay him a midnight visit and teach him a lesson for hurting Trey.

"No thoughts about maiming the asshole," Trey retorted as he pulled away from Luke to wipe away the tears from his cheeks.

A grunt was Seth's only reply. Trey was very attuned to him and Luke some days. It was kinda scary. And wonderful.

"Better?" Luke placed a chaste kiss on Trey's temple.

"Yeah," he huffed out a breath. "Renji..." He chewed his bottom lip.

"He may not fully understand how you feel because he's never had to deal with this sort of situation before. Not like all of us have," Luke said. "But it doesn't mean he loves you any less."

"I know," Trey whispered. "He…he was so angry after that meeting. He took it so personal."

"Of course he did," Seth remarked. "He loves you. Your pain is his pain. Your joy, his joy. The same for you."

"Yeah." He smiled sweetly. "We talked afterwards. Last night especially. Once I'd had a few days to process it all that is. And…he doesn't want to wait till the end of the year to get married."

"Ah. Wants you in the family fold sooner, huh?" Seth chuckled. "Good call I say."

"When's the big day?" Luke asked.

"End of next month." Trey's grin was wide and bright, cheeks flushed with happiness. "Sango-san said it was the earliest she could arrange everything to her satisfaction," he giggled.

"Yeah, let's not deprive Sango-san of making sure her two sons are wed properly," Seth snickered.

"Well damn, that is soon," Luke laughed.

"It is and well…" Trey chewed his bottom lip again, looking between Seth and Luke with a wary expression.

"What is it, hon?" Luke pet that golden head.

"I want…that is, I would very much like my twin brothers to walk me down the aisle and give me away."

Seth blinked once then stared at Trey with total surprise. He knew Luke had the same look on his face.

"Well?"

There was such hope in those gem bright eyes. And Luke, it was clear he was about to bust with happiness. Seth had to admit he was just as happy.

"We would be honored, Trey." Seth leaned in and placed a chaste kiss on Trey's cheek.

Luke did the same to the other cheek then hugged Trey close. "Love you, little brother."

"Love both of my big brothers." Trey reached out and brought Seth into the hug.

They enjoyed the moment until Renji peeked in, letting them know breakfast was ready. Trey untangled himself, giving Seth and Luke a quick peck on the cheek, then jumped out of bed.

"And hurry. Me and Renji have a surprise for ya'll." With a wink he was gone.

Not about to pass up that mystery, Seth and Luke quickly used the bathroom, washed up a bit, and dressed in comfy lounge pants. When they made it to the kitchen, they noticed everyone was dressed the same, Trey too, and the large table was loaded. Including Marshall's signature buttermilk pancakes.

"Hell yeah!" Seth rubbed his hands together in anticipation as he and Luke joined everyone at the table.

Wasn't much said after their plates were filled. The only sounds were the clinking of silverware on dishes and groans of approval. Then again, it was kind of hard to talk while shoveling in such awesome pancakes.

Finally coming up for air, Seth sat back in his chair and pat his stomach. Luke refilled his coffee cup then his own, also done with his meal. Seth passed the creamer, making note that Luke had truly ate his fill. Luke gave him a sweet smile while Seth sipped his strong brew. Older by ten minutes Luke might be, but Seth was the more dominant and would always see to it Luke was taken care of. It was a holdover from their childhood that Seth couldn't break. Even if he was so inclined. Luke placed a hand on Seth's thigh and he relaxed, relishing the comfort and their circle of close friends. Well, family really. It's what Marshall and Gary had told them from the first day they were hired. Takeda Security was a family. Best damn decision he and Luke had ever made.

"I'm sure you're both wondering about the surprise Trey mentioned?" Renji spoke up, cradling his own coffee cup.

"It did cross our minds, yes." Seth nodded with a grin.

"Well, after the feeding frenzy came to a stop." Luke chuckled.

"It's the pancakes," Trey snickered. "They're like crack."

Everyone agreed with sated expressions.

"What can I say," Marshall boasted, puffing out his chest. "I'm a master at the craft."

Gary leaned over and gave Marshall a quick peck on the lips. "That you are," he leered.

"Hey now. We just ate," Seth said with a mock frown, holding his stomach.

"Ass." Gary threw a napkin at him.

Seth caught while everyone laughed.

"As I was saying," Renji continued in a louder voice to get everyone's attention. "Trey, Gary, Marshall, and I were talking about our sooner than planned wedding and a thought occurred." He reached under the table and brought out a little black box. He then placed it on the table and pushed it toward Seth. "Take it."

Looking over at Luke, Seth saw that his eyes were wide, expression one of shock with a little anticipation mixed in. He motioned to Seth to take the box.

With trembling fingers, Seth reached for the box then opened it between him and Luke. A gasp left them both.

Nestled in black velvet were two identical wedding bands with a rectangular cut emerald in the center. The bands were platinum, setting off the deep green of the stones. They were absolutely stunning.

"Renji?" Luke choked out, his fingers clutching at Seth's thigh.

"We all know that no matter where you two go, getting legally married will be impossible." His dark eyes held sadness at that but his smile was warm. "Gay marriage is difficult enough these days for the rest of us."

"Fucking nosey, hypocritical, bible thumping politicians," Trey muttered angrily. "Need to be beaten with that damn book. Repeatedly."

"And with much prejudice," Gary added.

"Amen." Marshall saluted with his coffee cup.

Renji chuckled then moved on. "Since that's the case, I'm sure neither of you have even thought of being married, have you?"

"No." Seth shook his head, tearing his gaze from the rings to look at Luke. "We know our relationship is considered taboo. Even wrong and disgusting. So having more than what we have now hasn't been possible. Though truthfully, we're just happy to have each other in an environment where we don't have to hide."

"Not that we've really cared much about outside opinion," Luke added. "It just meant being more careful to conceal what we have so we could stay safe. Marriage was never even a thought, really. But yeah, we're happy now. It's been more than enough." His smile was radiant.

"Not for me," Trey stated as he leaned down then stood with a medium size package in his hands, bringing it over and standing between Seth and Luke. "I don't think it's fair that the rest of us can finally have what you two are still being denied. So, while it's not exactly legal, here." He handed the package to Luke.

Taking it, he looked over at Seth who gave him a slight nod. Carefully, Luke tore the paper off to reveal a picture frame with a fancy document inside.

"Is this…" Luke's eyes welled with tears, handing Seth the framed contents.

"It's a real marriage license, notarized and everything," Trey explained. "Unfortunately, it can't be filed with the state of North Carolina because you're blood related. Fucking law."

There, in black and white, was Seth and Luke's full names, stating they were wed by North Carolina law. It had been dated two days ago. Trey and Renji were witnesses, their signatures bold on the document and an authentic North Carolina seal embossed in the corner.

The scraping of a chair and Luke's hand leaving his thigh made Seth look up to see his brother grab Trey in a fierce hug, his shoulders shaking with silent sobs. Standing as well, Seth carefully placed the frame on his chair and embraced Luke and Trey, shedding a few happy tears himself.

"Thank you, little brother," Seth croaked, the black velvet box clutched tightly in his fist.

"Love you, guys," Trey sniffed as he pulled back. "Want you happy."

"I'm so happy I'm about to bust," Luke laughed as he wiped his wet cheeks.

Seth felt the same as he too wiped his tears away.

"What would make me happy is seeing if those rings fit," Gary smirked, Marshall's arm over the back of his chair. Both their blue eyes showed a little wetness too.

"The rings, yes!" Trey stepped away and went to Renji, sitting in his lap. "Okay, go." He waved them on.

"I feel like the main attraction at the zoo," Seth joked as he took both rings from the box.

"Get on with it ya big ape," Marshall goaded with amusement.

Luke snorted as Seth placed the empty box on the table. When he turned to Luke, gazing up into those green eyes, it was as if they were the only two people in the room.

They moved as one, their foreheads touching as they came together. Seth gave one of the rings to Luke then took his left hand, kissing the fourth finger reverently.

"You are my heart and soul, the very breath in my body," he whispered, the words coming from the depths of his being. "Always." With another kiss to Luke's finger, Seth slipped the ring on. It fit perfectly.

"You are the reason my heart beats. The light in my darkness. My joy, my love, my home," Luke whispered as well, taking Seth's left hand and placing his lips on the fourth finger. "Always." With another kiss, he slid the ring on Seth's finger. It too fit perfectly.

"I love you, Luke. My brother, my husband."

"I love you, Seth. My twin, my husband."

They sealed their troth with a blistering kiss.

The sounds of clapping and whistling broke them apart. Seth looked around to see everyone on their feet and coming their way.

"Congrats, guys," Marshall told them." Now you can be an old married couple like the rest of us."

"Feels good, huh?" Gary winked.

"Yeah." Luke gazed down at his ring then adoringly at Seth. "It does."

Seth gave him a quick peck for that. His brother never looked more gorgeous. He was practically glowing.

"And the gifts keep coming for the newlyweds," Trey said happily as he passed over a set of keys to Seth.

"What are these to?"

"The house."

"Huh?"

"We're giving you guys a little honeymoon," Trey explained as Renji cuddled him close.

"But –"

"It's alright, Luke," Renji stopped him with a smile. "It's only for four days while I take Trey to meet Ranmaru in Miami," Renji clarified. "Perfect timing, actually. Ran's out for the summer and Trey's never been to Miami before. We can see the sights and shop while Trey and Ran get to know each other."

"It also gives us a chance to check on Yana and her guys," Marshall added. "They've got a few potential employees for us to meet with as well."

"Will you have enough protection?" Despite the thrill of having Luke to himself for four, whole uninterrupted days, he and Luke were still responsible for Trey's safety. A job they took very seriously.

"Not to worry," Gary placated. "Raul and Thomas were given the sit-rep. And the guys we're meeting are ex-FBI and CIA with military backgrounds just like Raul and Thomas. Trey will have plenty of protection."

Luke relaxed at Seth's side as Seth blew out a breath. "Okay." That made him feel a little better. Raul and Thomas were good. Not as good as himself and Luke, but would do in a pinch. "Are ya'll heading out today?"

"In the morning," Renji answered. "I made reservations for us at that nice restaurant in Charlotte for later tonight to celebrate your nuptials."

"And I made sure the kitchen has been fully stocked," Trey added. "As well as having my uncle's two vintage Harley's and Ford truck filled up in the off chance you feel like a road trip when you come up for air," he smirked.

"If they come up for air," Gary muttered with amusement.

"Did you?" Seth challenged with a grin.

"Hell no," Gary laughed. "We didn't even bother with clothes that entire week."

Now that was an idea he could get behind, Seth thought as he gave Luke a heated smile. Luke gave one of his own, a promise in those leaf green depths.

"In the meantime." Trey chuckled. "You two go nap. The reservations are at seven, so we'll need to leave around three. No telling how bad traffic will be."

"It'll be shit the closer you get to Charlotte," Luke retorted. "You know that."

"Why do you think I said we needed to leave so early?" Trey snorted. "Now shoo. We need to get the kitchen cleaned then I promised Yana I'd Skype to give her the details about all this."

"Not too many," Seth said with amusement.

"Yeah, right," Marshall harrumphed. "You're just lucky she didn't want pictures and video."

"Jake and Cole weren't so lucky," Gary snickered.

Seth merely rolled his eyes then took Luke's hand. "Thank you, Trey. Truly."

"Love you, little brother," Luke said.

"Love you guys, too." Trey smiled warmly. "And really, no thanks needed. We're family, remember?"

A little choked up, Seth nodded then led Luke, his husband, back to their room. When the door was finally shut, they undressed each other and climbed into bed. They faced each other on their sides, sharing sweet kisses and basking in the glow of their new bond. Seth took Luke's left hand, staring at the ring.

"This is so surreal," he murmured then gazed into his brother's eyes. "But I hope you know that if –"

"I know," Luke placed a finger over Seth's lips. "We've been so focused on staying together and keeping safe that anything more didn't register. And I've been fine with that, Seth. Then getting hired here, it made being together without having to hide more than I could possibly hope for."

"It's been our dream." Seth kissed Luke's ring. "Then we meet a little rebel twink and…" He had to swallow the lump in his throat.

"He's made all our dreams come true." Luke smiled. "Even one we didn't even know we had."

"Yeah. The little shit." Seth chuckled softly.

"And look at it this way. We haven't had to agonize over the rings. Getting the license," Luke smirked. "Invitations, a banquet hall, or any of the other million things to do to get a wedding off the ground."

"Hmm...you have a point." Seth leaned in close, kissing Luke's jaw. "Seems we got the better part of the deal."

"Exactly." Luke gasp as Seth nibbled on his neck. "We can enjoy the perks without all the...fuss." He groaned when Seth suckled his earlobe.

"Perks." Seth pulled back with a leer. "I do like perks."

With a laugh, Luke said, "Yep. So, four whole days with my new husband." His smile was mischievous. "Any idea what we should do?"

Quickly rolling atop his twin, his husband, Seth reached between Luke's legs and slowly eased out the plug. He replaced it with his aching erection.

"Seth!" Luke gasped with pleasure.

"I'm sure we'll figure something out." He grinned wickedly before taking Luke's mouth in a molten kiss.

Yeah, no clothes the entire four days was a perfect idea, Seth thought as he lost himself in his brother, his twin, his husband's body and love.

Fin

Printed in the USA
CPSIA information can be obtained
at www.ICGtesting.com
LVHW020927291023
762474LV00024B/332

9 781516 953592